The Tristan Chord

The Tristan Chord

Bettina von Kampen

Enfield & Wizenty
(an imprint of Great Plains Publications)
420 – 70 Arthur Street
Winnipeg, MB R3B 1G7
www.greatplains.mb.ca

Great Plains Publications gratefully acknowledges the financial support provided for its publishing program by the Government of Canada through the Book Publishing Industry Development Program (BPIDP); the Canada Council for the Arts; as well as the Manitoba Department of Culture, Heritage and Tourism; and the Manitoba Arts Council.

Design & Typography by Relish Design Studio Ltd.

Printed in Canada by Friesens

FIRST EDITION

Library and Archives Canada Cataloguing in Publication

Von Kampen, Bettina, 1964-
The Tristan chord / Bettina von Kampen.

ISBN 978-1-894283-85-4

I. Title.
PS8593.O556T75 2008 C813'.6 C2008-902984-4

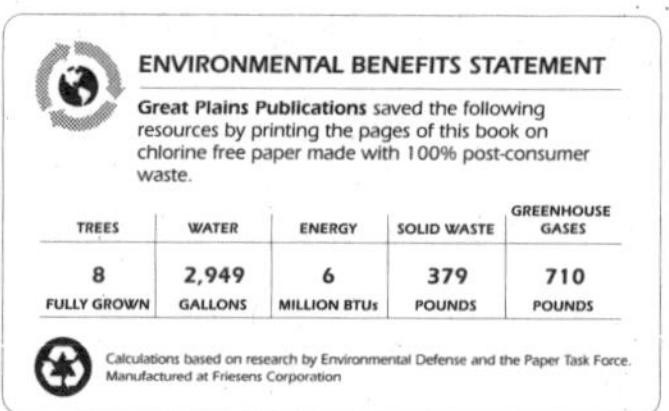
ENVIRONMENTAL BENEFITS STATEMENT

Great Plains Publications saved the following resources by printing the pages of this book on chlorine free paper made with 100% post-consumer waste.

TREES	WATER	ENERGY	SOLID WASTE	GREENHOUSE GASES
8 FULLY GROWN	2,949 GALLONS	6 MILLION BTUs	379 POUNDS	710 POUNDS

Calculations based on research by Environmental Defense and the Paper Task Force. Manufactured at Friesens Corporation

For Ricki

"Without music this life would be madness."
—Friedrich Nietzsche

Overture

Bayreuth, Germany, 1944

The first thing the officer noticed when he stepped off the train at Bayreuth was the air. It made him dizzy to breathe the clean, fresh, country smells of the Bavarian countryside where they still grew grapes to make wine. An elderly couple along the tracks even tended a vineyard. Were those people really going to harvest grapes and make wine? It astonished him to discover that there were people about not in uniform and not fighting. After Dachau and the rank air that surrounded him there, the earthy smell of the trees was like a drug – one he wasn't used to. For hours that first day he walked the streets, through the public gardens, doing nothing but breathing and smelling the air. Though untended, the flowers were in bloom and there were blossoms on the apple trees. He sat on a bench and listened to the birds. The warmth of the sun felt wholesome and pure. There were ducks in the river that swam over and quacked with anticipation, but he had no bread and they soon swam upriver to find someone who did. He settled back onto his bench and stretched out his legs. Two women pushing strollers came towards him, laughing and talking. As soon as they saw him, saw his uniform, they quickly turned their carriages around and walked the other way. Bitches, he muttered under his breath. The German people had become bitter and ungrateful. This war divided the country and he somehow had become the enemy. The sweet air around him dissipated. He rose from the bench, straightened his uniform and returned to his room.

• • • •

May 14, 1944

Am writing this on the train to Bayreuth. I'm surprised at the number of civilians like me on board, although most of them are old. Left Berlin at seven this morning and ate my bread and cheese ages ago and now must wait until we arrive. The trains don't run with any regularity now and there certainly is no food on board. Am trying to ignore the roaring pit in my stomach and take in the rolling countryside. There are stretches of lush green fields complete with caramel coloured cows and waving fair maidens. A beautiful ride even in the middle of a war. Karl is snoring on the seat across from me. Right now the train has stopped in the middle of nowhere for no apparent reason. There is a vineyard outside and a man and a woman are tending the vines. They are both elderly and permanently stooped, trying their best to carry on as usual. The grapes grow every year. No sense letting them go to waste and we need a little wine now more than ever.

We have been stopped for nearly twenty minutes and the porter just hustled by not looking left or right in case somebody dares ask him to explain. Oh, here we go. On the move again at a quarter normal speed but moving forward anyway. We'll arrive late and eat cold sausages and hard potatoes. It doesn't matter. I'm too hungry to care. Ah, we are picking up speed. Hopefully this time the train will keep moving until we reach our destination.

We just pulled out of Nürnberg after a quick exchange of passengers. Saw Julius get on down the line. His face was drawn with the effort of lugging that cello on board, or perhaps it is the strain of the war, which I am sure can be seen on all of our faces. Maybe I'll stroll down through the cars later to see him. The cars are emptying out and I assume this train is now full of musicians only. A few SS officers are on board. They never seem far away. Can't live with them and can't shoot them, as the joke goes. Another thirty minutes and this tedious journey will be behind us. I'll wake Karl in a moment. We may have to walk to the Gasthaus Schinner. Poor Julius with his cello. With any luck he'll find a baggage cart. We can all load it up and trek over to the hotel.

There is still light in the sky. Such long days now. Eight-thirty and I can think of nothing but food.

May 15, 1944

Back in Bayreuth, where I will once again spend the summer rehearsing and preparing for the festival. The trip from Berlin was painfully slow. After five hours we finally arrived and ran into Julius on the platform wondering where he might find a baggage cart. We tried to help him find one for his cello. We scoured the platform and Karl even checked the washrooms but everything has all been chopped up for firewood by now. So we ended up hauling our bags and instruments through town in the rain.

Helga had my room ready for me. The sight of the warm, heavy eiderdown on the bed and the fat raindrops splattering against the window made the room warmer than it was. Here, I always feel welcome. Gasthaus Schinner has not changed much since last year, although Helga looks thinner. No doubt the strain of the war and a shortage of butter. I checked under the balcony and the bicycle I used last summer is still there, dusty and with flat tires. I'll get round to fixing it up in the next few days. When the rain stops I might make some use of it. Karl is in the room across the hall, down and out with the flu. No doubt the endless trip on the train with nothing to eat but dry biscuits did him in.

I have a small writing table by the window where I can work. I have laid out my paper and pen. The libretto I finished over the winter and now here where the spirit of Richard Wagner permeates every cobblestone and keg, I will pen my own magnum opus! I hope to make some headway this summer, between rehearsals. If I can't find inspiration here, then there is none to be found. I lugged about ten pounds of manuscript paper with me from Berlin, not knowing if there would be any to be found here. Why the war would result in a shortage of manuscript paper I don't know, but the strangest things become scarce these days. Needless to say we were happy to see Helga on her stoop awaiting our arrival. She rushed into the street and hugged us all in turn. Julius straggled behind, much winded on account of his cello's heavy case. "I should have taken up the flute when I had the chance," he said, wheezing, when he finally collapsed in the kitchen.

Helga had food ready for us. We feasted on fried potatoes and herring and she even had a case of beer from somewhere and so we fell into bed sated and exhausted. We spoke in hushed tones about the war, the only thing anyone discusses these days, and Helga gave us a rundown of the things that were hard to get this year that she had no trouble finding last year, like almonds and bananas. She showed us her radio in the sitting room and told us we could use it anytime. Beethoven's Eighth Symphony played on the German broadcaster. She turned it up and then she whispered for us to be careful. The BBC broadcasts could be received here and she didn't want anyone to be caught. And with running a hotel, you never knew who would be listening at the door. There were informants everywhere. We sat up and listened to Beethoven – quietly – and drank a schnapps to the end of the war.

I took a walk through town this morning. Spring is in the air. I strolled through the public gardens. There is no one to tend them, but the flowers bloom and the birds sing anyway and there is usually a bench in the sun to sit on. I made my way over to *Die Eule* to check the tuning of the piano. It's not too bad. A few of the notes stick. Hendrick, the proprietor, told me it hasn't been played much since Christmas time. I'm not very good at the piano and will recruit the first person to show some aptitude to help me out with my score. The town teems with musicians, but not a competent pianist among them. There's Steeger, the chorusmaster, but he's got enough to do already without helping a young hack write an opera. There are a few ideas rattling around in my head and I have to give them some form and depth.

I imagine this year's festival will be much the same as last, with the 'Guests of the Führer' in attendance. When the war broke out we all thought the festival would be closed but Hitler ordered it to continue. The red and black flags are all looking a bit bedraggled and dusty, a reflection of everyone's waning enthusiasm for this war. I caught a glimpse of the soldiers from the Viking Division rehearsing on the balcony of the theatre, bleating a fanfare. It rankles us that the SS has been called in to fill out the chorus. With everyone off fighting, there are not enough musicians left in the country to perform *Die Meistersinger*, and so we resort to this.

It's bad enough we have to endure the parades and propaganda they shove down our throats, but to have those cretins stomping on Wagner's stage in their jackboots is really more than most of us can bear. I was surprised to receive the letter that called us back here again this year. With the Allied planes flying overhead, dropping bombs like confetti onto the big cities and the Americans and Russians itching to storm our borders, we wonder what our great Führer is thinking to stage an opera festival during these terrible times. According to Wieland Wagner, the director, we are to uplift the spirits of the munitions workers and wounded soldiers who are invited to attend the performances. If he feels any sense of irony in this, he doesn't show it. Uplift, indeed. Everybody knows they have no choice but to attend. Everything is paid for: the train, their lodging, their food. And in return they fill the unforgiving wooden seats for five hours of opera.

The parades and processions have turned into a thin masquerade. The country used to turn out in droves for these events, but nobody is interested anymore. Only once in a while can you see a tribe of children marching alongside them when there are no sound-minded adults to pull them away. Even now, when you would think all soldiers should be off fighting, they parade around. There aren't as many of them so they go around in endless circles to make it appear that there are thousands of them, singing the "Horst Wessel Song" at the top of their lungs: *Die Fahne hoch, die Reihen fest geschlossen!* It is undeniably catchy – that damn song. I'd be happy to write something as tuneful for the chorus to sing in my own opera.

May 22, 1944

Today is Wagner's birthday. Karl and I will go to *Die Eule* later and raise a glass to the master. It's the least we can do to honour the man whose presence in Bayreuth has been overshadowed by the Nazi party. They have claimed this town as their own. I wonder what Wagner would think of these wartime festivals?

Especially, I wonder if he would welcome the presence of the SS as we are expected to. I'm sure he would agree with our renaming his house from *Wahnfried* (peace from delusion) to *Wahnsinn* (insanity). Not too original but perhaps inevitable.

Surely Wagner would shudder at the sight of his town today – nothing much to do with opera and everything to do with Nazi propaganda. It's astounding how one diminutive man with a screeching voice can change the face of a nation in so short a time. Years ago, before the outbreak of war, I attended a rally in Berlin. The rally itself was spectacular. It was night and large fires burned into the sky. Spotlights shot beams of light into the air. There was music, "Die Meistersinger Overture" of all things. Thousands of troops marched in tight formation. It was as though all of Germany had been mobilized to perform one massive choreographed number. Hitler spoke for an hour and by the end of it I thought I belonged to the greatest nation on the planet and was ready to prove it to anyone. Such was his power. I hardly understood most of what he said, but he had the crowd in such a frenzy that we all knew something very powerful was at work and that our nation was ready to take on the world.

Later – drunk and tired. My pillow beckons. We celebrated with lots of beer, Karl and I and a few other orchestra members. When the beer flows, we don't stop to wonder where it comes from. More and more things are rationed and so far beer remains plentiful. The evening's mood was somewhat muted by a table of SS officers who were loud and rude and had no idea it was Wagner's birthday. The least they could do is pay attention to the task they have been assigned. Or do they hate being taken away from shooting and terrorizing people? One of them spat at our feet on his way out. A weak gesture to cover his contempt. He knows we are free and he has tied himself to that uniform.

• • • •

Bayreuth was so different from Magdeburg where the officer grew up. Here he was in Bavaria. The Alps were near. If it weren't for the Swastikas hanging from every balcony, it would seem this town was untouched by the war. But Hitler would never allow for any German town to be forgotten.

The war was hard, had made him hard. But he was an officer under the Führer's command and now he had been called upon to sing. This evening in *Die Eule* he spent most of his time scowling in the corner of the bar at the musicians who celebrated Wagner's birthday and played cards for beer. A few hours ago he had sung his heart out in the rehearsal hall. But he knew the civilians assumed a professional singer had been replaced with a typical SS soldier: no more than a bully and a braggart. He spat at the feet of the musicians on his way out. Because he could get away with it and he hated how they made him feel.

• • • •

May 26, 1944

Rehearsals are well under way. Even though we have performed this work for the past three years it is still an awesome experience. What musician wouldn't dream of performing here in the very theatre built by Richard Wagner?

The strangest thing has happened. Last night I was in *Die Eule*, drinking a beer with Karl and discoursing on my opera. I know this bores him, but I have to talk to somebody. I was trying to explain the difficulty I was having with a duet between the lead soprano and tenor, as I want the soprano to be singing off-stage and I don't think I can convince a diva to perform from the wings. The reason for this set up is because the tenor is hearing what he wants to hear from the soprano. She is not really present in the scene. It's all in his imagination so I don't want her on stage. I got caught up in the technical problems with the acoustics and the projection of her voice and Karl's eyes glazed over.

I needed to play it for him but one of the SS officers was at the piano, tinkling away meaningless notes, or so I thought until I recognized what it was he was strumming over and over: F, B, D-sharp, G-sharp – the opening of *Tristan and Isolde* – Wagner's famous story of yearning and agony. He was drunk, or so I thought, so I ambled over and asked if he was through. I didn't dare try to strike up a conversation and pretended I hadn't recognised what he was playing. He immediately got up and stumbled away as if I had disrupted a trance.

So I sat down at the piano to try to play for Karl the two parts I had been trying to explain. Suddenly he was back – the SS officer. He stood directly behind me and was reading the music as I played. Well, this made me very uneasy, not just for someone to hear my lame attempt on the piano, but one of the detested SS at that. I thought maybe he was angry that I had shooed him off the piano. Much to my surprise, he offered to play the piece for me. It was not hard to tell I was missing most of the notes. It turns out this fellow plays the piano masterfully. He sat down and played the entire duet through with the same ease as he drank his beer. There was a hush over the entire room. Nobody could quite believe a brute such as he (we assume they are all brutes, their jobs demand it) could play with such passion.

I stammered a thank you, took my music and went back to Karl, my heart thumping and my palms slick with perspiration. The officer sat at the piano awhile longer and played a Beethoven Sonata. When we attempted to applaud he shook his head at us and closed the lid of the instrument.

Do you have any more? he asked, again looming over me as I cowered. I didn't want to strike up much of a conversation with him. There is a line there that neither of us wanted to cross. They are armed and we are not and for the most part we musicians only carry the Nazi Party membership cards so we can work. They carry it for far different reasons. His hand rested on his gun, I don't know why.

The thing is, this fellow could probably play for me all I have written. I never know exactly what I have orchestrated because I can't play all the parts at once. I ran this by Karl who was quite drunk by the time this all came about and he thought I was crazy to have anything to do with the SS man. He was probably right, but if I can find someone who can play my music for me it will be an immense help and I might actually get somewhere this summer. I held back and simply said I was at *Die Eule* most nights and if fate should have it that he was there too then perhaps he could help me out. I didn't want him to think he had any authority over me in the bar, although clearly he does.

• • • •

His gun and his uniform allowed him entrance. Immediately, he was drawn to the piano. His fingers twitched at the sight of the keys, a remote and distant thrill returning to them. The violinist that had disrupted his reverie hadn't even recognized the Tristan Chord – or maybe these musicians were no longer moved by the genius of Richard Wagner. The musician probably wanted the piano to himself so he could play a piece of music from a hand-written manuscript for his friend. The man was writing an opera and wished to hear what he had written, but his fingers fumbled for the notes. The officer longed to have his fingers on the keys and offered to play the piece for him.

His presence made them nervous. The man gestured with his hand for the officer to sit and slid off the bench. He knew his uniform gave them little choice. He had to play well. For a moment his eyes scanned the page – B flat major. A duet orchestrated for strings, winds and a single horn. He opened and closed his fingers to calm the nerves, took a swallow of beer and struck the first chord. The sound filled the room, which had grown silent behind him. The piece was melodic, gorgeous high tones through the cello section. To fill in the sound further he improvised a counter melody he thought would suit the horns. The officer reached the end of the piece and a smattering of applause rose from the room. Swiftly he spun around and waved it away. He nodded curtly to the composer and turned back to the piano. Not knowing what to say, he played a Beethoven sonata and hoped it would take the place of any words expected of him. His throat tightened. It had been many years since he had uttered any kind or pleasant words to anyone and none came to him now.

Once he finished the Beethoven, he mustered some courage and asked the man if there was more music for him to play. As soon as the words left his mouth, he regretted them. It was clear the man and his friend did not want him near. He could feel them bristle in his presence. Instinctively his hand reached for his gun, though there was no reason to use it. He returned to the table where his fellow officers were sitting. One of them clapped him on the back and said something that caused the lot of them to laugh raucously. The young officer drank his beer in silence. Rather than uplift him the way it used to, playing the piano tonight caused an ache to settle in his heart. He regarded his comrades, their laughter, their talk, their drink, and knew it mattered not if his chair sank forever through the earth or if he remained seated there. For he and the chair shared a common insignificance.

• • • •

June 2, 1944

We listened to the BBC tonight, sitting quiet as mice in Helga's sitting room. The Allies are organizing over in England, preparing to invade the continent. It is just a matter of time now before America is among them. We will almost welcome them. This war has dragged on for so long and all the hope and furor for a new Germany has passed. Most of us would settle for the return of the old Germany. Of course, Hitler will never surrender. The "genius" has turned out to be completely out of his mind. The fireworks and frenzy of the early days of the regime seem so long ago. The only fireworks that light up the night sky these days are the efforts of our enemies to annihilate us. Not really a cause for celebration.

He was there again last night, as I expected, shuffling his feet, a little drunk. I was still a bit irritated at his inventing a new part to go with my duet. Of course it sounded better. I hadn't had time to explain that everything was not complete. Maybe he had been waiting there awhile. Karl and I didn't get to the bar until after nine. He won't tell me his name. It's almost as though he is mute or it pains him to speak. Maybe he has forgotten the art of conversation and is only able to bark out orders. I told him I would call him Beckmesser, one of the roles in *Die Meistersinger*. It doesn't seem to bother him, this made-up name. He was eager to play – took the music right away and sat at the piano.

Once again, all I could do was sit by and try not to be too pleased at what I had written. Again, this Beckmesser filled in some of the parts that were only sketched in. It was as though he knew exactly what I was after. I don't need to know his name, not when he plays like a man possessed. I can only hope my opera sounds as *bellicoso* when played by a real orchestra. He hammers out the bass parts like a prizefighter pummels his opponent into submission. And although he doesn't say much, his voice is sublime! It gives me great hope to hear him sing my music. I sat with my eyes closed and imagined the stage upon which it one day will appear. Why haven't you written more of the libretto? he asked and I gave a lame answer about the libretto being written after the music was complete. He didn't question this. Clearly, he is no composer. Were he to see exactly what he was helping me with he would have cause to shoot me for treason.

> There was only the one piece to play and he looked disappointed. Play something else, I urged. He closed his eyes and played *Träumerei*, by Schumann. Not a note was missed or an ornament cut short. I stood him a beer. It was the least I could do. I could see he was hesitant to accept it, but I left it on top of the piano and Karl and I left as we have an early start tomorrow.

• • • •

The composer said his name was Paul. Paul asked the officer his name and when he saw his reluctance to tell him, he christened him Beckmesser. The book Paul wrote in made the SS man suspicious. It was a journal and he guessed there were things in there about him and he didn't want his name in the book. And he had lied about the libretto, Beckmesser could clearly see through that one. Again, the composer asked him to play, this time, a section for the chorus. The brief exchange over his name had ignited a fuse and his stomach boiled with an ill-defined rage. He would rather have been back at Dachau than here. Being here was madness. To sing in an opera when there was work to be done. Years they had been at it and still the trains brought the people to the camps. When would they be rid of them all? How could they justify being here in this tiny Bavarian town at such a time? He was a trained soldier and this was what they asked of him – to don a costume and prance around as a villager in the 16th century!

He had never seen the glory of battle. His work was in the camps, maintaining order and following commands. For years he had not been expected to think. And here the orders continued: when to sing, when to appear and when to exit the stage, through which wing. His mind was rotting away, capable only of basic sensory functions and co-ordinating the physical moves required of his rote participation. But, at the piano, this changed. He played the chorus and sang the tenor part. There were few words but the melody was powerful and filled with passion. There was a glimmer of an ancient light, a corner of his memory illuminated, a brief shiver of delight. It unnerved him to feel this unusual and jarring sensation – something that long ago he took for granted. This time it was undeserved – a relic of another time that had given up its place in his heart. When he finished the chorus Paul told him he had a strong voice. Impressive, he said.

The young officer didn't turn around. He played another piece – Schumann, the way he used to when his mother was listening. His eyes closed, his fingers remembered the notes. The sound rippled through time as he was transported back to the study in his house, where he practised while his sisters played outside. Back to a time when the future beckoned. When wishes could bloom in his imagination and he was free to follow his heart. Those times seemed impossible now. The Schumann came to an end and he was forced to open his eyes and feel the fragile thread of his heart's desire dissolve away, back to nothing. There was a beer on the piano for him, from the composer. It took a moment for his eyes to focus, his mind adrift on sun drenched waters.

• • • •

June 10, 1944

Karl and I rode out to the forest today. There was another bicycle in the shed with matching flat tires to mine. We pumped up the tires and rode out to pick mushrooms for our supper. The sunshine felt glorious and hot on our backs. The sandy trails through the forest were well packed down and made the riding enjoyable. We met a couple of girls who were out on their bicycles and stopped to talk. Inge and Brigitte. Lovely girls who shared their picnic with us and laughed and called us typical men who ride out into the woods for the day with nothing but bottles of beer to sustain them. We passed around the bottles and accepted their offers of bread and cheese. There was even chocolate, five years old, they admitted, but heavenly all the same. They wanted to come to a performance but regrettably they were not wounded soldiers and there was no other way to gain admittance. They thought this was a strange premise on which to stage a festival and we had to agree.

We felt so far removed from any war while we were out there, the wind gentle through the pines, the scent of the forest as sweet and bewitching as ever. No planes roaring overhead or tanks rumbling in the distance. Just the four of us sitting on a blanket in the sun sharing a picnic and then dozing off for a nap while flies buzzed around the empty beer bottles. The girls went off and picked posies to take home. Karl and I decided Helga would enjoy some wild flowers and we managed to convince Inge and Brigitte to stay awhile longer and search for mushrooms. Already we had frittered away most of the day and the promised mushrooms had not been gathered. We rode our bicycles further up the path. The light was disappearing behind the trees. In a shady grove we found enough mushrooms for all of us to fill our baskets.

Much to our anticipated delight, the girls kissed us on the cheek and then allowed us to kiss them on the lips before we parted and watched them ride off in the opposite direction. That is one thing about the war. People seize the moment. They will forget the regrets of the past and the worry for the future and embrace the present. Helga fried the mushrooms and scrambled them with some eggs. We excitedly told her about the girls and our picnic and in a surge of maternal instinct she reached over and pinched our cheeks, exactly where they had been kissed earlier.

June 13, 1944

It seems we are moments away from catastrophe at every turn. Yesterday a light came crashing from the rigging and just missed the prop master's head as he was nailing a table in place. They will have to find a new table somewhere and the light is useless now. There is no money to replace such things. The sets and props have been used so often, some of the pieces are missing and the prompters, who hide behind them to whisper their cues, are having a hard time staying out of sight.

We rehearsed in the theatre today. Abendroth gets utterly frustrated with the acoustics, which are outstanding but a hellish trick to coax from the stage and he has moved rehearsal from the rehearsal room to the pit way before we need to be down there. The sound from the pit bounces off the cover that hides the orchestra from view and is first projected onto the stage before it reaches the audience. We must play slightly ahead of the singers in order for the sound to reach the audience at the same time. It is the task of the conductor to keep the singers and the orchestra together. Abendroth pulls that enormous handkerchief from his pocket and mops his brow and spends half the rehearsal shouting to his assistant about the flutes whose pretty phrases go unheard in the journey from beneath the stage to the back of the hall. The old man, we call him, as we nearly perish under his tempo for the overture. He loves a long and drawn out adagio. It's like he's dragging it on as long as he can. Karl timed it the other day and he takes a good five minutes longer than Furtwängler.

Every day as the temperature rises we thank Wagner for his ingenious idea of hiding the orchestra under the stage. During performances we sit in shirtsleeves. We may sweat like pigs but at least we are not in the usual black suit and tie. Even the conductors grab their jackets at the last moment for their curtain call and otherwise roll up their sleeves and sweat right along with us.

If Abendroth has it tough then Steeger will have it ten times tougher with the SS men roaring in the chorus. The regulars in the chorus are professionals and quite used to following a beat, but my guess is that the SS have not had much experience under a baton. They like the finale best of all when they are urged to sing as loud as they can.

• • • •

It was like no music he had ever heard. It was nothing like when the troops sang Party songs at rallies. The gramophone in the living room at home did not prepare him for this. The sound of two hundred voices in the rehearsal room exploded into two thousand restless spirits singing for their lives. His body quaked at the thunderous sound. A pang of emotion pierced his chest and he had to take two breaths before he could manage to sing again. The chorus master waved his arms wildly and then tapped the stand. His face reddened with the effort of teaching the music to the newcomers. The tenors were late on their entry again. They had been at it for two hours already. Herr Steeger closed the score and tapped the stand. *Wachet auf!* He said. Baton up, voices ready and the sound swells and makes the young man's heart thrill. It is a sound he will never get used to and never forget.

He joined early in the movement. Once issued, he wore nothing but the uniform. His mother took in the seams of the pants for him, but could not look him in the eye when he tried them on. His parents were not pleased, but it was Adolf Hitler to whom he listened, not his parents. The Nazi movement gave him purpose. It was something he believed for a long time. Surrounded by others who believed the same thing. He revelled in their camaraderie and companionship. There were hundreds of thousands of them, mighty and willing to do whatever was needed for Germany. When it was over and Germany had been restored and established as a great nation, he would march home and his mother would finally say how proud she was of him. By the time he got to Bayreuth he had been away from home nearly four years. It was difficult to mail and receive letters and he hadn't heard from or seen his family in a long time. He was a boy when he left, just seventeen and not yet shaving. The army had made him a man.

• • • •

June 18, 1944

The authority of the SS is felt everywhere. There's a clever fellow in the bass section who can draw caricatures of any of the clowns, Hitler, Goebbels, Himmler. Potty humour to be sure, but good for a laugh. Hitler and Goebbels sitting on opposing shitters and sharing a roll of toilet paper. Lots of ass kissing and boot licking. Well, when one of these gems fluttered from his music folder and settled at the toes of a pair of jackboots, you could see the fear in his eyes. He knew the bastard could do anything. There was a tense moment there with us standing around, pasty musicians with ill-defined biceps ready to tear the soldier off our bass player if he decided to do something. He twisted his heel into the drawing and walked away. It was enough. No one dared even pick it up.

Karl and I have to be careful what we say. If my friend Beckmesser knew we huddled around Helga's radio every night and listened to the reports on the BBC he would have reason to shoot us for treason right there in Die Eule. And he always looks like he's itching to shoot something. They broadcast in German for us so we can compare their reports to ours. There is a marked difference. Propaganda is a powerful tool. According to Goebbels we are well on our way to victory. There is talk of a V-bomb that will surely end the war in one swift flight. Just a few days ago the Allies landed at Normandy. Had they heard about that when they aired the report on the V-bomb? In a way it was a relief to hear it. Maybe soon there will be an end to this war. But what will be left of Germany when it is over? They are coming at us from all sides. The war distracts us from our opera and the opera is meant to distract us from the war.

Die Meistersinger has been performed at the festival since 1888. Not every year like it has been lately but there have been dozens of performances. Most of us were here last year and a few, including myself, were here in 1933 when it was performed, back in the good old days before the war besmirched the face of this site. As much as Hitler wants these things to go on, there's no money for these productions. The other day, Hermann was racing around trying to get his hands on some grease or oil because anytime the sets are changed there erupts a horrible squeal from the winches. I believe he finally found some lard and used that. It's a heartbreaking thing to see all the old stagehands, the ones who have been involved for years, trying their damnedest to put on a professional production in the midst of all this. It's difficult with the insolent presence of the SS people who do nothing but scoff at our efforts and laugh at the whole thing. We all know it's a farce, but this is all we know. It must seem trite to them, mounting a musical production when they have been fighting a war. We will no doubt remain on either side of our artistic beliefs throughout these next few weeks.

June 12, 1944

Beckmesser sang an aria of mine today. My hands are still shaking. I told him he had a voice equal to most of the tenors I have heard on the Festspielhaus stage. It was difficult to gauge his reaction, since he rarely looks at me and his response to most of what I say is to take a drink of his beer and smack his lips. Then he'll say into the air, "What's next?" You can tell he's transported when he's playing but as soon as he stops he acts as though it's an unpleasant chore. But nobody gets to play at that level thinking it a chore. He is gifted and I told him so. If only he would look at me once and grunt! Anything!

• • • •

He did not want to hear it. 'You have a good voice.' It rattled him, to hear kind words. What was he supposed to say? Paul was an amateur composer.

He knew which instruments blended well and the types of phrases and harmonies that the human ear finds pleasing, but his ideas were rudimentary at best. The choruses were stirring – gentle, quiet melodies. But, the words to tell him so would not come. He did want to tell Paul something, that his music was calming. That the moments in the bar when he was playing were the only joy he had felt in years. They would scoff if he were to say those things. It was foolish and weak to be overwhelmed with emotion at a few notes strung together. It made no sense. He was a soldier, strong and brave. 'What's next?' were the only words he could utter.

• • • •

June 21, 1944

There is one month of rehearsal to go. Some of the soloists are here already, working on their stage movements and spending hours in costume fittings. So many shapes and sizes, the costumes have all been altered a million times. The sets and props are all a little ragged. Wieland and his mother, Winifred, huddle in the middle of the theatre, always in a hushed and heated discussion over whether to spend money on paint or lights. They stand in the aisle and stare at the stage and point and shout at the stagehands to move things around. Much practice goes into changing the sets. If those mechanisms are going to give way now is the time, before the seats are filled.

In a few weeks the entire cast and crew will be here, the same ones as last year, here to sing the same roles yet again. When I decided to become a musician these were not the kinds of performances I thought I would be giving. It becomes mechanical, sometimes playing bars on end without paying any attention at all and realising in a panic that you have lost your place. But I suppose even the most dazzling jobs can become mechanical and tedious over time. They don't pay us much, but I suppose we are lucky to be excused from military duty to perform here.

Who will return this year? Many have had the good sense to make themselves unavailable and have instructed their agents to keep them busy in America for now. For the most part there will be two performers per role. We in the pit have our favourites of course. Jaro Prohaska, our cavalier Sachs with his wavy dark hair and finicky moustache. Hours spent in the make-up chair just to get the right degree of curl. Even Jaro in the third act can't help but smirk when he cries "*Wahn, Wahn, überall Wahn.*" (Madness, madness, everywhere madness.)

Maria Müller, a sweet and innocent Eva, trademark red cheeks. With Erich Witte as David the two of them look more like Hansel and Gretel than tormented lovers. Greindl will be back to play his lean and mean Pogner. Hopefully his moustache will go or nobody will know the difference between him and Prohaska. And everyone wishes they would stop using Zimmerman for David. He's the alternate and looks like Eva's father and brings an uncomfortable flavour of incest to the stage. Ah, we in the pit know how to pick apart the cast. But they bring it upon themselves with their tantrums and fits. Don't they know there's a war going on? Can't they sense the unrest in the audience? Wounded soldiers shifting uncomfortably in their seats for what must seem an eternal five hours. There has often been discussion about upholstering the wooden seats but the Wagner family will never compromise the fine acoustics for the comfort of their patrons. I suspect that many of Wagner's staunch followers would rise up in revolt if the seats suddenly absorbed even a fraction of the sound.

• • • •

The stage was a good place to hide, the officer discovered. Out of his uniform for the first time and in a costume. Here he could act, become someone else. Here he was a member of the Guild of Master Singers. Far from his real life of standing guard over row upon row of prisoners, authorized to shoot at will. On stage he did not wear his pistol and it unnerved him the first time he was without it. But soon he felt safe on stage. There were no threats here to national security. He did not need his gun in the village of Nurmberg. But as soon as the curtain fell and he changed back into his uniform, the gun was back in its holster by his side. The musicians didn't like it, that they were here. They all steered clear of them. Except for Paul who needed someone to play the piano. The officer wasn't sure what he had started that day. It was impossible for him to pass by a piano and not reach out and touch the keys.

At home he would play for his youngest sister and her friends. Nothing spellbinding; they were too young to be impressed. All they wanted was to hold hands and dance around in circles while he played faster and faster and they would spin out of control on the living room floor until they landed in a heap, dizzy and giggling. As soon as they recovered they sprung to their feet and demanded he play another. Childish songs played for children. His other sister – now there was a voice. She would sing professionally one day, he was sure. A voice like water flowing over thousand year old stones. He missed her most of all. Their voices resonated at identical frequencies when they sang together creating a singular sound belonging only to them. Through their voices flowed a common blood by which they were connected, each fulfilling in the other what no one else could ever replace.

Now he was committed to this tenuous friendship, though he knew Paul did not want to be friends. He already had friends enough. But, friendship did not matter to the young man. It was the esteem of having been selected to play. To have been invited into the circle of musicians in this town made famous by music. For when he played the young man stood out. He was no longer one of hundreds of thousands but only one.

• • • •

June 28, 1944

I try to get him to talk, but he's always got that gun and I know he's used it before. Eleven years the party has been at it, cleansing the nation, and these are the men they have recruited to do it. First they went after the communists, then the social democrats and now the Jews. Next it might be second violinists so I had better watch it. I've asked about his family, his hometown, how he likes being here to sing. That one he answered and said Steeger was an idiot. I told him he was probably the first person to call him that. And then before I could stop myself I said, "That opinion means nothing here, coming from you."

He rose and towered over me and said, 'I could shoot you right now for saying that.'

Well shit, if he was going to shoot me I would have said a lot more than that! But it's true. His choice was evil and mine was beauty. How could he not see it? But now I know where he stands. It has something to do with my journal, that outburst. He saw me writing in it and when I stuck it back into my satchel he had a peculiar look on his face and then we had that exchange about him shooting me. Oddly, it did not scare me, though I do take it seriously. He's probably shot people for lesser reasons.

I wonder if he wishes he could change his mind. But he's already done too much killing to take it back now. It must eat away at him. How could it not? You'd have to be delusional to believe that killing for a cause is noble. They can't possibly all be certifiably insane. I would love to get that gun away from him and find out what he really thinks. It's his playing, and his singing. I refuse to believe he is one of the truly evil ones and yet it's what he wants me to believe.

I overheard the chorus rehearsal the other day and Steeger was trying to get the troops to breathe together between phrases. Sad for him, a man who has built his career muscling and massaging this chorus into the finest in the world, only to have it infiltrated by these bastards who won't give up the authority they think they have over everything. I wanted to blurt this out to him but he already knew what I thought.

July 1, 1944

Today I invited Beckmesser to come with me for a bike ride. There were no rehearsals scheduled and in a way I wanted to give him a way out of what he said the other day, the threat about shooting me. I knew he would never apologise but I could sense that he was sorry he had said it. There is a farmer just beyond the town who gives Helga a few eggs every week and occasionally a chicken or a rabbit. Much to my surprise Beckmesser said yes. Karl thought I was crazy and was sure I would end up shot and left for dead in a ditch. We rode out and I asked him to tell me his real name. 'You know, when they write my biography they will want to know who the talented pianist and tenor was who helped me with my masterwork.'

For the first time ever, a smile crept across his face, probably because he was laughing at me. 'I think I'll keep Beckmesser. It's growing on me.' He lit a cigarette. It was the first time I had seen him smoke. With a voice like that on him he couldn't possibly have the habit for real. He offered one to me, which I accepted, even though I haven't smoked in years. I took it as a peace offering and we passed a few silent moments as the smoke swirled around us.

We got on our bicycles and he pedalled off like a madman and then lifted his feet from the pedals and coasted down a hill. I thought I heard him laugh but the wind in my ears could have fooled me. When I caught up to him he had his feet back on the pedals and rode beside me, his face utterly blank.

'Are you going to tell me anything about yourself?'

'Today is my birthday.'

Well, I nearly fell off my bicycle. I reached over and clapped him on the back and yodelled Happy Birthday. I think I was the first person to wish him a happy birthday in years. I reached into the basket where there were apple tarts for the farmer from Helga, in exchange for what he would give us, and handed one to Beckmesser.

'You have to have something sweet on your birthday.' I did not expect a tear to come to his eye, and it didn't. But I don't think I ever have seen a deeper look of gratitude. His eyes shone with delight and he ate the entire tart in two bites.

He still didn't say much, but I could tell he was happier for a while. And he didn't shoot anything at the farm, even with all those warm-blooded animals skittering around. We rode back with two chickens and six eggs. The farmer thanked us for the tarts, looking a bit uncertain about the presence of an SS officer at his farm.

I was dying to use this light moment to ask him a million questions but I knew it would bother him and didn't want to ruin his birthday. We met later again at *Die Eule* and I bought him a beer and Karl shook his hand and it was very nearly a birthday party. Except that since I had left him after our bike ride, he had become gloomy. I had written a new chorus for the start of the second act but he did not feel like playing. He glanced over the notes and tossed the pages back onto the table where I sat. He finished his beer alone at the bar and left without so much as a nod.

• • • •

The bike ride in the country electrified the SS man. For a fleeting moment as he coasted down a hill he felt such a surge of joy jolt him he thought it would stop his heart. He quickly came to his senses once Paul caught up with him. At a loss for words and to deflect any other questions he told Paul it was his birthday. It felt queer to tell someone such a thing and he had to brace himself for the enthusiastic response. The apple tart was a complete surprise and as he ate it he feared he might fall over from ecstasy, so delicious was the taste of the sweet apples and pastry. The tart was as sublime as the first notes he struck on that piano at *Die Eule*. And then the black curtain fell and all happiness disappeared behind it. The sugary sweetness on his tongue turned to acid. The rush of the bicycle ride lingered only as a faint nausea. Later at the bar, Paul wanted him to play through a chorus, but the black veil had not lifted and he knew he could not play tonight. The happiness of the afternoon had affected him like a bad drug and he now hung in its grey shadow.

• • • •

July 3, 1944

Helga goaded us into picking berries for her today with the promise of gooseberry cake and whipped cream. I have no idea where she will find the cream, but Karl and I are happy to help her. Later we will have our coffee and cake in the garden where we can breathe in the scent of the rose bushes and listen to the birds. It is a sanctuary, back there in the sunny garden. A place untouched by the war.

Rehearsals are steaming along. We know the music so well by now. We have performed nothing but *Die Meistersinger* for the past four years. They did Tristan and Isolde a few years ago but it was then decided the story of unbearable yearning, loneliness and death would not be suitable for an audience of suffering, forlorn and wounded soldiers. Besides, the orchestra needed for *Tristan and Isolde* is twice the size of the one needed for *Die Meistersinger*, so this is a prudent choice.

The soloists arrived today and already Maria Müller had one of her snits and stormed off the stage and held things up for an hour. A war does not put a stop to a diva's fits. And all Abendroth wanted was for her to follow his beat. He waved his baton at her and yelled, 'Have you never seen one of these before? Follow the stick, you must follow the stick!"

And that was enough. I don't know who eventually coaxed her out of her dressing room. Wieland no doubt was stuck with that task.

July 7, 1944

Work on my own opera proceeds quite well. I think the story is sound – Christina the Astonishing. Thought to be dead, she rises from her coffin only to find the stench of human sin so overwhelming that she flees to the rafters of the church, frightening everyone except the priest. There are her two sisters, the Count Louis of Looz – a potential love interest, nuns and townspeople. Plenty of suitable roles for an opera. There is Christina, an indestructible saint whose mission is to pray for souls in purgatory. Christina's first aria is sung from high up in the lofty church, the priest listening, interjecting here and there to try to coax her to come down. She sings with the French horn to accompany her and finishes with swells from the strings. The audience will be spellbound, afraid to even unclench their fingers from their armrests. The story carries on with her life of devotion and strange behaviours. Not a glamorous role for a diva, Christina is like a wild thing from the forest, barefoot, clothes in rags and twigs in her hair. Witnesses see her hidden in ovens or immersed in frigid rivers for hours. She suffers torture from those who fear her and mercy from those who pity her.

The opera will end the way it began, at Christina's funeral. Everyone would come to see another miracle. But no, there would be no divine calling this time. The Agnus Dei would be sung to the end. Accompanying the subdued chorus would be the oboe and horn. The last note of the opera would be a subdued E flat, held and sung in unison, with two flutes and a cello.

Christina is an allegory for Germany. Sadly, I see no other outcome other than this country brought to her knees in defeat.

I cannot very well let Beckmesser know this. The SS men are all still ardent believers in victory, poor buggers. The war will end and the landscape will reek with the stench of human sin. The opera is a story of Germany's rebirth. Christina's ability to endure long hours in icy waters or to survive nights in hot ovens and emerge unscathed is what Germany will have to endure in the years to come as the world watches and judges to see what will arise from the rubble. It gives me shivers to even think of it. I just wish I could make the music reflect what I feel. There's the rub! The libretto was the easy part. But the notes! Where are they supposed to come from? Damn that Beckmesser. He plays it the way I want it to sound, before I even know how I want it to sound. He has changed since his birthday. I think the apple tart poisoned him against me. He still will play whatever I place on the piano in front of him, but he is surlier than ever.

• • • •

Ever since news of the Allied invasion at Normandy the seeds of doubt stirred within him. With those doubts he looked to the future, but he saw nothing. The end result had always been firm and clear in his mind. At the end of the war there would emerge a new Germany – one where he would have a prominent place as a soldier who fought valiantly for victory. But now with the possibility of defeat looming, the edges of that delusion peeled away. He thought of his role in the war: to stand watch while thousands of people huddled in long lines, stripped of their clothing and all belongings. To make sure none of them stepped away from the line, or ran for the fence or wailed too loudly, because that would cause panic. He had killed many of them right there. What did it matter when they were all going to die anyway? He had the authority to kill as many as he liked. And he did. He killed people who were waiting to die. It wasn't even his duty. He was just there to keep order. There were no commands issued to him to shoot those people. It was just that nobody said he couldn't. He wasn't sickened by his acts. He was in no way remorseful about what he had done.

All he saw now was the futility of his actions – that in the end, his role in the war was meaningless. He had lost every human urge. They were, all of them, reduced to animals, prisoners and soldiers alike. His gut churned with bitterness at being thrown into a beautiful setting and asked to perform music meant to move people when he himself had lost the capacity to be moved. To be told he had a beautiful voice, that he was gifted, caused him to nearly go blind with rage. There was no future for him. He had spent his lot in the last six years on an illusion. He had been eager to be swept along, thrilled to be part of it, blind to the delusion. The future that had been promised to him, for which he willingly stripped away his humanity, was not to be realised. In the end, when they all lay panting among the corpses, they would realize it was all pointless.

• • • •

July 17, 1944

First performance today. I am exhausted. We started at three and it is now nearly midnight. All went well, the audience applauded for a good twenty minutes and even shouts of Bravo here and there. Tomorrow I will have to ask Beckmesser how he liked being on stage. A change has come over him. He is moody much of the time and since I haven't written much new there is nothing for him to play. He has stopped shaving and his dark beard gives him a sinister aura that I don't trust. I wonder if he is dreading returning to his usual duties once the festival is over. The rest of us get to go home and wait out the end of the war but I expect he will be called back to duty. But then, as a soldier and one who voluntarily signed on, one would think he would rather be fighting than performing in an opera, especially right now as the front advances ever steadily towards our borders.

July 23, 1944

Beckmesser is out of commission. Something triggered his temper yesterday and he smashed his hand through a wall and broke two fingers. I suspect it may have something to do with the failed attempt on Hitler's life. Already word is out that the traitors – any and all of them – are being hunted down to be hung. We heard it on the radio late last night. Hitler ranted and raved for a good hour and by the end of it only one thing was clear. There will be no surrender. He will remain at the helm while the country goes down in flames. This is not leadership – it is suicide. For the first time I feel dread for what is to come. Maybe, for the first time Beckmesser does too.

Our days are consumed with the performances and so I had nothing for him to play. He hasn't gone near the piano in weeks and until last night I hadn't seen much of him at *Die Eule* either. I don't think this is why he's smashed his fingers but I could have guessed he would have punched the wall sooner or later. Now he has to appear on stage with his cast covered with rags to make it look more authentic. Hopefully nothing else will set him off because he could knock somebody out cold with that cast.

Had a few too many after the performance tonight. Karl is passed out in his room too. These days we sleep until eleven and straggle to the kitchen for coffee. We have completely disrupted Helga's meal schedule but she doesn't mind making us breakfast at noon. She sits down with her soup and watches us try to wake up. I try to get out for a walk everyday before the performance begins because I know I will be five hours in the dark under the stage. It is a steady and welcome routine in these uneasy days and the music sounds brilliant night after night, whether our esteemed audience recognises it or not.

• • • •

The SS officer was growing morose with the end of the festival drawing near. Paul stopped composing because of the heavy rehearsal schedule, so his evenings were long and lonely. Most nights he stayed in his room and watched a spider rebuild a web that he tore down every day. The animal's industry astounded him. Destruction of its web was an inevitability of life – the spider didn't brood for days, pondering why this travesty has befallen it. Undaunted and without fail the spider set to work and constructed a new web to ensure its survival. He sat and contemplated the animal's strength and knew he didn't possess even a fraction of that kind of resolve.

His hand was broken, an embarrassing testament to his lack of composure. He could feel himself unravelling from the inside. He had lost all faith in the war and the Party. He did not want the festival to end, nor to return to Dachau. But it was Germany's certain defeat that scared him most of all. Even Hitler's speech did nothing to rouse his patriotism. His indifference confused him. It all used to be so clear.

The performances bored him. For the finale, when they all were called to be on stage, the audience applauded and he stared out at the rows of soldiers who had fought for the past five years and wondered if they could pick him out from among the real singers. After the first few performances he didn't stick around for the final curtain but left by the stage door and stood in the dark. His eyes adjusted to the light of the moon where it fell on the fields beyond the theatre – the land he had been fighting for. The land that soon would be in the hands of the enemy.

• • • •

August 9, 1944

Last performance tonight. Everybody feels numb. Will this really be the final performance here? And if so, what an awful way for it to end, with these cretins on the stage and the audience bored to death. But, for the last time I will tune my violin with the rest of this fine orchestra and we will all give the performance of our lives. Musicians are a dedicated bunch that way. The music always is the most important thing. Wieland and Winifred do their best to maintain an atmosphere of professionalism. They continue to work diligently and take this festival as seriously as the last. They lead by example and hope their respect for us will translate into the passion they expect from their performers and stage crew. It is their family legacy that is at stake – the festival has been in the hands of Richard Wagner's descendants since its inception. If they harbour any feeling that the festival is over, they do not let on. I think of them whenever I get disillusioned with our task here. Nobody thought it would come to this. Performing in the dying days of a war, with the world poised to defeat us. I play for Wagner, for the glory of his genius, and I play for my country. When the war is over, it will be festivals like this one that will mark the dawn of our rebirth as a nation. No matter what is left of this country, music will prevail to lift our spirits once again.

• • • •

It is over. The applause died down. The houselights went up. His hand throbbed. The cast was loose now that the swelling had subsided. He changed from his costume back into his uniform. It was worn at the cuffs, the collar of his shirt stained. It had been months since they were issued new ones. The musicians were in great spirits and were gathering at *Die Eule* for one last drink to celebrate the close of another successful festival. Paul asked him to come along. 'And to hear you play once more, Beckmesser.' He waved his cast in Paul's face to remind him. 'Come along anyway, Beckmesser. It's our last night here. I have something for you.' Always when he heard that name he would think of Paul. But the young SS officer declined the invitation. He was tired, he said.

But he was not tired. The latest orders were to destroy the barracks, to blow up the incinerators, to dig up mass graves and burn the bodies, to burn the paperwork. They were preparing for the Allied invasion and they wanted no evidence to remain of their work. This was what he would be doing after tomorrow when he returned to his post. It was not lost on him that he had worked throughout the war in a prison camp while others had walked free. All he had worked for had been a colossal farce. He was only twenty-one and his life had come to nothing. He chewed the inside of his cheek until it bled and he spat the blood on the ground. This experience had shown him what his life could have been. He could have been a professional musician. Paul had said so.

He waited outside Paul's hotel, in the shadows along the fence and smoked a cigarette. He heard him coming half a block away because Paul was whistling. He would have to use his left hand. It was no problem. Sometimes he shot people with his left hand for practice. It worked just as well. He stepped out of the shadows. There was no need to hide. 'Hey Beckmesser,' Paul said before he saw the gun. There was something in his satchel he was trying to grab. The shot hit on target and Paul instantly slumped to the ground. A second shot was rarely needed. His was a trained hand, whether right or left. Paul's satchel fell to the ground beside him. The journal flew out and skittered along the ground, followed by pages of manuscript paper that spilled out onto the street and fluttered listlessly in the night air. The pages didn't put up much of a fight as the young officer gathered them up and stuffed them back into the satchel. Two steps away he retrieved the journal and secured everything back in the satchel. He left Paul lying there, blood running into the street, his eyes wide open and the bullet hole gaping in between. The young officer slung the satchel over his shoulder with an air of authority and strode away. If this war deprived him of his future, then all Germans would be deprived. They would all pay.

Act 1

Toronto, Canada, Present Day

CHAPTER 1

Robert fired the envelope from Bayreuth into the garbage and leaned into the back of his chair. If he were a cartoon there would be a black cloud scribbled over his head. He could practically feel it there – "Gloom Descending" – an undiscovered lugubrious companion to Vaughan William's "Lark Ascending."

He scratched his neck and stared at the discarded envelope. This would be the third year in a row that he was unable to get tickets to the Wagner festival and the random fashion in which they handed out tickets was beginning to irk him. The first time he'd attended was back in 1985 when James Levine had conducted *Parsifal*. Spellbound, he'd sat in his seat in the twentieth row as the music held him captive across Wagner's mystic abyss. It was a dream come true for him, to be able to sit in the very theatre that Richard Wagner had built. He'd gone early so he could wander up and down the rows and up to the balcony. He swept his hand along the backs of the seats, knowing that at some point in the past the hand of Richard Wagner also had grazed these surfaces.

Earlier, he sat on the steps of Wahnfried, Wagner's home in Bayreuth and stood where he was buried, right behind the house with Cosima and his beloved dog, Robber. The paths in the public gardens were unchanged from the days when Wagner wandered the same paths while contemplating his work. He ate his meals at *Die Eule* along with other Wagner scholars and enthusiasts. On the walls of the restaurant were hundreds of photographs of musicians and performers who had spent their summers there. There was an old piano in the corner that according to the owner had been damaged in the war and a sign rested on the closed keyboard that read: DO NOT TOUCH.

A small upholstered bench in Wahnfried had to be covered with a plexiglass box because everybody who sat on it picked away a bit of the thread in order to have a souvenir to take with them. Robert knew he would have been one of those people. Back in the day when Cosima Wagner still lived there, thieves had taken a pair of Wagner's glasses and a set of wooden shoe impressions right out of the library. What Robert would give to have those glasses sitting on his desk right now. He often wondered where they might have ended up. Instead, as homage to Wagner, he carried his reading glasses in a lilac case, much like the one Wagner used for his glasses.

Robert absently spun the globe on the stand beside him – the world when Ceylon and Siam still existed. His mind drifted … *Parsifal*, Bayreuth, 1951 … the first festival to be staged after the war. Knappertsbusch conducts. The stage, nothing but a shimmer of light, a cavern of shadow. And the music begins, billowing from the hidden orchestra pit like sacred smoke. Wagner's music and the town of Bayreuth resurrected after the war.

Later, he would have to tell his mother about the tickets. She would be happy he wasn't going. She abhorred Wagner. "Wagner and I don't get along," she always said. "We clash."

When she said it like that it sounded like a joke, but Robert knew it was no joke, even though he didn't exactly know why.

• • • •

The telephone rang. He carried it over to the chaise longue, still ringing, kicked off his slippers and stretched out his legs.

"Hello?"

"Robert?"

"Yes."

"When will you be here?" It was Johanna, his mother, calling to make sure he remembered that tonight was Tuesday and he'd agreed to come to dinner. He wiggled his toes in his socks. His feet itched.

"I just got in." He tugged at the toe of one sock and then the other and stretched his legs out and wiggled his toes again in the fresh air.

"Six?"

The clock read ten to five. There would be time for a quick shower.

"Sure. Six will be fine."

"You can come earlier if you want."

"I'm going to have a shower." His fingers absently tapped a Bach fugue on the arm of the chair.

"Bring my containers back."

"I will." They said goodbye and Robert rested his head. Light dappled the parquet floor. He gazed over at his piano that took up most of the dining room – a gleaming baby grand Steinway with a book of Strauss *Lieder* open on the stand. Perhaps tomorrow he would buy some pale roses to place beside the bust of Wagner that glowered at him from a bookshelf. Roses were Wagner's favourite flower.

He made his way to the kitchen to wash out the plastic containers his mother wanted returned. The curtains matched the placemats – a gift from his mother, hand-sewn in the second bedroom of her apartment. The fabric was pale, checked gingham, like a southern belle's school dress. There were mornings he sat and stared back and forth from the curtain to the place mat while his toast and peanut butter went cold – and could not imagine coming up with the idea to match those things.

• • • •

At five to six he waited for the elevator, dressed in fresh pants and a clean shirt. He carried his jacket over his arm to hide the paunch that had surreptitiously appeared above his belt in the last few weeks. Tonight he'd finally conceded a belt hole to accommodate it. Behind one door was the sound of a basketball or hockey game. It didn't matter which it was. All sportscasts sounded the same to Robert. The hallway smelled of yesterday's roast. A dog yipped ferociously behind another door. It was the miniature Dachshund that barked and growled at Robert whenever he had the misfortune of riding the elevator with it and the pudding-armed woman who owned it. He turned his head when he heard another door click open. His heart raced and he willed the elevator to hurry before she had a chance to get there. But the wait could be interminable for the elevator as it was now, and Marcelline, beaming, swooped into position beside him. She had to make a pass behind him to get on his left side. That she was deaf in one ear was one of the very first things she had told him, as they were standing waiting for the elevator the day after she'd moved in.

"I have no idea what that means," he had said, quite in earnest and she collapsed against the wall in gales of laughter.

"Deaf," she cried and pointed at her left ear, one that was adorned with two thick steel hoops. "You know, deaf."

"Yes, I know deaf," he said defensively. "What I mean is do I have to treat you a certain way because of it? Do you have special needs?"

This was when she punched him in the arm and said, "Does it look like it? You're funny, Robert."

There was a dragon tattooed onto her neck that breathed fire into her deaf ear. He rubbed his deltoid where her bony knuckles had connected and felt an instant, unnerving attraction to her. On their way down on the elevator she stood right beside him with her good ear cocked in case he should say something. "Beethoven was deaf in both ears and probably never told a soul," he offered.

"What?"

Three weeks after he had moved into the apartment his mother was astonished that he had yet to meet any of his neighbours. Since then he'd been able to tell her about Marcelline. It always made his mother laugh, the way he described her. Marcelline smoked marijuana – the smell drifted from under her door along the entire corridor – and she listened to classic rock music. The messy way she put up her hair to reveal her slender neck and fire-breathing dragon made Robert squirm. She wore tight t-shirts with rock logos and had that flirty, unabashed manner that so many young girls had these days. Every time she saw him she mentioned piano lessons. He could only imagine what people would think if they saw him, a forty-year-old man, leaning over a twenty-one-year-old girl as he guided her through a Bach Invention and tried to avoid looking down her shirt. "I've never had private students," he told her. And it would stay that way.

• • • •

"Hi Robert." Dressed in black jeans, heavy black combat boots and an ill-fitting tattered black sweater, her hair still wet from the shower. Over her shoulder was slung an army surplus backpack which looked like it contained a week's worth of survival supplies. He clutched his jacket to him.

"Hello." He turned to the elevator and pushed the "down" button. "Damn thing."

"You only have to press it once. Pressing it like that all the time means you feel like you're losing control. They've done experiments with rats."

"Is that so?" He pressed the button again. Pulled in his stomach. "Why rats?"

"I don't know. They always use rats." She giggled in a way that reminded Robert of bubbles rising in a glass of champagne. For some reason she giggled at most things he said.

"Were the rats able to express their feelings of loss of control to the scientists? Why don't those scientists station themselves beside a real elevator and ask real people? What can a rat tell them?"

"Lots," she said in a tone to indicate she wasn't stupid. If her hands weren't full she would have punched Robert in the arm. "Something in their brains changed. They got all stressed out."

Robert sighed. Stressed out indeed. His stomach relaxed. "Maybe they should play light classics for the rats while they wait. Maybe *Hooked on Classics*. See if their brains still zing uncontrollably."

Finally the elevator arrived and they both got on. Marcelline adjusted her backpack. Robert deduced that she had a change of shoes in there and probably a science fiction paperback with druids and bright colours on the cover. It was a tattered old canvas bag that had been written on in ink, no doubt by all of her pot-smoking friends. He was pretty sure she had a fat cat in her apartment, judging by the clots of hair that were always stuck to her pant legs. She worked at a restaurant called The Cocoa Bean on Lakeshore Boulevard and had suggested more than once that Robert come for breakfast when she worked the day shift. In fact, every time they rode the elevator together, she mentioned it. He braced himself.

"Next week I'm on days again if you want to try the all-day breakfast." She made a motion with her hand that was meant to nudge his arm but she stopped short. Why she kept asking him, he had no idea. His friend Leonard maintained she was flirting with him and didn't understand why Robert didn't just go for breakfast one day. He had been by the restaurant. It was a typical hippie hangout and he imagined the air smelled of incense and the menu featured tofu, whole foods and herbal tea infusions.

"Do they have brownies? I'm not much of a breakfast eater."

"But it's all-day. Come when you're hungry. You must get hungry sometime. It's all organic." She laughed again as they got off on the main floor. "Of course there are brownies. But no funky ones, if that's what you're wondering."

And she ran off to catch her bus, waving goodbye to Robert, her boots clomping on the sidewalk. You're no gazelle, he thought.

• • • •

In the car he listened to the Dvorak cello concerto. The extra he'd spent on the stereo in his car was worth every penny. It was almost as good as the sound he got out of his Rotel stereo in the apartment. He had to be careful what he listened to while he drove because it could put him into a trance. Beethoven's *Ninth* was out of the question. How could anyone concentrate on the road with that piece of music in the air?

He pulled into the visitor parking and sat in the car while the piece finished. Frank, the doorman opened the door to the building for him and then scuttled ahead of Robert to get the elevator.

"Good evening, Dr. Turner." Frank was a stout, wheezy man who had a crush on Johanna. It concerned Robert that he hadn't been able to get a straight answer out of his mother regarding this crush. There was a possibility she didn't mind it.

"Good evening, Frank."

"Heading up to your mother's?"

"I am. Would you like me to return some of those containers for you?" Robert could see there were a few on Frank's desk – no doubt from Johanna. Robert remembered that his were on his kitchen counter.

"Oh, no thanks. I've got to wash them out first."

"Hmm. I see." Sneaky little runt, Robert thought.

The elevator came and Frank pressed the button for the seventh floor. Thankfully a taxi pulled up and Frank did not ride the elevator up with Robert.

"Did you bring the containers?" Johanna could see that he hadn't. Robert shrugged. "I forgot. I tried to bring Frank's up but he wouldn't let me."

"Have a scotch. I remembered to get some. Goodness, your hands are dirty."

Robert regarded the ink on his fingers for a moment. From the papers he'd started grading before he left. He shrugged and looked at the drinks tray as his mother disappeared into the kitchen. She had purchased a bar scotch for him, oh well. He poured one for himself and a Canadian Club for her. He sniffed the air – coq au vin. And perhaps a cake? He couldn't tell.

The apartment, a sprawling twelve hundred square feet, faced the lakeshore. Windows all along the south wall, a long balcony with all-day sun. A pleasant view to the east, sky and water, and on a clear day the skyline of Toronto. Hamilton's smokestacks on the far shore to the southwest pumping white plumes of smoke high into the sky. At night there were orange and green flames visible at their base. Directly below the building was a bicycle path that stretched all along the lake towards Hamilton and right below the balcony stood a three-story house that served as a private preschool. Morning, noon and night there was a constant parade of minivans and mothers delivering and picking up their preschoolers. And in between an unbearable uproar, as high-pitched preschool voices shrieked from the garden as their minds painfully expanded.

Felix, his mother's cockatiel, squawked at him from his perch. "Shut it," Robert said.

"Shut it," Felix said back. Robert smiled.

"Smart ass."

"Smart ass," the bird echoed from between the bright orange patches on his cheeks. Felix's big plume crested off his head, like a cream topping on the bird's white body.

Robert took his drink out to the balcony and gazed at the lake. It was a deep blue today and dotted with sailboats. He sat down. There was a strange object on the table beside him. It was a purple butterfly fashioned out of bits of dusty glass and shiny metal inside of which sat an unlit tea light.

"Where did you get that *objet d'art*?" He pointed at the butterfly. Johanna had come outside for a moment to look at the view.

"Oh, something Pearl bought for me off the shopping channel. It's quite pretty, really."

"Really?"

"Oh, Robert. Sometimes people want to do nice things. She hasn't got anybody, you know. It's sad."

"If you say so." He tipped his head back and pretended to shake the last drops from a bottle into his mouth.

"Oh, come on. She doesn't drink that much."

"You're right. She drinks just enough." Robert took a sip of his scotch. It didn't matter to him. Pearl was just one more person Johanna ministered to. "I ran into Marcelline on the elevator. She thinks rats would enjoy classical music."

"Mmm, I'm sure. Where is it that she works again?"

"The Cocoa Bean."

"I'd like to take Pearl to lunch tomorrow. After we shop."

"I don't think the place is licensed."

"Stop it. You're no saint either." She refilled his glass. "I have to check the rice."

"Do you want me to set the table?"

"It's already done. We can eat in ten minutes. What do you want for your birthday?"

"That's not until next week."

"I know, but I need to plan. I thought maybe a ham. You like ham."

That he did. With sweet mustard sauce. A recipe she had learned from her mother-in-law years ago.

"I'll make scalloped potatoes too. Is that okay?"

"Sounds perfect."

"And it will heat up nice after."

She left Robert outside where his eyes rested on the lake and he wondered if those sailors knew that they could only get as far as Rochester. No serious seafaring would occur on those waters. Just once around the bay and then back to the marina for martinis and canapés.

At the dinner table the dishes of food all gravitated towards Robert. Johanna pecked at her plate while Robert took a second helping of the chicken.

"I heard from Bayreuth today. No tickets again this year."

"Oh. That's too bad."

She didn't raise her head and kept shuttling grains of rice around on her plate. Many times they performed this dance – steadying hands clasped to proverbial shoulders, a few awkward and clumsy steps and then back on sure footing and balance once again restored.

"I made a cherry torte for dessert. Do you want some now?"

She was on her feet and clearing away the dishes while Robert leaned back and patted his stomach. "I'll wait a minute."

"Do you want coffee?"

"Sure."

He got up and carried a few things into the kitchen. On the counter Johanna had placed a couple of containers. Robert eyed the pot and estimated there would be enough for him and Frank and Johanna to have some leftovers. The coffee machine gurgled. He leaned over the cake and breathed in.

"There will be enough for you to take some home."

"There always is."

CHAPTER 2

Once Robert had left, Johanna cut the cake into large slabs – one on a plate for Pearl and another into an empty yogurt container for Frank. It was only eight o'clock so she slipped on her shoes, stepped out into the hallway and knocked on Pearl's door. Johanna heard Pearl's slippered feet shuffling towards the door. "Coming," her voice called. The thin sound of the television could be heard. The television was always on at Pearl's.

Pearl was wearing a worn lilac sweat suit, her feet shod in equally worn slippers. Johanna made a note that slippers might be a nice gift for Pearl's birthday. Her neighbour smelled of alcohol.

"Oh, Johanna," she drawled. Her voice sounded faintly like she was from the deep South. Her face lit up when she saw the cake. Her fingers, painted a while ago with pink polish, clasped the doorframe as she steadied herself. "You baked again. I don't know how you do it."

Johanna proffered the cake and the door was immediately held open to her. She shook her head. "Robert was just over and I have to clean up. I just wanted you to have a piece while it's fresh."

"Will you be shopping tomorrow?"

"Sure, I thought we could have lunch too."

"Oooh," Pearl pursed her lips. "I don't know if I'll feel up to it. I don't need much. Just some milk, and maybe a bit of Cheese Whiz."

"Well, then it won't take very long."

It was important for Pearl to get out once in awhile. Johanna knew she drank all alone in her apartment. Sometimes she offered Johanna a glass of apricot brandy that she accepted so as not to make her feel bad. It was easy to get drunk when you had nothing else to do. She noticed that Pearl got flustered in the grocery store and bought a lot of processed cakes and instant noodles. This was what happened to people who spent too much time alone. They forgot how to cope.

"That's awfully nice of you but it would probably be easier if I gave you some money. I'll just slow you down."

"You can pay me after if you're not going to come."

"You always say that and never take any money. It makes me feel bad. Here." Pearl fumbled in her change purse and produced a folded bill. She handed it to Johanna. "I think that's a ten. Can you check?"

Johanna took the bill from her. "That's fine. I'll bring some bread, too, and a few bananas. They're good for you."

Pearl beamed. "Maybe you'll have time for coffee tomorrow."

"I'll knock when I get home," she said and backed away towards her own door. "Good night, Pearl."

Tomorrow she would knock at the door again and insist Pearl come along. Sometimes people didn't know what was best for them. She was sure once Pearl got a little fresh air and activity she would feel better. Besides, Johanna wanted to be out of the house when Barbara called. She would be back from her trip to Germany and Johanna anticipated the phone call with a shudder. Barbara would have stories and greetings from all the friends and remaining relatives she had seen. She no longer asked Johanna to join her on these trips. At first it was easy to refuse. Magdeburg had become a part of the Russian sector – East Germany. Johanna couldn't be bothered with the visa application and the hassle that travel to East Germany entailed. When Barbara went she had to present herself at the police station to say she had arrived. They demanded twenty-five dollars a day be exchanged for East German marks. It would be fine if there were anything worth spending the money on, but even Barbara said she was hard pressed to spend it all and she was not allowed to take it with her when she left. The shelves in most stores were empty. Barbara described lining up at the bakery in the morning along with kindergarten teachers, all vying for the same loaves of bread and buns. Once everything was sold, the bakery closed for the day. They only made so much and when it was gone, it was gone. The Intershops, where Western goods could be bought, required Western currency. It all sounded absurd and pointless to Johanna, even after unification.

It had nothing to do with the past, the way Barbara always insisted. Johanna's home was here now, in Canada. There was nothing to go back there for. Barbara and her husband Ferdi used to like to go to the German Club on the weekends to dance and eat fatty sausages with sauerkraut and gossip with the other Germans about their trips to Spain and Norway. They discussed where to buy the best beef roast for their *sauerbraten* and which shops sold the German language magazines. "It's like a little bit of home. Everybody speaks German. We have all been through the same experience – the war, then immigrating to Canada and settling here. It's nice to talk to people who understand."

They may have all been in Germany at the same time but Johanna doubted the war was the same for everyone. It would be a long time before anyone could claim to understand what she had been through. She had ceased trying to understand it many years ago when she made the decision to settle here and leave the past to someone else.

• • • •

Felix scuttled back and forth on his perch, wanting a treat before she covered him up for the night. She plucked a grape from the bunch and fed it to him through the bars of the cage. "What do you say?" She asked. "Say JoJo."

The bird blinked and pecked at the cage, impatient for the grape. "Come on. You talk for Robert. Say JoJo."

Finally, she gave up and let the bird have the grape. Robert only taught him silly things to say. She couldn't understand why the bird refused to learn her name. She finished tidying the kitchen and went to bed. Tomorrow she would go to the mall and find a gift for Robert's birthday, maybe new towels. Men never bought those kinds of things for themselves. As she brushed her teeth she thought of Pearl – all alone. In one sense humans were the only animals that took in and cared for those failing to thrive. The weak weren't left behind to die as nature intended. On the other hand there were so many poor souls that had no one to care for them. They lived in isolation and hardly managed to feed and bathe themselves. The hospital was full of frail, lonely old people who had nowhere to go and lived out the days that were left them in pyjamas and diapers, reliant on kind nurses to feed them fruit and watch that they didn't choke on their Ensure. Nobody's life should end that way, yet so many did.

• • • •

Back in his parking garage, Robert gathered up his briefcase from the passenger seat of his car. He had bought his silver Mercedes 230E used, but it was fully loaded and in excellent condition and the ride was incredibly smooth and quiet. The alarm bleeped when he aimed the remote and locked the doors. Inside the elevator, he pushed the button for the eleventh floor. The elevator stopped on the main floor where a gruff-looking man got on with an unruly dog. This was what people resorted to for company. Robert stiffened in their presence. Thankfully they got out on the third floor. He managed to grunt when the man wished him a good night and took a deep breath once the elevator doors shut.

Inside his apartment he secured the door's two locks and the security chain, put his food away and then settled in his study with a stiff dollop of Laphroaig and placed a CD in the stereo.

Robert tapped his baton on the coffee table, the score to Wagner's "Tannhäuser Overture" open in front of him. Rehearsals with the faculty/student orchestra began tomorrow and he knew that this early in the season the musicians would be rusty. They would chatter non-stop and try his patience. But he looked forward to getting back to it anyway. The tall speakers angled towards him and he raised his hands and waited. The distant harmony of the brass rolled across the room. He cued the cellos in the right speaker with a quiet motion of his hand. Then the violins, soaring octaves. He waved the pulsed beat with his left hand and then the theme swelled, carried by the brass and the strings. He swept his hair from his brow. The horn took up the theme again and he cued the trombone. On his feet as the last bars neared and he conducted now with his eyes closed and fists clenched. As the last chord faded he flopped onto the sofa and gasped for breath. Wagner's music never failed him. It pulled his heart up and right out of him and reached for infinite horizons. It made him weak in the knees – the most whole music he had ever heard, the orchestra, the voices, all blended into sublime perfection. It was as astonishing as an orange or a rose. Such perfection could not possibly be man-made. It had to come from the earth itself.

The first time he'd heard Wagner was during one of their summer visits to see his Aunt Barbara and Uncle Ferdi and his cousin Albert in Calgary. The boys played in the basement during the hottest days. Albert had been given a record player but the only records he had were his father's classical records. Naturally the boys decided that the one with the soldier in armour on the cover would be the most to their liking. They dressed up in soldiers' costumes, played the opera music loud, and pretended it was a soundtrack to a war movie. Albert, with twenty pounds and three years on Robert, would always end the scene by sitting on Robert's chest with some sort of weapon pointed at his head as the music came to its dramatic end.

At home, his parents' musical tastes included The James Last Orchestra and Perry Como. Years later, when he was a teenager, he and his friend Leonard were browsing in a record store for Pink Floyd and Led Zepplin records. Robert came upon a recording of *Lohengrin*, and remembering those summer holidays, decided to buy it. Had his mother reacted with indifference he may never even have listened to it. But when she saw it, her face twisted and it bewildered him that she would become upset at such a purchase when other kids were buying Black Sabbath albums.

"What on earth do you want with that?" He remembered her exact words, her face contorted in an effort to remain calm.

"Albert and I used to listen to it. I bought it for the memories." A cheeky brat at fifteen.

"Albert… I should have known. Ferdi probably had them just lying around."

That Wagner should not be left lying around like porn magazines shouldn't be made so little sense to Robert that he listened to his recording many times, trying to hear whatever it was that was so sinister. The music grew on him and he bought several more Wagner recordings. While he sat downstairs in the rec room, he read the liner notes and soon was bringing books home from the library and every time his mother made a face he grinned and said, "Hey, it could be worse. I could be a mass murderer."

It was a comment Johanna didn't find funny at all, not that he'd expected her to. Soon, in order to better understand what he was listening to, he asked for piano lessons. At school he played trombone in the band, so he had a bit of a head start. His father deferred the conversations about piano lessons to his mother, who had a way of avoiding the topic the way some parents never brought up hockey because they didn't want a lifetime of exorbitant costs and early mornings.

After his father died, Robert knew that Johanna was eager to steer him along a virtuous path. When Robert asked again it was so reasonable a request that she could hardly refuse. "I'll think about it. But no Wagner. At least not when I'm home."

"Why not? Does it have something to do with the war?"

She did not answer right away and Robert watched her knitted brow for clues as she wrestled to find an answer. To dislike something so strongly and then not be able to explain it was odd. Robert waited, curious. "It's so loud," she eventually claimed. "There's nothing refined about it, just a lot of bellowing and huffing. I like music to calm me."

"Is it because Wagner was played so much during the war?" he persisted. It was maddening the way she never told him anything about the war when she had been right there and probably had plenty of stories to tell that would interest a fifteen-year-old. Sometimes he thought that he knew more than she did.

"I never heard any Wagner during the war."

"Hitler loved Wagner."

"Where did you hear something like that? How does a child know what Hitler liked and didn't like?"

"I'm fifteen." Boasting now. "At those rallies they used the overture from *Die Meistersinger* all the time. You should know. You were there. Albert told me. He knows a lot about the war from Auntie Barbara and you never tell me anything."

"There's nothing to tell. It was a terrible time. You should consider yourself lucky to be growing up in this country. War does awful things to people. Perfectly normal people go crazy."

"Like Uncle Heinz?"

Her face blanched. "What did that Albert tell you about Heinz?"

"He killed people. Jews. Six million of 'em." Such a sassy brat when he wanted to be.

Johanna's breath quickened and she clamped her hands onto his shoulders and shook him. "You listen to me. Nobody knew about those things until much later; the things that went on there. Nobody knew."

"That's what they all say," he cried, twisting away from her grip. "Hitler kills millions of Jews and nobody notices? Come on!"

"No piano!" she blurted out. "It's out of the question."

"Fine! I'll pay for the lessons myself." He shouted at her, not noticing her hands trembling or her eyes blazing with fright. "I can practise over at my Jewish friend Leonard's house."

"Wait," she lowered herself to a chair. "You know I like Leonard. He's a fine boy. And such nice parents." His words had stunned her like he knew they would. He might as well have slapped her across the face. Instantly he felt ashamed. But he couldn't understand it. Ever since he'd been friends with Leonard she grew visibly alarmed at the sound of his name. "You know I have no issue with Jewish people, but what must they think of us?" she had said "They make me nervous, that's all. I don't know what's expected of me when I am around them."

Robert paused, then sat down. He didn't like to see his mother upset.

"Your father would have wanted you to have lessons. I'm sorry." She reached for his hand. "We will get a piano and you find a teacher, okay?"

Robert nodded, a lump in his throat. It is a poor son who makes his mother cry. Johanna got up and stirred their ground beef and tomato dinner. "Dinner's in ten minutes."

After that, Johanna hardly spoke to Barbara for a long time and Robert felt terrible for blurting out all that about Heinz. He wanted his mother to be able to talk to her only sister without getting angry.

• • • •

Robert's dining room/study was decorated to reflect Wagner's taste. The piano was the centrepiece. Colourful Turkish rugs lay on the floor and heavy drapes on the windows. On the wall beside the window he had framed the words: "Here where my delusions have found peace, let this place be named Wahnfried." The same words Wagner had inscribed above the entrance to his house in Bayreuth. There was also an engraving of Wagner's house, and of course, the bust of Richard Wagner himself. Robert sat down at the piano. His fingers thrummed a G minor chord while he stared at the stone face of Wagner. Stern, genius, unrelentingly productive – what Robert would give to be able to compose such music.

He stretched his hands out in front of him and settled on the bench. Play from the beginning and see what comes. Determined to sit at least an hour, even if nothing came, Robert shifted the manuscript papers to the Allegro he had been working on and played it through. It was not bad, perhaps a bit too plaintive, but the human ear had a resonance with those kinds of sounds. Perhaps he should write the last movement and then return to the Adagio. A rondo would work well with the oboe and horn, he thought. The cello and horn could simply echo what the violin and oboe began. Like a fugue in rondo style. Or a rondo in the style of a fugue. Yes, that was it. He plinked away on the piano and within the hour had a fair sketch of the last movement and a good idea of the theme for the Adagio that would lead into the Rondo with no break. Sometimes working backwards was the best way to move forwards. These compositions were a hobby. Nobody would ever hear them. Occasionally he wrote out the parts and had the orchestra try them. He joked about it at rehearsal in case what came out sounded simplistic and childish and often it did. Works in progress he called them no matter how much time he had spent on them. Some of the pieces he had written were not too bad and one year at a performance he had dedicated half the concert to his work.

After two hours at the piano, a stiff back forced Robert up and into the kitchen. He drained the juice from a can of salmon into the sink. Brain food, his mother would say. Robert scuffed at the floor with the tip of his slipper while he waited for the toaster. Irises on floor tiles, an idea someone had come up with. People all over, thinking and coming up with ideas and getting paid for their efforts. Were irises on floor tiles as satisfying as deciding on the oboe and horn for the rondo? Possibly. The toast popped. Robert carried his plate to the kitchen table and listened to the news on the radio. At the table he leafed through the score for "Firebird Suite" and imagined the tempo for the first section. He'd have to beat in twelve for the bassoons to get their parts. He flipped to the "Danse Infernal" and became suddenly anxious. What had he been thinking? They would never pull it off. It was too difficult, but he had a strong wind section this year and wanted to show them off. He stared at a section where the winds were playing in three and the strings in two. It would be conducted in one, leaving it up to the players to watch and count. The back of his neck prickled. Catastrophe loomed behind every beat. The piece could shatter at any moment into a million dazzling shards, sending the audience running for cover. He wondered how many rehearsals it took Stravinsky with his orchestra to get the piece right.

The sun was bright and bathed the balcony in gold light. Robert stepped outside to warm up. He leaned against the railing and gazed into the sun. There was a man who lived in the building across from him who stood out on his balcony every evening. Often they would both be out at the same time. Robert was acutely aware of their shared solitude. Both of them alone on separate balconies, sharing the view. It was how he often felt with his mother while growing up. She often seemed to be out of range, emitting a weak and distant signal that was somehow meant to connect them. When he was young, he would amuse himself at the playground in the sandbox surrounded by other children while Johanna sat alone in the middle of a bench. The other mothers sat together and talked. After they scolded their children they laughed. But Johanna never scolded him. She sat and read a paperback until he had played enough and asked to be taken home. At times her loneliness stifled him and he preferred to be taken home rather than witness her isolation. He would gather up his toys and pack them into his playground bag and demand she take him home.

"Why don't you talk with the other mothers?"

"I prefer to read when I have a chance. I spend all day at work talking. If I have an hour to sit in the park, I like to be quiet."

Reasonable questions and reasonable answers. He was a child. He believed everything she said. He did not yet recognize when she was being evasive. He learned that later but he also learned not to press. Something about his mother demanded caution. She had an inherent fragility, like a pretty egg that would surely shatter if cracked.

CHAPTER 3

Johanna spotted the flashing light on her answering machine as soon as she got in. Without stopping to undo her scarf, she pressed the retrieve button. It was Barbara, letting her know she had arrived home safely and would call again later. Even without Ferdi she continued to make trips to Germany. When Ferdi died of a heart attack five years ago, Johanna was not surprised and had to dig deep to muster up some sympathy for her sister's loss. To Johanna, Ferdi represented everything she abhorred about her native country. Just another fat, loud-mouthed German, she thought. When Barbara had excitedly called her to tell her that she was getting married to him, Johanna had to steel herself not to say anything. But it angered her that Barbara would bring him into their small circle. Johanna had worked hard to bury her past and now every time she visited Barbara there was Ferdi to contend with. Opinionated and crude, he drank endless bottles of Wahrsteiner beer and Barbara cooked pork hocks and dumpling dinners that left Johanna bloated and dull.

She hung up her coat and glanced briefly into the hallway mirror before carrying her bags into the dining room and depositing them onto the table. She pulled her shoulders back and stood up straight. More and more she noticed a stoop to her posture. It would not suit her to turn into one of those bent-over older women. Her silver bangs were getting long. Maybe next week she could book an appointment. Her lipstick had worn away at the centre, leaving only a ring of pink at the outside edge. No need to reapply it now when she was about to eat lunch.

Felix squawked when he saw her. "Just a minute, Felix." She unpacked the towels she had picked up for Robert and decided he would like them after all. She had taken a long time deciding. There were so many to choose from. The ones she finally settled on were white with two shades of green stripes. It was hard to believe he would be forty-one in two days. It made her feel like she had lived a long time.

For her lunch she ate two slices of bread with Swiss cheese, a scoop of cottage cheese and four tinned sardines. She ate at the dining room table and watched Felix try to get her attention by rattling the mirror with his beak. He would pick it up and fling it side to side so that it clapped against the bars. He really was a clever bird. She just wished he would learn her name.

"Okay Felix. Here I come." Johanna opened the cage and pressed her finger against his chest. The parrot, excited by the prospect of freedom, quickly hopped onto her finger and clucked with pleasure. "Jo, Jo," she sang to him. "Jo, Jo." He bobbed his head at her but wouldn't talk.

After she left Felix on his favourite vantage point on the bookcase, Johanna stretched out on the sofa and shut her eyes. The pillow rested at an uncomfortable angle under her head. But she did not adjust it fearing she might fall asleep. At three o'clock she wanted to bake cranberry-bran muffins to bring to the hospital tomorrow when she had her volunteer shift. The girls all liked her baking. They took turns bringing in treats but usually the others picked up Tim Hortons donuts or store-bought cookies.

The telephone rang and Johanna jumped to answer.

"Johanna?" It was Barbara, calling again from Calgary.

"You're back."

"Yes, I'm back. What a wonderful trip," Barbara said in German. Johanna frowned. She wished Barbara would speak English to her. After all this time Barbara still sometimes mixed the two languages when on the phone. "Were you sleeping?"

"Just resting." Johanna replied in English. "I have to bake muffins for tomorrow." Johanna picked at the pilled fabric on the arm of the sofa. "How are you?"

"Good, good. I walked by Tante Ilse's house. The people living there now have put in all new windows and ugly shutters. The rose bushes are still blooming, but everything else is so modern now. All the houses look different."

They had lived with Tante Ilse in West Berlin after the war. It was easy before the wall was built to travel with the S-Bahn or U-Bahn from East to West. To leave East Germany permanently you either stayed in a refugee camp or with relatives in the West. They hadn't taken much with them when they fled Magdeburg and had not told anyone they were leaving. It was better for those left behind if they could truthfully say they had no idea where the girls had gone. It was in Berlin that Johanna did her nurse's training and Barbara finished school. If there was anyone in Germany Johanna might have wanted to see, it would have been Tante Ilse. Without her, they couldn't have come to Canada. Johanna always made sure to give Barbara some money for a bottle of schnapps for her.

"Albert is coming for a visit. Just a short one – a couple of days between shows." Johanna listened to Barbara prattle on. She never seemed to run out of things to say.

"That sounds lovely. When was the last time you saw him?" Albert, Johanna's only nephew, sang professionally for Gilbert and Sullivan productions and travelled most of the year. Johanna rarely had a chance to see him anymore. They chatted awhile longer about nothing in particular. Barbara asked about Robert.

"It's his birthday next week. We'll have dinner."

Felix chirruped at her from his perch. His feet scratched along the spines of books and scattered dried bird droppings onto the floor. Johanna held the phone between her shoulder and ear and clapped her hands at him. He scuttled to the far corner and cooed. There was a knock at the door.

"Someone is at the door," Johanna said. "Just let me see."

Johanna knew it would be Pearl knocking at the door looking for her groceries. When Johanna had knocked that morning she hadn't answered even though Johanna knew very well she was in there watching *The Price is Right*. She let Pearl in and indicated to her that she was on the phone. "Barbara, I'll call you back. Pearl just arrived for a cup of coffee."

"Ja, gut. Bis später."

Johanna hung up. "My sister."

"Oh, the one in Calgary?" Pearl stuttered towards the sofa and sat down with a sigh. Johanna did not smell any alcohol on her today. She didn't drink every day, or maybe she had run out. Pearl never asked Johanna to buy her liquor or cigarettes and Johanna never offered. Once in awhile Pearl took a taxi to the liquor store and the convenience store and bought what she needed.

"Yes. She calls sometimes. We call. Would you like a sandwich? I've got leftover sardines."

"Mmm, that sounds good. I haven't eaten a sardine in years."

When Johanna brought her a plate, Pearl poked at the bread. "Look at this stuff. I didn't know bread could have so many seeds."

"It's a hearty rye. It's good for you,"

"Sure. How can it not be?"

Pearl ate while Johanna watched. What Pearl ate was of great concern to her. Alcoholics typically suffered from poor nutrition. The call from Barbara had thrown her off and Johanna had a hard time listening to Pearl's stories about her television programs and the news of her one nephew who called her once a month from somewhere in the States. Baltimore? It was always Barbara who called her. Even though they shared a past, there was not much to say in the present and Johanna had a hard time thinking of reasons to call. Before she knew it, time slipped by, the phone rang and it would be Barbara again. She swept up the little pile of pilled fabric from the arm of the sofa and dropped into the waste paper basket beside her desk. Johanna hated to admit it, but she had felt relief when Pearl had rung the doorbell ending the phone call. Even when she and Barbara talked about their sons, the conversation centred on music since they both had chosen musical careers. Barbara had no idea how these talks upset Johanna and would have been utterly shocked to hear that Johanna would never have wished the gift of music upon her son or her nephew. There was such a gulf there between the two sisters. Two people on opposite sides of the country, their voices strained through the turbulent air.

When Pearl left she packed up some cake for her. She saw her to the door and rode the elevator down to bring a piece of cake to Frank.

• • • •

Frank leapt to his feet when he saw Johanna in the doorway with cake for him. "Johanna, not again!"

"Don't pretend you don't want any. I have to make muffins yet so you might as well have what's left of this."

He cleared the newspaper off a chair and Johanna sat down. There was a bank of monitors in his small office. The building had several security cameras set up around the perimeter. On his desk lay a half-eaten sandwich and a thermos of coffee. No matter what the time of day, Frank always seemed to be in the middle of a sandwich. His sketchpad was closed, three sharpened pencils on top.

"Any progress today?"

"I'll get to it later. I have so many versions of that view." He pointed to the tree on the boulevard. "I need to move my office."

"Soon it will be winter. That will change the view."

Frank screwed up his face. "Don't say that. Not yet."

Johanna had said to him once that he had the best job of all, to be able to see what was happening outside from inside. He could see who was coming around the corner before they could see him. "That's what security is," he agreed.

A few art reproductions hung in his office and Johanna liked to look at them when she sat here. Frank was an unlikely art enthusiast, in brown uniform and stiff hat. But there they were: a Monet, an A.Y. Jackson and an abstract by Kandinsky.

"What is it you like about those?" she had asked.

"The colour. All day I stare at these black and white monitors. I have those in here so my brain doesn't forget that there is beauty to be seen. I don't want to get to a point where I am incapable of recognizing beauty."

"I guess that's the purpose of art. To remind us of that." Johanna stared at the paintings. Her eyes saw brushstrokes and colour and she knew beauty was the intent, and she waited for some feeling to well up inside of her as she looked at them, but it didn't come.

"You can buy those anywhere. And they sure make a difference in here."

"I see," she said. And she wished she could.

• • • •

Robert packed his briefcase as he prepared for rehearsal. His stomach rumbled with discontent. There had been no time to pick up anything from the takeout counter at the grocery store and all he had in the fridge was a small container of peach yogurt. He supposed that would be better than nothing. His plate from lunch sat in the sink with a sprinkling of water on it.

A hesitant tap at the door stopped him. Through the peephole he saw Marcelline and his heart lurched, a sensation he only ever attributed to fear, although what he had to fear from this young girl he hardly knew. One chain and two deadbolts and there she stood before him.

"I brought you a lamb chop from the restaurant. I hope you haven't eaten." She held a Styrofoam container towards him and the aroma that come from it made his stomach rumble.

"I haven't." He stood there stupidly in the doorway, not sure how to extricate the food from her. "Have you?"

"Yeah, I usually eat at work before I come home. I never feel like cooking after work and I'd never be able to cook food like this anyway."

The statement made Robert instantly suspicious. "I'm surprised they serve lamb at your save-the-whales restaurant."

"If it's organic, they'll cook it up. Try it."

"I was about to have yogurt for dinner."

"Oh." She giggled. "So you do eat healthy food. Well, here. Enjoy."

"Thank you." He took the container and noticed Marcelline looking past him into his apartment. He started to close the door.

"Can I try the piano?"

He turned around as though he didn't know what she was talking about. "Oh, that. I thought you didn't play."

"I don't know how to read music, but I like to play. Everybody likes to play."

There weren't many people he'd had to his apartment, but they inevitably were drawn to the piano. There was art that hung on the walls and books stacked on bookshelves, plants, windows, but it was the piano that drew people in. Not one person ever walked by it without reaching out and touching the keys.

Something in the way he adjusted the door against his shoulder left enough room for Marcelline to slip past him and suddenly she was inside, her backpack deposited by his feet. She smelled faintly of sweat. Her blouse was rumpled and stained with something yellow she had spilled. A loose thread dragged from the hem of her pants. He let the door swing shut and followed her clomping boots in.

Only Johanna disproved Robert's theory about the piano. She never went near it. When he finally got a piano to go with his lessons, it was moved down to the basement where he imagined playing to ghosts that came out of the walls to listen. In the winter it took nearly an hour for his hands to warm up enough to play anything fast. He never heard any music come from his mother, except once he heard her singing when she thought he wasn't at home. She had left the door open and he had heard her from outside. The melody was not familiar to him and the sound of her voice, singing, was even stranger. To this day he had never come across that song but the melody stuck in his head. He had written it out long ago, the way he remembered it. Standing outside with his cheek pressed against the screen, he could only make out the melody, not the words. When he had transcribed what he remembered it was a guess. Over time he had committed the simple melody to memory and often sat at the piano and played the eight bars over and over, like a mantra.

Marcelline had settled onto the bench and her fingers found the notes to "The First Noel."

"Maybe by Christmas you'll have that perfected."

"Oh come on. Why don't you play something for me?"

"I'm about to eat," he said, holding the container up to remind her.

Marcelline plinked gently at some of the keys. "I wish I could play. Why don't you teach?"

"I teach at the university." Did half-deaf mean tone deaf? He was dying to find out.

"A professor?"

"Yes, a professor." She left the piano and wandered aimlessly around his apartment, looking at his books and touching things.

"A music professor. Like in *The Music Man*." He blushed a little at her attempt to impress him.

"With a capitol P that rhymes with T that stands for Turner." Robert turned in the middle of the room as he followed her meanderings around his apartment..

"Professor Turner."

"Well, Doctor actually. But yes. Turner."

"Who's this?" She asked and patted the bust of Wagner on the head. Robert flinched.

"That is Richard Wagner. He is famous for the operas he wrote."

"Opera! All I can think of when I hear opera is Bugs Bunny."

Robert took a step towards the piano and closed the lid while Marcelline was on the other side of the room. "Look, I actually have to leave for rehearsal in half an hour. Maybe I'll stop by the restaurant this weekend and try that breakfast."

"Oh, sure. That would be great."

Great. He was only trying to manoeuvre her out of his apartment, but he could see by the gleam in her eyes that there would be no getting out of it. She flipped her hair back and her fingers played with a thin leather strap around her neck.

He opened the container and held it up to his nose. "Thank you so much for dinner. You've really saved me tonight."

"I thought you might like it. Wait till you try the breakfast. Have a good practice, whatever it is." And she sallied forth to her own apartment leaving Robert in a wake of her sweet scent. He picked up the lamb chop and gnawed off a good chunk. There were tiny roasted potatoes and baby carrots with it and he ate the entire meal with his fingers standing in the middle of his apartment, ill at ease with the invisible boundary that had been breeched.

• • • •

The rehearsal room was in its usual uproar of noise as the musicians warmed up. It was one sound Robert never tired of. Amidst the cacophony Robert discerned the oboist practising her solo, a second violinist hacking through some difficult triplets, and one of the hot shots in the firsts sawing through the opening bars of the Brahm's concerto for no reason. The second French horn trying to hit the high C needed in the second movement. It sounded all right now but when the time came it could come out as anything. And the basses, his beloved basses were thumping out some improvised jazz beats. That was fine – they always knew their parts, even though they fussed about their cues. "You're paid to count," Robert told them even though they always were given their cues. No need to take senseless risks.

He clapped his hands to get everyone to stop playing, the concertmaster took over, and the orchestra tuned. "*Tannhäuser*," he barked. "I'll beat a full bar before you come in, but just this once." He tapped the stand, raised his arms. The horns weren't ready. "Any time in the next three hours would be great." He stood motionless until he could see their eyes. A few people giggled. Four times he started the horns, out of tune and out of time. It had to be perfect, that intro. It sounded nothing like the Berlin Philharmonic, but with practice and persistence, it would come close. The octaves in the strings were a mess but that would be sorted out at the string rehearsal. It better be. It was all texture, that part. Shimmering light dappled across a clear lake. It sounded like sludge right now.

He sweated for the duration of the Stravinsky but much to his amazement the bassoons kept it together. It was not up to the tempo in parts that Robert would like. He may have to compromise – clarity for *vitesse*. There was always the dress rehearsal in the hospital auditorium to try things out. He came upon the space there a few years ago when he had dropped by to pick up his mother. It was astounding to him that a hospital would have such an acoustically wonderful hall that was used for almost nothing but annual general meetings and the children's choirs that visited at Christmas time. His mother had been non-committal when he first asked her and eventually he had found the person to talk to on his own. His idea was well-received. Karen, the volunteer supervisor, thought it would be tremendously uplifting for the patients to hear some music. His mother was not so sure. "It's a lot of work for the volunteers to bring the patients down there."

"Karen said a lot of them could make their own way down. What can you possibly have against these people hearing some music? It's proven that music is a healing thing. Besides, that room is underutilized and the orchestra can use the practice in front of an audience."

She didn't argue with him. "I have nothing against them hearing some music. I just don't see what good it will do. Those heavy classics you like. Why can't you play something light?"

"Like Gilbert and Sullivan?"

"Yes, something like that. Something that might make a person in the hospital feel better."

"I don't see the point in playing music that makes most cultivated people want to throw a knife at someone."

"Well, that's the kind of music most people like. Your cousin Albert makes his living off it because it's so popular. That other stuff is too depressing."

And so it would have carried on had Karen not come up to them just then and proclaimed how marvellous it was that Robert's orchestra was going to start giving performances. She was off to prepare a template for the poster. And Robert was not in the mood to hear another word about his celebrated cousin. The thought of Albert making a living by belting out that insipid music made Robert want to vomit. And by the look on Johanna's face and the way her hands clutched her stomach, he knew she had heard enough as well. He knew she wasn't keen on the idea but she could keep herself busy in the gift shop tidying the sympathy cards if she didn't want to listen.

• • • •

After rehearsal he drove to meet Leonard at the Ivy Room. Leonard had been away for two weeks on a cruise and another two weeks had passed before they both had the time to get together. Robert stepped into the warmth of the room and scanned the tables. Large ceiling fans circulated the air,

Miles Davis played on the sound system. There was a lot of dark wood and polished brass. There were several business types lingering at the bar. Leonard was already seated at a table, sipping a gin and tonic. Robert ordered a Laphroaig.

"Welcome back." Robert clapped his friend on the shoulder, eased into the chair and stretched out his legs. "Rehearsal was a mess tonight."

"Hopeless?" Leonard asked. His eyes wandered beyond Robert's head to the bank of women at the bar.

"Oh no. I'd never say that. It will get sorted out."

Leonard nodded. "Slim pickings here tonight."

"How was the trip?"

"The trip was fine. The women – all beautiful and on the arms of pasty-faced men with British accents. Here, I brought you something."

From his pocket he produced a palm tree fridge magnet.

"I have just the place for it."

"That's your birthday present."

"I got your postcard."

"Did I send you the porpoise or the sea turtle?"

"Sea turtle. Very nice." After a brief pause Robert added, "Marcelline brought me dinner tonight."

"Oh? What was she wearing?" Leonard liked to tease Robert about Marcelline. It was his impression that she was fishing for Robert to ask her out.

"Don't give me that," Robert replied, "I'm old enough to be her father."

"Well, yes. But a young father."

"Yours is a twisted mind. If she's after anything, it's free piano lessons."

"Your mind could stand to be a little more twisted. What did she make you?"

"Lamb chop, from the organic restaurant. It wasn't bad. She wants me to come for breakfast."

"Sounds like a date to me." Leonard signalled the waiter for two more drinks.

"At the restaurant. I doubt she can cook." Robert did not want to fuel Leonard's imagination. "Besides, she's deaf in one ear. You'll never meet her, so forget about it."

He spied a petite brunette in a tweed skirt at the far end of the bar. She cast a glance around the room and smiled when she saw Robert looking. "Hey. There's a brunette over there who's been looking at you."

Leonard whirled around. "Which one?"

"The one at the end."

"She's not looking now."

They sat awhile in the dim light with Robert flipping through a few photos Leonard had taken on his trip. "I'm thinking of doing the Barber 'Adagio for Strings' for the spring concert."

"Oh dear," Leonard made a high-pitched hollow screeching sound to mimic what the strings would surely sound like.

"We'll be doing the whole thing *mezzoforte*."

"Sounds delightful. Very stirring."

After their second drink, Robert slipped away, leaving Leonard behind to chat up the brunette. On the way home, Robert's thoughts flashed back to the time one summer when they were teenagers and in an attempt to rebel, he and Leonard had roamed the neighbourhood setting things on fire. It started innocently enough. Twigs and leaves. Small fires they could easily put out, usually by dousing the weak flames with spit or pop. Then they started on piles of lawn and yard clipping. Lighting them with the Bic lighters that they got at the corner store, no questions asked. Most of the time the flames fizzled out. No fire trucks or police searches for arsonists. Except for the last time. When the pile of twigs and leaves caught on fire and spread to a garage. They panicked and ran away when it became obvious that they wouldn't be able to put the fire out. They were sitting in Robert's backyard, about twenty minutes after they left the scene when they heard the sirens. They both looked at each other, feeling sick. They had to go look, like true criminals returning to the scene of the crime to revel in their destruction. The fire was huge. Thick black smoke billowed high into the air, followed by flames shooting up and threatening the elm trees. There were a number of people standing by watching, but the police officer spoke only to them. Picked them out of everybody in the whole crowd. Later, Robert wondered what their faces must have looked like at that moment to give them away so unmistakably.

"You boys know anything about this?"

"No."

"You sure?"

A terrible feeling had come over him. His insides felt ice cold. He thought he was going to throw up. The police officer steadied him with his big, official hand. Leonard was no better, swaying side to side and finally leaning up against a garbage bin.

"We didn't do it," Robert squawked. Tears threatened to flow.

"Show me what's in your pockets," the officer demanded.

Both of them had instinctively plunged their hands into their pockets at the first sign of trouble. There was no getting out of it. Leonard brought forth a lime green Bic lighter. Seeing this, Robert produced his as well. This admission was taken very seriously and both boys were questioned by the officer. They were youths and so only would be written up, their parents talked to. Both showed remorse and blubbered about it being an accident and the first time they had ever done anything like it. Leonard said they had tried to put it out and had run away when it became clear the fire was growing. This seemed to help their cause. A couple of naïve kids, good students, never in any kind of trouble before. Robert raced all the way home, wanting to get to Johanna before the police officer did. She was in the kitchen, something sizzling on the stove. He slammed through the door breathless, pale and sweaty.

"Robert, what is it? Is someone after you?"

"No."

"What's wrong? Are you hurt?"

"No." Then he began to cry. He didn't mean to. But the tears just spilled out of him. "I did something bad."

Hearing this and seeing how upset he was, Johanna hesitated. "How bad?"

"Pretty bad," he gulped. "The police might come here."

Her face grew ashen. It wasn't the reaction he'd anticipated. He thought she would be angry or disappointed. But his mother's eyes were wild with fright. "What did you do?" She whispered, wringing her hands in her apron to keep them from shaking him.

"I'm sorry," he wailed.

"I feel sick." She spit the words at him and he shrank back against the kitchen wall. Her lips had turned pale and trembled. "You tell me. I want to hear it from your mouth, not the police."

She spoke with such vehemence that Robert for a moment wondered if she thought he had killed somebody.

"Tell me!" She yelled, taking a step towards him. "You tell me what you've done."

"I set some grass on fire." He blurted it out, hoping she wouldn't hit him. "We thought it would just go out. We tried to put it out but the flames got too high. The grass was really dry and then the garage caught on fire. The police were there and knew it was us. I'm sorry. It was an accident."

"My God," she said and lowered herself onto a kitchen chair. The fear in her face melted into relief. She pulled him towards her and held him. "Of course it was an accident. You wouldn't do such a thing, Robert. Not you."

He felt her heart pounding against his ear where she held his head. He felt relief at this sudden and unexpected absolution and he let her cling to him as long as she liked, there in the kitchen while their pork chops sputtered on the stove. He was still punished – she made him take a cake over to the people and apologise and offer to do their yard work for them for free. They did not want anything to do with him. They accepted the cake and that was the last he saw of them. But no punishment would make him forget the look on his mother's face that day. Something had terrified her. Something about him and Robert had never figured out what it was.

CHAPTER 4

A white Ford Expedition cut in front of her and Johanna had to stomp on the brakes. On the back seat was a Tupperware container with muffins that Johanna had baked for the volunteers. These lurched forward with the sudden stop and Johanna cursed under her breath. "Kitten," read the license plate in front of her. It was her supervisor Karen, or Kahreen, as she insisted it be pronounced.

Angela had coffee ready when Johanna arrived. "Any sign of the queens yet?"

"Only Karen. She nearly made me lose my muffins when she cut me off."

Angela burst out laughing, as she often did at things Johanna said. Angela called Karen and her friends the urban warrior queens because they zoomed around town in their SUVs with leather interiors and satellite tracking systems. As far as Johanna was concerned Karen was just another randomly chosen person in a position of authority who had no idea what to do other than to loom over everyone and make people nervous for no reason.

Johanna hung her coat in her locker and pulled the pink volunteer smock over her blouse. Her nametag was still clipped to the collar from her last shift. Dressed in a skirt and blouse and low-heeled sandals Johanna wondered if it would elicit a comment from Karen, who had taken Johanna aside one day to tell her she didn't need to dress so nicely 'just to volunteer.' The other volunteers wore slacks and cotton polo shirts and running shoes but Johanna kept her formal style.

Johanna pulled a plate from the cupboard and arranged the muffins. Angela brought her a cup of coffee and sat down at the table. "There's a meeting on Wednesday. At least I think it's Wednesday. Karen's experimenting with a new font again and I could hardly read it."

Johanna smiled. Angela was so easy to get along with. The world could use more people like her. There was a box of donuts already on the table and Johanna saw that Angela had already eaten one. She tried to bring healthy things in for them to eat since both Angela and Marg were a bit overweight.

Johanna wet a rag and wiped down the refrigerator and the cupboard doors where they got sticky. Then she rinsed the rag and started on the microwave. As far as she knew, she was the only person to do this. There was a rotation for cleaning the lounge but most people thought all that meant was doing the dishes and emptying the coffee filter.

"Johanna!" Angela scolded. "Sit down for one minute and have a coffee with me."

"I hate a sticky fridge. You can have the first muffin."

"The first one? I'm going to have the first seven!" Angela pulled a People magazine towards her. "How's Robert?"

"Oh, fine." Johanna finally sat down and took a sip of her coffee. It was a bit weak. "He's disappointed he didn't get tickets to the Wagner festival."

"Ooooh, *Vaaaaaagner*."

Johanna smiled. When Angela mentioned Wagner all Johanna had to do was pull a face and it was accepted that she didn't care for it. Angela agreed with her, even though she admitted she had never listened to any *Vaaaagner*. She never asked why Johanna didn't like it. To her it made perfect sense not to. "You and me, we're more for Mozart. Refined music."

"That's exactly what I tell Robert. He can keep Wagner for himself."

"When is the orchestra performing again? I might sneak away and go listen. He's always happy for an audience."

"Hmm," Johanna pretended to think, even though she knew there was a rehearsal coming up. She once told Angela that Robert didn't like her coming to the rehearsals and that he preferred her to come to the performances. That Johanna rarely attended either was something she didn't say. It was different when Robert was a boy and his teacher had the children perform recitals twice a year. Set up in the teacher's living room with all the parents seated on an assortment of chairs and sofas, Johanna would sit with her entire body tense as she waited for it to be over. The way Robert sat at the keyboard, slouching, his hands and wrists slack and his fingers dexterous and precise on the keys made her recoil at the similarity. The older he got the more disturbing the resemblance became. Even the music he liked to play, heavy and dramatic, brought back unwanted memories of the music she used to hear coming from the study in their old house in Germany.

Marg arrived with more donuts. "I thought it was my turn. Oops," she said when she saw the tray of muffins.

Karen, followed by Brenda, flourished a box of almond cookies from an Italian deli and insisted that each of them should try one because the cookies would melt in their mouths. By the time the meeting was over only crumbs remained. Johanna was pleased that despite the extra food, everyone had tried one of her muffins. She gave Angela the extras to take home with her.

Johanna filled her volunteer cart. The lounge was empty again. Angela and Marg were working in the gift shop for the morning. Johanna took stock of her cart. Candy bars and mints, the daily newspaper. She filled the cart from the boxes in the supply closet room. Karen had finally agreed to let the volunteers have a key to the supply cupboard. "There have been incidences in the past," she said. Johanna had worked there longer than Karen and would have heard about any "incidences." If she meant that every so often one or two chocolate bars couldn't be accounted for, then she had a lot to learn about what constituted an incident.

Johanna wheeled the cart to the elevator and waited. People milled about the lobby, looking around uncertainly. Often, Johanna asked if they needed directions and gratitude washed over their faces as Johanna guided them to where they needed to go. "That's what I'm here for," she would tell them.

A few people got on the elevator with her. Johanna pressed the button for the tenth floor. She smiled at a woman with a baby on her arm. By the time she reached the tenth floor the elevator was empty. She expertly steered the cart into the corridor and started on the north wing. Most of the patients were in their rooms. Johanna knew a lot of them, as this was the long-term care ward. Poor souls waiting for a bed in a nursing home, the numbers of their friends and family ever shrinking. Johanna tried to remember what everyone liked. Mrs. Keenan bought scotch mints again, thinking her great-grandchildren liked them, even though Johanna had never seen these grandchildren.

In Mrs. Summer's room there was a large bouquet of flowers. The irises had wilted and the daffodils had drooped. The woman in the bed glowered at her. Johanna smiled. "Would you like me to freshen up your flowers? The carnations are still nice."

Without waiting for an answer, Johanna carried the vase to the sink, replaced the water, and rearranged the flowers. She used a pair of the nurses' scissors to snip the stems. Satisfied with the outcome, she returned the vase to the bedside table. "There you go. Aren't they lovely?"

Mrs. Summers didn't say a word. She never did. Her family had brought in an extra storage container in which she stashed chocolates and chips and anything from her tray she didn't eat. Many of the older patients had a tendency to hoard food. Johanna knew what it was like to never have enough. Once you experience that kind of hunger you take measures not to let it happen again. Johanna patted Mrs. Summers' hand and resumed her rounds.

Mrs. Summers was one of the fortunate ones. She had family. There were many rooms filled with people who had nobody. They had survived in dingy apartments and stopped washing and eating, instead drinking and smoking just to stimulate their senses. Nobody ever knocked at their door with a casserole or a slice of cake or a moment to talk. Only the landlord knocking for his money and he was usually the one who called the ambulance to come and take them away when they no longer were capable of getting to the bank with their cheque. Then they lay in their hospital beds, their bony arms and legs swimming in the blue gowns and adult diapers, knees and elbows black with months of dirt, the skin around their ankles dry and flaking, teeth and nails the same rotten colour of rust. Not even the nurses wanted to go near them. The doctors had no notion what to do with them but to feed them and try to get them strong enough so a nursing home would take them. Social workers tried to round up the next of kin – to find someone responsible for these poor souls, someone who might care. No one ever came forward. Johanna made a point of checking in on these patients. They had no money to buy anything and many of them had lost the ability to carry on a proper conversation. But she stopped at the foot of their beds and said good morning and, if they replied, she tried to have a little chat with them. Most of them didn't say too much so she straightened out their sheets, asked if they were too hot or cold and made sure their water was within reach.

She went to the sixth floor, her old ward. When she came to the hospital to apply for a job many years ago, Johanna told them she specialized in mental illness. With palpable relief they assigned her to the psychiatric lockdown unit and she never looked back. The war had probably gone unnoticed within those glossy eggshell walls and green draped windows. There were some old patients that had been there since the First World War. Shell-shocked amputees who bit ferociously if anyone got too close. She was used to those patients. They reminded her of the patients in the small hospital at home where she had begun her career. After the war it was nurses more than anything else that were needed and Johanna had been quick to apply for training. Nurses were needed everywhere. This meant she could go anywhere when she was ready.

Johanna glanced around the patient lounge. A couple of younger men sat in front of the television, harnessed to their recliner chairs. Their eyes no longer viewed the world with any comprehension. Even the most concrete object, the chair on which they sat, the spoon they propelled towards their mouths, held no meaning for them. And yet they would stare at the television and giggle maniacally along with a laugh track. It proved to her that a person's soul could die before their body gave out. Karen would never set foot up here. It made Johanna shake her head the way people were afraid of the crazy ones. Sometimes she thought it was the most rational thing in the world to let your mind go. Nobody ever bothered those ranting lunatics on the street or asked anything of them. They were given a wide berth in this world.

As she waited to be buzzed through the doors, she suddenly remembered that today marked twenty-five years since her husband Jim had died. An eternity really, though she remembered that day with cinematic precision. Gordon, the operations manager of the hospital, had come to tell her when she was in the middle of a shift. One look at him and Johanna knew. She allowed Gordon to usher her to the emergency department where doctors and nurses were making some effort to revive Jim. "Stop," she commanded. "Let him go if he's going."

They all paused and looked up, then stopped. Each of them slipped out of the room and left Johanna alone with her now dead husband. Their friends had called them JJ: Jim and Johanna. She had met him at the hospital on the floor that no one wanted to visit. He came up to the psych ward one day because the locks on the doors weren't working. It had taken maintenance three days to send someone up. That meant for three days the nurses had to watch the doors and make sure none of the patients got out. By the time Jim got there they had had enough. The head nurse had lit into him, yet he remained composed and quickly got to work. It wasn't his fault that the work order was late. Johanna felt sorry for him and told him it really hadn't been that bad, and offered him a coffee from the nurses' lounge. Soon they were meeting at lunch and eventually he got up the nerve to ask her out. His family had not been affected by the war in the way that many had and Johanna discovered if she didn't offer up any information he wouldn't ask. She agreed four months later to marry him, a real Canadian. She would be Canadian and her children too. It was what she had come for. The past broke away from the future and drifted back into the caverns of her mind.

His death had been a messy and preventable accident – electrical circuits switched on at the wrong time, Jim with a bundle of live wires in his hand. He wouldn't have known what hit him. As she stood there clutching his now lifeless hand, her thoughts were of Robert. Calm came over her. It would just be the two of them now. It simplified things. They would stay in the house. That was important – to give Robert a sense of stability. Losing his father would not make his world fall apart. She already worked, so he was used to that. And he was nearly nine and could be taught to let himself into the house after school and wait the half hour for her to come home. She enjoyed the thought of coming home to Robert. It was a selfish thought, but one she allowed herself in face of the tragedy – she would now have Robert to herself. They would take care of each other. "There is always a silver lining," she told Robert later that day. "And one day you will see it."

• • • •

Her shift ended at noon. Johanna's stomach grumbled. She stopped by the gift shop and bought a packet of roasted almonds from Angela to tide her over until she got home.

"Need a break before I leave?" she offered. Sometimes Angela had to get home to babysit her grandson.

"Oh, no. I'm still going strong." There weren't many people in the gift shop and Angela slid Johanna's dollar back across the counter. "Just take them. I love it when the numbers don't add up. It's fun to watch Karen sweat over sixty cents."

"You know I can't. Ring it through. I don't want to be blamed for missing almonds."

"You're too honest, Jo. Can't you see I'm trying to make a rebel out of you?"

Johanna waved as she wheeled her cart back towards the volunteer lounge. In her mind she did a quick inventory of her fridge at home and couldn't think of anything she needed. She tossed her smock into the laundry. Next time she would start with a clean one. The lounge was reasonably tidy. Johanna sat down and ate her almonds. Angela made her smile. A rebel. Just what the world needed – another rebel.

The door flew open. Karen entered with a stack of memos and a cup of coffee that she tried to balance. She teetered towards the table and put the cup down. "Oooh, that's hot." She shook her hand around and blew on it. Karen had cut her long blonde hair. It now lay flat against her head like Julius Caesar. There were brown tips throughout that made her head look like a spotted owl. She danced around and would not make eye contact. Johanna watched her a moment before she finally said, "You cut your hair."

Instantly Karen spun around, her hand reached up and patted down the plumes. "I did. It was time." She spoke in earnest. "I don't think women after a certain age should wear their hair long anymore. A mature woman looks better with her hair short. It says, 'Hey, I've been there and now I just want to simplify my life. Hair is not important to me.'"

"It looks nice," Johanna offered.

"Do you think so?" Karen asked. "Well, it feels good anyway. I think I did the right thing."

"Did something happen?"

"Johanna, I've turned into one of those people who turn the television on for company." She stood before Johanna, stern, hands on her hips, defiant.

"I turn the radio on for company sometimes."

"That's not the same thing." Her eyes shifted away. "I better go check on the girls in the gift shop."

The television was not the same as the radio at all. Karen was just lonely. Her husband had left her a year ago and Karen was trying on the role of divorcee. She had brought her friends on board so that she would have company at work. At first everybody understood, but more and more their presence was stifling. They acted like they ran the place. They all drove those enormous cars. They sat around Karen's office and even had a desk and computer of their own to work on. They wore cashmere sweaters and push-up bras and strode along the corridors with trays of coffee, always in a rush. Each wore her hair long and in a slightly different shade of blond.

They sat on committees and baked cookies for meetings. They organized fundraisers for sick children and spent their husbands' huge corporate allowances on expensive hairdressers and spa treatments and burned rubber to the best parking spots wherever they went. The roughest terrain their SUVs encountered was the speed bumps in the parking lot at the mall. From what she could tell, the blondes spent most of their time selling the things their children had outgrown on the hospital's Buy and Sell page. Karen's office was usually filled with toys and expensive children's clothing, waiting to be picked up.

Workers were digging up the flowerbeds in preparation for fall. The day was pleasant with the sun warming the air. Johanna made her way back to her car across the parking lot, licking almond salt from her lips. The way Karen had looked at her Johanna knew she wondered if Johanna had paid for the nuts or not. Either way Angela would get a kick out of detaining her for twenty minutes while she pored over the cash tape.

• • • •

On Saturday Robert woke and decided to have breakfast at The Cocoa Bean. He was in the mood for something sweet. Waffles came to mind. With berries and butter. The walk would do him good. He showered and then dressed in jeans and a short-sleeved shirt. The day was bright and The Cocoa Bean had a patio overlooking Lake Ontario where he planned to sit with the Saturday paper. Oddly, he felt a glimmer of cheer when he considered the look of recognition Marcelline would give him when she saw him.

He picked up a *Globe and Mail* on his way. The restaurant was busy and smelled of bacon and coffee. Robert's stomach rumbled. Maybe he would have an omelette instead. But eggs didn't always agree with him. A sign greeted him and told him to seat himself. There were tables outside under umbrellas. The lake was a deep blue and sailboats dotted the water. Robert claimed a small table and glanced around. Marcelline was taking an order and hadn't noticed him yet. A group of young girls sat at one table. They all looked a bit alike – scruffy hair, sloppy clothes and jewellery pierced through unusual places. Marcelline seemed to know them and made a stop there every time she passed by. Some friends of hers, he thought. Marcelline reached over and pinched one of the girl's faces. His heart thumped a few times, disturbing his composure. Short skirts were making a comeback, he read in the paper where he buried his head. He should have brought Leonard with him.

"Hi stranger," Marcelline stood before him, a crooked smirk on her face that he couldn't read.

"Good morning. I've come to try the breakfast."

She produced a menu from behind her back. "Can I pour you a coffee to start, sir?"

"Sure. That would be nice, um, Marcelline." He made a show of squinting at her nametag.

"I'm surprised to see you here. I thought you were a dedicated recluse." She turned over his cup and poured.

"I've been told it would do me good to get out once in a while and somebody recommended the breakfast here."

After she moved on to the next table, Robert sipped his coffee. The paper didn't hold much interest for him. There was an article about a couple of old Nazi collaborators, both in their nineties. It would set his mother off for a while. She would be reminded of her brother Heinz. She hated that Robert knew that her brother had joined the Nazi Party. But how could she possibly keep it from him? He knew she kept it from everyone else. That was her choice. It wasn't something he would advertise either. It didn't bother him that they didn't steep in their emotions whenever they were together, but there were certain things he expected to be privy to, and that was one of them. Hers was not the only family of Nazi supporters during that time. All Germans had been practically forced to comply, his mother said. "See Robert," he could hear her already. "They are still rooting them out. One by one, even if they are frail, useless old men, they want their revenge."

So what? Those old codgers knew when they came here under false pretences what fate might await them. What would they care anymore, with one foot in the grave? They've had the last laugh after all, haven't they? He was so far removed from that part of history and his mother spoke of it so seldom it was hard for him to understand why she felt compelled to react when these stories appeared. It wasn't like they were going to come after *her*.

"Are you ready to order?" Marcelline stood with her pencil pressed to her pad.

"I'll have the Belgian waffles with raspberries and cream."

"Coming right up." She reached over and squeezed his arm. "I'm so glad you came. I knew you would. I told my friends all about you. They think it's so cool that you're a classical musician."

She skipped off with her coffee pot to her table of friends and he blushed when he thought that she might be talking about him. There was a brief moment when he thought he should clarify that he was not actually a musician, but then he didn't want to veer back into the discussion of piano lessons. Robert resumed his study of the paper and then there she was again, placing an unordered glass of orange juice before him.

"It's on me. A mimosa."

"Oh." A surprise to discover champagne on the premises. "Thank you, Marcelline."

"You're welcome," she said in her singsong voice.

He sipped the mimosa and waited for his food. There was a brisk breeze off the lake. It invigorated him. Later he would go home and work on the arrangement of Gounod's "Sanctus" from the *St. Cecilia Mass* that he was preparing for the orchestra. He was rewriting it for the brass section. The trumpet would take the solo. It would work beautifully the way he heard it. The horns underneath, trombone in the low register and the tuba player would be thrilled with the part he'd written for her – the melody foreshadowing the trumpet. Sweet harmony in the tuba part of all things!

By the time his plate arrived his head was full of the blazing sound of his beloved brass section. He could feel it behind his sternum, the emotion welling up. He ate hungrily, accepted another coffee, and asked for the bill.

"Is something wrong?"

"No, I just have to get some work done today. When inspiration calls, I must heed."

"The bathroom's on the right."

"No," he said, suddenly embarrassed. "I have some work to do at home."

"I know that." She punched his arm and smiled. "You're so serious all the time. It's sweet."

A warm flush came over Robert, a split-second premonition flashing through his mind that he was about to kiss her. Thankfully he remembered the table of friends who thought he was cool.

"I'll get your change."

"No need. Thanks for the mimosa."

"Thanks for the tip."

As he walked home along the boardwalk, the raspberries sang on his tongue.

CHAPTER 5

Johanna was cooking carrot ginger soup, a new recipe she found in a free magazine from the grocery store. It called for lemongrass, something she had never used before, and fresh ginger, something she was trying to eat more of because another free magazine said it was good for her. She had invited Pearl for an early supper. There was salad and a nice loaf of dark rye bread. She would feel better knowing Pearl had eaten a good meal. Pearl's kitchen was stocked with just tins and frozen food. Almost everything she heated on a plate in the microwave. It wasn't healthy. And she ate far too many store-bought sweets. Her doctor had already told her she was borderline diabetic, but this didn't seem to bother her. "I don't know if it would do me much good to give up my Mars bars," she drawled. "Because let me tell you, Johanna, I am not already sweet enough." And then she laughed and coughed and covered her teeth with the back of her fist.

The carrots were all peeled and simmering in the chicken stock. There would be enough left over to give to Robert when he came for lunch on Sunday. If it turned out, she would send Barbara the recipe in the mail. She would write it on a small recipe card with a note folded around it. She should write to Barbara more. Then there might be fewer uncomfortable conversations on the phone. Barbara always had lots to say. About her trips or her clients at the salon where she still worked two days a week. For this Johanna was thankful. They should have lots to talk about but Johanna could never think of anything to say. It was the unspoken things that got in the way and left their conversations stilted and forced.

She cut the end off a carrot and carried it out to Felix's cage. The bird knew the trajectory of the path from the kitchen door to his door and started a dance across his perch when he saw Johanna approach. "JoJo," she tried again.

Felix clucked with delight. He hopped down to where the carrot had been placed and pecked at it. "Eat it. It's good for you. I know you like apples better but I don't have any apples today."

The telephone rang. Johanna thought it could be Pearl asking to come by early, wanting company.

"Hello."

"Aunt Johanna?"

"Albert?"

"Yes, it's me. Albert."

"Oh, Albert. It's so nice to hear from you. I'm just cooking a carrot ginger soup. I've got my neighbour coming over later. Does Lois ever cook with ginger?" Her voice was cheery as she puzzled over this call. Albert rarely called her. Sometimes he did, on her birthday or Christmas. Albert was slow to answer her.

"Sometimes," he said. Then there was silence.

"Albert, where are you calling from?"

"I'm in Calgary."

Johanna's heart skipped. "Oh!" Her voice came out a funny squawk. She waited for him to speak.

"I have some terrible news. Are you sitting down?"

Johanna's breath caught in her throat.

"Mother's had a stroke." His voice cracked and he said nothing more.

Johanna clasped the edge of the sofa and guided herself around, her legs suddenly unhinged and shaking. "Oh, Albert." She held her head and pressed the phone to her ear. "Is it really bad?"

"You better come, Aunt Johanna." Albert sobbed into the phone. "I'm sorry. It's just I feel so terrible. They tried everything they could, but it was too much, the stroke. Massive, that's what they called it."

Johanna felt faint. Barbara … "I'll come, Albert. When did she die?" He hadn't said it yet, that she was dead. Johanna strained to speak. Such unthinkable news and Albert upset and crying on the phone.

"She went to the mall this morning. At eleven o'clock the hospital called. I should have gone with her but she knew I was tired and went without me. It's just awful that she died like that. Collapsed in the mall."

Johanna was silent as she listened to Albert cry on the other end of the phone. He sounded like a little boy, his voice strangled and choked. She wanted to end the conversation, not knowing what else she could possibly say right now. She sat doubled over on the sofa as though she had been punched in the stomach. "I have to go Albert. Will you be all right? I'm so sorry." Her breath came out in short gasps.

"Don't worry Aunt Johanna. I booked you onto a flight tomorrow at eleven in the morning. I'll be at the airport to pick you up."

"Thank you Albert. That's very kind." She stayed on the sofa and held the telephone, making an effort to breathe. And she had just been thinking of Barbara. The soup in the kitchen – she was going to send the recipe. She remembered Barbara saying Albert was coming to visit. At least he had been there. Though she felt the wind had been knocked out of her, the grief had not yet hit her. Felix had become very quiet in his cage. Johanna went over and checked his food. The carrot lay at the bottom of the cage with tiny nibbles gnawed into it. The silence of the apartment engulfed her.

Johanna sat back down. She felt nothing. The soup would be ready and the stove had to be turned off. This immediate and tangible task guided her to the kitchen. The recipe called for a half can of coconut milk but Johanna thought it would be better if the soup cooled a bit first. She stood by the open balcony door and tried to let the cool air soothe her. The last time she had seen Barbara was last spring when she had helped plant her garden. Barbara still lived in her house and knew Johanna missed having a garden. They had planted rows of beans and tomatoes and pumpkins – of all things. Barbara had wanted to try growing pumpkins even though she had no use for them. "I just love the look of them in the fall. Outside the city in the fall there are fields awash with pumpkins." She had laughed at this – a field being awash with pumpkins.

That was Barbara, always jolly and laughing and seeing the bright side. She had sent Johanna a picture of her garden "awash" with rotting pumpkins. None of them had grown to her expectations but then Barbara didn't mind. It had been an experiment – something to do just for fun. It was something Johanna could have put on her recipe card. 'I tried this soup just for fun.' But Barbara would have known. She was always telling Johanna to lighten up. It was one of her favourite sayings. In Barbara's mind, when something wasn't going right all you had to do was lighten up. It had been her answer for everything.

• • • •

Robert set his fountain pen and manuscript aside and lay on the chaise longue. The sun spilled into the room and warmed his full belly and soon he was asleep. He dreamt of walking in the public gardens at Bayreuth between acts, having a long discussion with Arturo Toscanini about Wagner's awareness of the *Festspielhaus* acoustics when he wrote *Parsifal* and how much it differed from his previous work. He could see that the maestro was impressed with his knowledge and as Robert strolled along beside him, his hands clasped behind his back, he hoped he would next be invited to a party or a rehearsal. But in the distance a bell sounded and Toscanini had to race back to the theatre. The bell sounded again and again, which did not fit since the end of intermission at Bayreuth is usually announced in a more refined manner, with a brass quartet playing a fanfare from the roof of the balcony. Robert's mood immediately darkened when he awoke to the telephone ringing.

"Hello." Fully expecting the bank, or insurance sales, or some charity to save thieving children, Robert put on an impatient tone. Just because they had caught him at home didn't mean he wasn't busy.

"Robert, it's your mother." She too had an impatient tone. "Barbara's dead."

"What?" He wasn't sure he had heard. "Dead? What did you say?"

"I can't talk right now. Pearl is coming for supper."

"Wait, Aunt Barbara? What happened?" He sat up. Aunt Barbara, his mother's younger sister – the last one alive.

"She had a stroke. It was quite sudden. I haven't set the table."

"Can't you cancel your dinner?" This attention to the immediate and trivial things was something Robert had witnessed often. He imagined the whir of activity in her brain right now. If harnessed it could provide electricity to the city for a month.

"She needs a good meal. She's practically anorexic."

"Can't you take it over to her?"

"I don't know if she eats it when I just drop it off. I want to see her eat."

Robert ran his hand through his hair. It was getting to be just the length he wanted – like Herbert von Karajan, but not yet grey. "When are you leaving?"

"Tomorrow morning. Albert booked it for me."

"Hmm." He picked up his manuscript. He made a small notation at the key change to listen for the intonation in the flutes. Those fifths never came out right. The first flute had a tendency to play sharp in that range.

"Do you have time to drive me or should I book a car?"

"I will drive you, of course. Should I come by tonight?"

"There's nothing for you to do. I will be busy getting ready. I've got laundry to do and a suitcase to pack. Pick me up at seven."

"Seven?" There was no surprise here. On time meant at least an hour early. The conversation passed so quickly that the gravity of the news didn't sink in until Robert hung up the phone. Barbara, the only remaining sister, had just died and though his mother was acting like it had happened to someone else, she was flying to Calgary to help out. To process the event would take too much time. Acceptance seemed to establish itself immediately. It was more important to get on with things that had to be done.

Albert was booking her flight. Something he, Robert should be doing. But his mother rarely asked anything of him. Robert hadn't seen Albert in years. He recalled a chubby eight-year-old covered in mosquito bites always whining that he was hungry. They hadn't forged much of a relationship as adults. Cousin Albert, chubby when he was young, had grown into a portly adult. Now his mother was dead.

Robert tried to concentrate on his work but there was a stitch in his side. He hoped the cream he had dolloped all over his waffles wasn't bad. Just in case, he took a swallow of Pepto-Bismol from the bottle he kept handy in the door of his fridge. A thought came to him and he picked up the phone and called his mother. "Would you like me to come with you?" he asked.

"Where?" She sounded out of breath.

"To the funeral?" It pleased him that he had thought of it, to offer. He knew what she would say.

"No, no. You're too busy. Besides, I need someone to take in the mail and feed Felix."

"What about Pearl?" He braced himself.

"I can't ask Pearl. She's not well. Besides, people snoop. Can you do it? Frank can take the mail, but can you take Felix? It will save you coming here everyday. He needs to be fed twice a day. And you have to cover him up at night. He's no trouble, really. It'll be company for you."

Maybe he could teach Felix a few more words. "Sure. I can do that."

"Are you sure?"

"Of course." There. He was doing something to help. It made him feel better.

• • • •

It was an awful feeling, this gap where her family should be. Alone in the void, everyone out of reach. Before the war there had been such happy times. Everything was so normal and idyllic. Her father worked as a professor of linguistics at the university and her mother stayed home to take care of the house. The children played endlessly in the huge garden. In the summer they were allowed to splash in the sprinkler. There was always enough food and their beds were warm. Friday evenings they played games together with marzipan prizes for the winner. Her father would play records on the gramophone, he and her mother would drink schnapps, and she and Heinz and Barbara were given hot chocolate. Sometimes her father would play the clarinet and Heinz the piano and the rest of them would sing. She remembered it so clearly. Then the war came and changed everything.

Johanna went to bed, not knowing what else to do, feeling empty and anxious. Even when she thought about something else, there was the flutter of nerves that signalled distress. Her body ached with fatigue but her mind was on the flight, the arrangements for the funeral, Albert, Felix, Pearl. They had eaten dinner together after all. Johanna didn't know what else to do. Johanna tried several times to tell her, because after tomorrow she was sure to notice she was gone, but the words got stuck in her throat time after time and the evening passed and she hadn't said a word.

In the morning she would have to knock on Pearl's door and let her know. And Frank – he would be there in the morning. She could tell Frank then and ask him about the mail. What a terrible thing to have to tell everybody this horrible news. They would offer condolences and try to console her. It would draw unwanted attention. They would want to discuss her family. Johanna kicked the covers aside, suddenly hot and agitated. She wondered if Albert had started sorting through Barbara's things. A swell of fear rose up in her that he would find things that she would have to explain, though what kinds of things she couldn't imagine. Her stomach turned and she sat up and remained at the side of the bed until she was sure she would not be sick. She trod towards the dining room where she slid open the balcony doors and stepped outside. The night was dark, no moon. She stared out across the water. There was no horizon, just infinite space. She pulled her robe around her and stared into the darkness adrift in odd memories. People plucked from her life with no warning. She and Barbara left alone. Johanna had no choice but to look after her younger sister. Barbara was only sixteen at the time, and Johanna just twenty. Johanna took her west as soon as she could. She made sure Barbara finished school while she worked and trained at the hospital. They waited for their visas. Johanna feared every day she stayed in Germany that something awful would happen and they would never get to leave.

There was an urgency to her actions that Barbara couldn't understand. The aftermath of the war weighed heavily on Johanna. While growing up, their parents tried to shield them from the fanaticism that Hitler preached. But it became increasingly difficult as the Nazi Party demanded more and more involvement from the German people and its power seeped into every pore of daily life. As children they knew nothing different. The message was everywhere: the newspapers, the radio, school – all instilling in them a sense of nationalistic pride. They cheered at rallies and attended parades. They proudly wore the uniform of the League of German Girls. Heinz was also completely swept up in the enthusiasm. Johanna thought later how devastated her parents must have been when he joined the SS. But it was young men like Heinz at whom the propaganda was aimed. So many young men like him were lured from their homes to fight for an unattainable ideal. It was deliberate the way young Germans were targeted.

It stunned Johanna to think of it later. To remember how proud she had been to be German. Germany was the most exciting and powerful nation on earth and she was a part of it. Hitler was a magician who would turn the country around. Until the very end, the newspapers resounded of victory. Even when the tanks circled Berlin, troops could be rallied to mount a counter attack. The message remained the same: Victory would be theirs. Long live Germany! When the end of the war came, the magician who had masterminded it vanished and the country's pride turned to shame. Her only brother Heinz had been part of it. She never would forgive him for the guilt that bled onto her. Expecting a hero's welcome he had come back and launched into composing an unfinished opera that some poor violinist had given him along with a journal filled with notes. It was all so meaningless after what had happened. To this day she did not understand what it was in that endeavour that he found so important.

As soon as it was possible she made arrangements for herself and Barbara to leave Germany and all the awful memories and associations. They would go to Canada. At first Barbara didn't want to go. She was young. All her friends were in Germany. She didn't understand the desperation with which Johanna implored her. "I can't leave you here and I can't stay. You can't stay either. They will make us pay, all of us. This isn't our country anymore. It belongs to the Allies."

Finally Johanna convinced her by telling her she could live near the mountains. Barbara was unfazed by the awful legacy left by the Nazis. "I don't see how we could have helped it," she said. "They really gave us no choice."

"Even Heinz?" Johanna asked. "Even the things he did?"

"Yes, even Heinz had no choice."

This had always been the unspoken cause of the tension between them. That Barbara had forgiven Heinz and Johanna had not. They didn't talk about it. Not in all the years that had passed, and now Johanna wondered if there were things she should have told Barbara. But too much time had passed. Besides, she was sure she would never be able to explain.

The ship had sailed from Bremen to Calais on a brisk and sunny day in May. Work would be waiting for them. Johanna as a nurse and Barbara a hairdresser – it sounded strange but those were among the jobs that were needed overseas. Without them they would not have obtained their visas. She and Barbara stood on the deck of the Castel Felice with all the other passengers and waved and watched as the ship chugged into the Atlantic Ocean and the shores of Europe dissolved into the horizon. Barbara loved the trip. There were dances every night, shuffleboard, lots of food and wine. Johanna smiled at the memory. Barbara did know how to make the best of a situation. As for Johanna, she spent most of the passage seasick and wrapped in blankets on a deck chair, able only to eat dry buns and sip tea. But they were sailing away. Each day took them farther from the past and closer to their future.

Now Johanna couldn't fall asleep, awash in memories. At five in the morning she gave up and made a pot of coffee. The sun rose over the horizon. Johanna pulled on a sweater and took her coffee outside. Traffic hummed in the distance. Birds rustled in the trees, the air damp. Her flowerpots were overgrown and the plants all drooped. She had planned to clean them up this week and now they would have to wait. If she sat there forever, it would have suited her, with her mind and body numb. But inevitably the turmoil churning her insides started up again and she didn't know how to make it stop. Her thoughts bounded over the terrain of her once quiet mind and uprooted everything in their path. Hidden facts that were once securely anchored now lay vulnerable and exposed.

• • • •

Her doorbell rang. Robert stood in the doorway, shifting awkwardly from one leg to the other. He motioned to hug her but she backed away and pointed at the scarf he had tied around his throat. "Do you have a cold?"

"Not yet. I have a scratchy throat though." He rested his hand on the back of her shoulder. Her muscles felt tense. "Did you sleep?"

"No, not much. Do you want coffee?"

Robert shook his head. Johanna had a list of what he was to do with Felix. "You best come and get him later on and take him to your place." She peered through the bars of the cage and cooed.

"Bye-bye Felix. Say bye-bye." The bird blinked and scuttled across its perch.

They made one stop at Pearl's. Johanna gave her two pots of frozen stew and a loaf of bread. Pearl clutched her arm and shook it. "You take care now, Johanna. I'll sure miss you."

Frank spied the suitcase right away when they reached the lobby.

"You didn't tell me you were taking a trip, Mrs. Turner."

"I didn't have a chance to, Frank. My sister in Calgary died. Quite suddenly and I have to fly there to meet my nephew."

Frank clutched his hat. "Gosh, that's terrible news. What happened?"

Johanna pursed her lips. "We weren't that close."

"I lost my brother last year." Frank wrung his hands around his hat and then put it on his head. "We were never that close either but once he was gone it felt like we were closer than I knew. Sounds strange, I know. Do you have ... another sister, or something?" He quickly fell silent, fearful that he was saying too much. Johanna stood rigidly by the door and waited for Robert to pull the car around.

"Well, these things happen. I'll just be gone a short while." She remembered last year when Frank told her about his brother. For a whole week there was another security guard. Johanna had asked him where Frank was but the man hadn't been told. "They just tell me where to go," he said and laughed loudly. When Frank came back he said there had been a death in his family. "My little brother," he had said and it made Johanna sad to hear him say it that way.

CHAPTER 6

When Robert returned for Felix, he checked the fridge and saw that his mother had left a few containers of soup for him. All the fruit and vegetables were packed in bags and ready for transport. She didn't want anything to go bad. He knew that within all the items there was a meal, but how to put it all together was confounding. Perhaps Leonard could help. He was always impressing women with his cooking. Crepes St. Jacques, Veal Piccata, and usually something flambé for dessert.

The one thing that he did not want to happen inevitably did and Marcelline joined him, and Felix, on the elevator at his block. It had been a week since he'd seen her. The blanket covered the cage so the bird would not get upset.

"Robert, did you buy a bird?"

"It's my mother's. She's away on a trip." He didn't feel like explaining.

"How sweet of you. You're babysitting."

He rolled his eyes. "Yes, I am. And look at all the food I'm supposed to feed him." He held up the bags of groceries.

"Really?"

Robert snorted. "No, it's extra food from my mother's fridge. What kind of a bird eats Camembert?"

"Well, I don't know. Some might." She moved to punch his arm, but didn't.

Felix moved inside the cage and it felt suddenly heavy and awkward. "I've got to get him inside. He's getting restless."

"At least you'll have some company." They paused. Robert could not make out her tone. The grocery bags were getting heavy. Marcelline started down the hall. They were both at their own doors, keys in hand. They each stepped inside and latched the doors.

Robert set the cage onto the living room side table and lifted the blanket. "There you are, little one," he said. "Maybe some Bach will help calm you down."

The bird cowered at the bottom of the cage and wouldn't look at Robert. "C'mon Felix, make it snappy." It was one of the first things he had taught the bird to say.

But, even Robert's squawking wouldn't rouse the bird. It took the first few bars of the "Goldberg Variations" on the piano. It pleased him when Felix jumped up onto his perch and cocked his head towards him as he played. "You never get to hear anything like that at home, do you?"

He played the first sonorous bars of Beethoven's "Pathetique Sonata," the second movement. His left hand lingered on the low notes. Felix cooed quietly in appreciation. All the lights were out except the one over the piano. The walls fell away and Robert was alone on a stage, all eyes on his hands and all ears perked and quivering in anticipation. Mendelssohn's "Song Without Words," some Erik Satie – such simple notes and yet utterly compelling. The music pulled at him like a centrifuge, drawing him in closer and closer to the core. It was impossible to overcome its power. For about an hour he played into the darkness to his imaginary audience. His mother never asked about his playing. She never asked to hear him. When he was growing up she was always busy doing something when he practised on the piano at home and she never commented on any of his playing, good or bad. The lessons, he understood, had been a sacrifice, something he never asked about in case it reminded her that she didn't want him to play. One day, when he played through a Bach Invention with no mistakes for the first time, he shouted, "Mom, I played it with no mistakes. The first time!"

His mother was in the kitchen baking Christmas cookies. "Play some Christmas music," came her reply. She hadn't heard it. Had not been paying attention.

"Why don't you care how I play?" He stood leaning against the kitchen door and watched her brush chocolate glaze over some gingerbread stars and trees. His voice was changing by this time and he had grown thin sideburns that he groomed carefully every day.

"What do you mean?" Her focus remained on the cookies.

"You don't care if I play well or poorly. I can sound like a dog's breakfast or like Horowitz and it makes no difference to you. Doesn't that strike you as strange?"

"I suppose it is a bit odd. I've just never really cared that much for classical music. It sounds nice, what you're playing. Do you know any carols? I'd like to hear some."

Christmastime was the only time anything remotely German happened in their home. It had mostly to do with the cookies and the carols. Robert played carols for her while the aroma of gingerbread filled the house. At least they could share that.

• • • •

He didn't feel like working and settled into his chair with a biography of Mahler and a glass of single malt. In the corner Felix scratched at the bottom of his cage. Every so often Robert glanced over to see what he was doing. It did feel different with another warm-blooded creature close by. Usually it was just himself and his things.

Eventually he wandered into the kitchen and unpacked the food. The kitchen was well-equipped but rarely used. A complete array of spices in decorative pots lined the cupboard above the stove. An exorbitantly expensive set of chef's knives sat in their block on the counter. All the things he had bought when he moved into this place, determined to cook at least twice a week. There were seven cookbooks, all with easy-to-follow recipes. He pulled one down and leafed through it. But it seemed too much effort. It was unusual for him and his mother to be apart. He did not like how her absence made him feel so attached to her. He opened a plastic container of soup and placed it in the microwave. In three minutes it was hot. He buttered two pieces of toast and opened a bottle of Spanish red wine. He set a place across from Felix and hunched over his soup while he tried to make the bird talk to him between bites.

• • • •

The flight was full. Johanna tried to smile at the steward who checked her boarding pass, but her mind was on getting to her seat through all the people who clogged the aisle as they rummaged through their carry-on luggage and stashed things in the overhead bins. Johanna only carried her purse and a paperback she knew she wouldn't read. There was an elderly man in the middle seat. Johanna indicated to him that hers was the window seat and he leapt to his feet to let her by.

No sooner was she settled, her gaze fixed out the window and she heard the man next to her: "Are you off to visit family?"

She turned and tried to look as though she had misheard him.

"I've got a new grandson." Undeterred by her silence, he reached for his wallet and showed Johanna photos taken at a studio of two children, one three years old and one just a baby. There was a backdrop of fall foliage behind them. In another photo the parents were added, looking wooden and unsure that the children were not simply props.

"Very nice." She balled up her sweater and jammed it between the seat and the window and rested her head. The woman who claimed the seat on the other side of the proud grandfather would be the next one to hear about the grandchildren. Thankfully this person seemed more amenable to chatting and Johanna drifted off to the sound of his long-winded family history that began somewhere in Poland. His gravely voice with a thick Germanic accent lulled Johanna into a hazy half-sleep. Too many memories swirled around her head. The summers. Those had been idyllic. Two weeks by the sea, all of them together, the whole family. The long walks along the sand dunes where the sharp edges of the tall grasses whipped at their legs when they passed. Tirelessly they swam as the white sun blazed in the sky. Every day they enjoyed the same luxurious pace. When the weather turned cool they made excursions to see local artist studios or small museums. They licked ice cream cones on their way home and sat around the fire pit every evening where their father grilled sausages and they would dunk them in hot mustard, their appetites voracious after a day spent outdoors. The clothesline hung full with their beach towels and swimsuits ready for the next glorious day. *My parents died at Dachau.*

Johanna's eyes flew open. She turned to the old gentleman in the middle seat. His head rested back and his eyes behind wire-rimmed glasses were shut. The woman next to him caught Johanna's eye and smiled sadly. Her hand rested on the old man's speckled hand. "Lots of stories," she explained to Johanna.

Had she dreamt it? She clutched her sweater and squeezed her eyes shut again. She willed her mind back to the summer holidays but it would not go there. There were many such memories but they were hard to see clearly, tainted by an elusive shadow.

• • • •

Johanna nearly walked right past Albert when she arrived at the airport. He tapped her on the shoulder, startling her. "Aunt Johanna."

She spun around. "Albert?"

Relief washed over her when she saw him. His face had the same charming boyish features she remembered. He gave her a warm embrace. He was about to say something when Johanna spied her suitcase come down the chute. She removed herself from his grasp and pulled her suitcase off the carousel. It fell with a thunk at her feet. Albert was quick to retrieve it. They walked in silence towards the parking lot.

"Are you all right?" She squeezed his arm.

"Oh, I know I will be thankful that I happened to be here. The worst for me was coming back to the house after the hospital. Walking in the door of that empty house. I just cried and cried. I probably will when we get there today too. Don't be surprised."

"That's all right, Albert. It's good to cry."

"And you?" They were at the car – Barbara's Toyota Camry with the Hawaiian Hula girl gyrating on the dashboard.

"Oh, I don't quite believe it yet. After you called, I phoned Robert and then I had to get ready. Robert's taken Felix for me. I had to tell the neighbours. It's all a blur. I simply haven't had time to cry." Tears felt a thousand years away.

They drove awhile. Albert hummed. He hummed a song all the way through, not just a little bit of the melody. To hear someone virtually singing so close by made her uncomfortable. She tried to think of something else to say before he started again. "Have you seen her?"

"Her body is at the funeral home. Would you like to stop by?"

"I don't know." Johanna's eyes darkened. "I don't think I want to do that just now. Are you rehearsing for a show?"

"Yes. Funny – the timing of all this. I was called just two days ago to fill in for the production in your city. A three-week run."

"Really? Well, you must stay with me. I insist." The words came automatically. Johanna's mind was elsewhere. There was so much to do, so many things to think about. The thudding of her heart in her chest actually pained her. Her breathing became shallow and the motion of the car was making her woozy. She gripped the handle of the door until Albert turned onto Barbara's street and pulled up to the house. The house was a small white stucco structure with a peaked roof and decorative window shutters.

Every five years Barbara changed the colour of the shutters. They were painted sage green right now and the colour before that had been a cheery yellow. Inside, it struck Johanna how different Barbara's house was from her own home. Knick-knacks littered every surface. Every bookcase and cabinet filled to overflowing with papers and mementos. There were souvenirs from past trips everywhere: glass ornaments which blew snow around from her trip to the Rockies, wine glasses from a resort in Bermuda, a little toy mouse wearing a sombrero.

Barbara had given up asking Johanna to join her on her trips. Almost every other year she saved up enough money to go somewhere. Johanna didn't like to travel like that; to mingle on the deck of a ship or to mingle at poolside at a resort, surrounded by strangers who tried to get you to talk about yourself. Barbara thrived on it. She would sign on with bus tours where she would travel with sixty other people, all traipsing from the bus to the restaurant and back again in a country where they would travel to six cities in eight days. There were drawers overflowing with postcards from the friends she'd made along the way. Her address book was filled with addresses of people all over the world. How many friends did one person need? She couldn't possibly have kept in touch with them all.

On the other hand Johanna hardly kept anything. The same photos, paintings and ornaments had been displayed in her apartment for years. When she sold her house she cleared out a lot of useless things and the only new things were the occasional gift from Pearl or the women at the hospital when they had their Christmas party. She preferred space to clutter. Clean surfaces and neat drawers, where things could be found easily.

There were small piles formed around the living room and dining room. "I see you've started sorting."

Albert nodded. "I hope you don't mind. I thought it might take my mind off things. Stupid of me, really. As you can imagine, it had the opposite effect. There are a lot of memories in this house for me."

Johanna touched his arm. "I know it must be very hard. I can stay awhile and do it."

"Oh, it's not that I don't want to do it. I just get caught up. Every time I pick something up I spend ten minutes pulling myself together before I can look at the next thing. At this rate it will take me twenty years to go through everything. I'll stay through to the end of next week. That should be enough time. Then I'll come when rehearsals start."

Johanna found herself feeling at ease with Albert. He had a relaxed and easy manner. Johanna smiled. "We'll get through it. I hope you'll take whatever you want."

"I've scrounged around in the basement looking for empty boxes but there don't seem to be many."

Johanna sat on the sofa. "Will Lois be coming with the boys?"

"We talked about it. The boys are starting grade three and we decided since I was already here she should just stay put and get them settled into school. Less disruptive for them."

Johanna nodded. It was sensible for them to carry on, she thought. No need to unsettle things. "Am I supposed to get used to this? That she's really gone? I sit here expecting her to bustle out of the kitchen with a pot of coffee in one hand and her watering can in the other."

"And then pour coffee onto a plant."

"Yes, something like that."

"Speaking of which, would you like a coffee? I've figured out how the coffee machine works."

Johanna nodded and rested on the sofa while Albert disappeared into the kitchen. As he prepared the coffee he sang a song about a wandering minstrel. She wondered if he would sing the entire time. When he returned he carried with him an envelope. Johanna's heart leapt unexpectedly as Albert entered. Of course. Photographs. She could only imagine what was to come. "I had some questions about these, Aunt Johanna."

He held a photo out towards her. She didn't have to look at it to know what it was. It was of her and Heinz after she had won second prize in a singing competition. Heinz stood beside her making a funny face, and she held a large trophy, shy with the camera there. "Oh, Albert." She tried to make her voice calm. "I was young then. The war came. You know. Things changed after that."

"But mother said you had such a gift. She said what Heinz did in the war was detestable. But to punish yourself? That she never understood."

A bad feeling burned inside of Johanna, like a furnace that was dangerously hot. "Past is past. You are lucky you can make a living at it. To pursue a career in music back in those days would have been considered foolish. I became a nurse. There is always work."

"But, you never sang again. Not even in a choir or around the house. Does Robert know?"

"Yes, Robert knows. Why would I keep it from him? I used to sing and I gave it up. People give up on things all the time. Life goes on. You can't do everything. It's too much." She tried to sound cavalier about it. An era had passed since those days. It had not been a conscious decision. She physically could not make the sound come out even if she'd wanted to. It was buried way down inside her, lodged like a fossil in a layer of ancient rock. It took a long time before the sound of music didn't make her stomach roil. It was hard enough for her to endure Robert's infatuation with Wagner. Thankfully her son had no great aptitude for singing. That talent had gone to Albert.

They lapsed into an uncomfortable silence. The photograph lay on the table between them. Neither one of them dared touch it now. Albert put a CD on the stereo. "Not too loud please," Johanna said. "It bothers me when it's loud."

This incomprehensible need that people had for sound around them irritated Johanna. Music every minute of every day. At home it had been the same. Heinz had become a Wagner fanatic when he heard that Wagner was Hitler's favourite composer. Endless hours he sat in front of the gramophone and played *Lohengrin*. Then Robert had brought a recording home one day and it was all she could do to keep from throwing up. She knew that she had looked at him as though he had played a cruel and deliberate joke on her. She had to let it go or he would think she had lost her mind.

Johanna thought of the things hidden away in the storage locker in the basement of her apartment block. Dread seized her when she thought of Robert finding everything after she died – things that only she could reasonably explain. Suddenly there was an uncontrollable urgency for her to get back home. "I think we should call a realtor first thing in the morning."

"But tomorrow is the funeral. It can wait a day."

Johanna rose from her seat and paced around the living room. She dusted around some figurines with her finger. "I don't see any reason to wait. Do you? These have to be packed."

"She was my mother. I grew up in this house. I'd like to bury her first."

"Fine." Johanna picked up her coffee and carried it to the guest room. She sat on the edge of the bed and stared at the dresser. The music bled through the walls. It was always too loud. Albert probably thought she was in here crying when actually she was waging an internal battle to quell the surging memories of a brother she could not bear to think of and a sister she never knew.

CHAPTER 7

The sound of Mozart's *Symphony No. 40* washed over Robert. Karl Böhm conducted and the relaxed tempo of the first movement took Robert by surprise. He was just settling into it when the telephone rang. He was relieved to hear his mother's voice. "Mother," he exhaled into the phone. "How is everything?"

"Oh, we're fine here." We – she meant Albert. "How's Felix?"

He should have known it would be her first thought. Then he remembered. The cover was still on the cage. An angry protest erupted as the cloth was lifted. "He's fine."

Robert peered into the cage to view the numerous feathers that littered the bottom. Stress.

"Turn your music down. It's so loud. I can hardly hear you." He had been hearing those words his entire life. The music was never quiet enough. He pressed PAUSE and waited to see if his mother would say she could still hear it.

"That's better. Albert tells me the neighbours want Barbara's couch. I don't know what to do about that."

Her voice far away, Robert pictured her in her black sweater and skirt, on the sofa, picking at her cuticles. "Why do they want the couch?"

"Oh, you know people. Because it's there. Up for grabs. They probably don't even need it. Albert's already made arrangements for everything to go to the church sale. The neighbours can go and buy it there."

"I suppose."

"Did you call the hospital?"

Damn! No, he had not yet notified the hospital. "I'll call as soon as I hang up. I've had a busy day." His eyes searched for a bit of paper on which to write himself a reminder. "What's the number?"

"Oh," she sighed. "You'll have to look it up. I have it written down at home. Call and tell them I am visiting family for a couple of weeks."

"Visiting family?" Robert frowned.

"Well, I don't want any fuss. I'll tell them when I get back."

"If you were just visiting family wouldn't you have planned your trip and let them know ahead of time?"

There was silence at the other end. "Fine. Tell them it's a family emergency."

"All right." She sounded a bit upset. It was easiest for Robert to agree to whatever she asked. "When will you be back?"

"There's a lot to do here. Albert will help me go through it after the funeral but he can only stay a few days. He's got rehearsals.

Of course. To play Pooh Bah in *The Mikado* no doubt. A role he'd been playing for ten years. Non-stop. It was the only role he played anymore. Because he had gotten fat, Robert mused.

A dog yipped in the hallway. He thought maybe Marcelline was on her way to his door. His ear tuned into the sounds of the hallway but he heard nothing and there was no knock at his door. "If Felix is nervous you can give him a bath. He likes a warm bath."

"He bites my fingers. He knows I'm not you."

"He needs a bath."

"I don't think he's nervous." It was enough to remember to feed him.

"Just give him some apple then. Leave the peel on. It's good for him."

"Maybe I could eat the peel."

"Do whatever you like," she laughed a little. "I'll call after the funeral, Robert. Did you try the soup?"

"It was good."

"Not too spicy?"

"No. Very good."

They hung up. Johanna had sounded all right. A bit anxious, but that was to be expected. Robert placed the call to the hospital and tried to remember what it was Johanna had wanted him to say. He got a machine so he simply stated she had to fly to Calgary for a family emergency.

The bird danced nervously with Robert's approach; it was never the tall man, always the tiny woman who fed and cooed at him. Robert removed the small plastic tray and filled it with birdseed. "You don't want a bath do you?"

The bird cocked its head and blinked at Robert. Animals were so cunning. "I'm going to pretend I didn't see that."

• • • •

Just as Robert was sitting down to eat the chicken cordon bleu that he'd picked up at the takeout counter from the grocery store, the doorbell rang. Instantly, his heart jumped. It would do no good to pretend he wasn't at home. The first movement of Sibelius' symphony was blaring from the speakers. He was trying to decide if the orchestra would be able to manage the tempo of the third movement. There was only so much liberty he could take with it. It could not be kindergarten slow and if he took it at a proper tempo it would fall apart after the first two bars and the violins would never recover. There was a persistent knock at the door and Robert picked up his plate and trod towards the door. "Coming."

There stood Marcelline, holding out another Styrofoam container. "Oh," her face fell. "You're eating."

"Just started," Robert said eying the container she held and trying to deduce what was inside. Perhaps it was something tastier than his chicken.

"I brought you some lasagne. It's really cheesy."

"Hmm," Robert didn't care too much for lasagne. His mother used to make it sometimes but it was always runny and the noodles mushy. "That's very thoughtful of you, but I have my dinner. In half an hour I have to run out to rehearsal."

"Do you want some company? I'll eat the lasagne."

What an odd girl. Felix scuttled around on his perch and reminded Robert that indeed, once in awhile, he did want company. Perhaps this would be the perfect time. He did have to leave soon. "Sure, come on in. I'll get you a fork. We have to share the table with Felix."

"Oooh," she cooed. "So that's what he looks like. Aren't you a pretty little fellow?"

The sound of a female voice cheered Felix up and he bobbed his head up and down with delight the same way he did with Johanna and never did with Robert. Marcelline dropped her bag at the door and slipped out of her untied boots. They sat across from each other, each with a Styrofoam container steaming in front of them. Marcelline had her hair pinned back with silver barrettes. She wore her white blouse and black pants from work. The final movement of the symphony started and Robert watched Marcelline for signs of life as the strings soared and the brass blew their brains out.

"Is this your orchestra?" She was hunched over her container.

"No, this is the Chicago Symphony." What else could he say? He picked at his chicken with his fork. "I have a dress rehearsal tonight."

"Why do they call it that anyway?"

"It's meant to be a run through. No more rehearsing. Everything should be in place." He sighed. "Should be, but never is."

"Is this something they can play?"

Where to begin with a beginner? "I am trying to decide. Probably. The second violins always sounded like buzzing flies anyway."

"I took cello in school for three years. Then volleyball took over my life. I forgot everything."

"I see. And now? What takes over your life now?"

"Work. Just like it does everyone. I've been thinking about joining a volleyball league. Some of my friends play."

Robert pondered this. Rare was the time he thought of his work as work. It was what he always intended to do with his life. How do you end up waiting tables at The Cocoa Bean instead of doing what you wanted? So many people scratching their heads at the end of the day thinking there must be more to life than this.

"Come over here," he said and pulled the piano bench out. "We have ten minutes. I'll give you a short lesson."

"Really?" She let her fork drop and skipped over to the bench. Robert explained the keyboard to her and then made her find each C, each F and then each A, which she did with ease. She played for five minutes.

"Now, what are the black notes for?"

"We'll save that for your next lesson." He glanced at his watch. "Right now I have to go."

She looked disappointed as she continued to scan the keyboard. "When is my next lesson?"

"I'll let you know." Not sure what he had started, he suddenly added: "Say, would you like to help me out tonight? I could use someone up in the balcony to tell me how the orchestra sounds."

"What?" She wiggled in the chair. "I don't know anything at all about music, except what you showed me just now. Don't forget I'm half deaf."

"That means you can half hear. I just need to know if you can hear all the instruments." He didn't really need to know anything of the sort, and knew how ridiculous it sounded to ask her, but something came over him as he watched her at the keyboard, eager to learn. This was what he did – he taught people to appreciate music. He would not turn his back on what he had started.

On the way to rehearsal they listened to the third act of *The Flying Dutchman* in Robert's car. "Is this your favourite kind of music?" She asked. After dinner she had run to her apartment to change into a pair of old jeans and a green t-shirt. On her feet she wore a pair of sandals, little daisies painted onto her big toe nails.

"Yes, I suppose it is. And you? What is your favourite kind of music?" He braced for her reply.

"Classic rock. Like Pink Floyd, the Doors, Led Zepplin. All those old guys. My favourite though are the Grateful Dead."

"Hmm." At least it was something Robert had heard of. Leonard used to listen to that stuff. They would sit in his basement and smoke marijuana and not get high although Leonard claimed he felt it. Each of them had a couple of tie-dyed t-shirts that they made in art class at school.

"What exactly does that mean? Grateful Dead?"

"I think it's meant to be ironic, like once you're dead you don't have a chance to be grateful, or anything to be grateful for. So you better do it when you're alive. At least all their music sounds like they are happy to be alive."

"Or maybe they are simply grateful to be dead."

"Oh, come on." This time he deserved a punch in the arm.

Robert guided Marcelline up to the balcony where he deposited her in the middle of the first row. "You can see and listen from here. I'll ask you later how everything sounds."

"All right, but I'm sure everything will sound great to me."

The hall gradually filled as patients made their way along the rows of seats. This process took awhile as many of them had a hard time deciding where to sit. Others were wheeled in or guided by nurses. Robert stood in the wings a moment and watched this process. The dress rehearsals had become popular in the hospital. It was advertised on posters and through the hospital intranet as a concert series featuring the university orchestra. The concerts were held late on Thursday afternoons and Robert noticed over the past three years they had been performing here that more and more staff members attended, people who were not accompanying patients, possibly people who knew a thing or two about the music. He asked his mother once who they all were and she said a lot of them were the maintenance and housekeeping staff and some who worked in the kitchen. "*Die Menschen*," he had said and she'd scowled. It suited him to give free concerts to those people. They otherwise might never know what a live performance of classical music sounded like.

His mother sometimes popped in at some point during the rehearsal with her friend Angela but never stayed. There was one time during a performance of Gounod's "St. Cecilia Mass" that Robert left the stage in order to hear what the orchestra sounded like in the middle of the hall. As he turned and loped up the centre aisle he saw his mother leaning against the back wall, her arms wrapped across her body, and her eyes closed as though she were in a rapturous embrace. The sight of her like that stopped him in his tracks. He stared at her a moment while the orchestra played on. Usually when he caught sight of her in the audience she sat with a stiff and uncomfortable posture, almost wincing with anticipation of the sound. Quickly he turned so that she would not see him looking. After that performance she had again declared that the music was nice and gave no indication that she had been moved at all.

The musicians warmed up and tuned their instruments. They were all dressed in blue jeans and black t-shirts to give some semblance of order to their presence. Robert wore black trousers and a black turtleneck – casual but distinguished. Up in the balcony he saw Marcelline leaning over the railing. He wondered why she would choose to take up volleyball over the cello. He would have to ask her later.

The acoustics in the hall were remarkable and the orchestra had been spoiled with the sound it created. The brass hardly had to touch their lips to their mouthpieces for the sound to fill the hall. Robert reviewed the score and cringed when he heard the shriek of the piccolo struggle to force out a tricky exposed passage. The concertmaster tuned the orchestra and then Robert strode to the podium and bowed at the smattering of applause. Marcelline beamed at him from on high. He raised the baton and gave it a 'hurrah' twirl in her direction. Then he turned and faced the orchestra, instruments up and players ready. This was the moment. He looked at the faces before him and nodded with a smile. Here is where you and I must connect – he sent the message telepathically. Two wires touch to create a spectacle of colour, smoke and fire. The last rehearsal had been terrible and he let it be so. Sometimes there was nothing more motivating than a terrible rehearsal to rouse the fear of God in people. His hopes were high that tonight the group would shine.

He raised his baton and began the Stravinsky. In the audience the patients shifted uncomfortably. They didn't like it. It was too bizarre for them. In the middle of the "Berceuse" the fire alarms clanged, slowly, oddly fitting into the music's strange beats. He carried on with the piece. Those alarms never meant anything. The piccolo player played her sweet heart out and clashed with the ringing alarm. Robert beamed at her. Finally, something that sounded worse than her. With one ear he listened for the announcement. There, it came: Code Red – C6. Nowhere near them. Probably burnt toast.

As they left the hospital and made their way for the car, they saw it had rained. Light drops continued to fall. He paused and scanned the lot. All the cars looked alike. Marcelline remembered where Robert had left the car and he dutifully followed her. On the way home they listened to the radio and Marcelline asked if he would like to listen to some *modern* music at her place.

In her apartment Robert found himself on the sofa with a glass of white wine in his hand. There was dust around the base of the glass that he swept at with his finger. Marcelline changed from her sandals into heavy hand knit socks. Her apartment was filled with tiny plastic toys and comic books and an enormous aquarium in which circled a one-eyed angelfish. A poster of Annie Lennox graced the wall.

"What happened?" He asked as he watched her feed the poor fish who couldn't always see its food as it made its way in an elliptical path around its home. A cat appeared and hopped onto a cat perch to watch the feeding of the fish.

"They didn't tell me at the store that an angelfish and a Siamese fighting fish wouldn't get along."

"The other fish poked its eye out?" Robert was amazed that violence would erupt between creatures so small.

"Yeah," Marcelline laughed a hiccuppy laugh. "He wasn't in there two seconds and wham – shark attack!"

Robert sipped his wine and tried hard to suppress a pucker. He swirled the glass out of habit.

"It's nothing special, that wine," she said. "I just like a glass after work sometimes."

"Hmm, I concur."

"That it's nothing special or that you like a glass after work?"

"Both, actually." Relieved that she knew what concur meant. The fact made him relax and he accepted a second glass while she played a Grateful Dead record for him. Another surprise – that she owned a turntable and six milk crates filled with every record she'd ever bought.

"Do you recognize any of it?" She sat in an orange beanbag chair and sipped her wine with little cat-like sips. He smiled and said he did. It was the kind of music that sounded instantly recognizable even if you'd never heard it before.

"Thank you, Marcelline," he said after the record ended. The last of his wine went down with a gulp. He was ready to go. "I'm glad you were there tonight. I don't often have anyone in the audience to tell me how it sounds."

"I was happy to be there. It sounded great." She stood with him and gave him a quick peck on the cheek. When he got home he briefly pondered the significance of the kiss. Then he inspected his own wineglasses and gave them each a wipe with a dry cloth.

• • • •

When Johanna woke up it was to the sound of Albert's voice as he performed his vocal exercises: low guttural growls followed by a series of strange mewling sounds, followed by a fit of coughing. He hummed scales like a buzz-saw. Once he was through with his scales and arpeggios he sang "Braid the Raven Hair" in a lovely falsetto. At first she wondered if he was doing it on purpose, given their conversation the previous evening. She lay in bed and listened to him. It made sense that he had to practise. This wasn't some childish way of rubbing it in her face.

But he would never understand. The decision was not hers to make. She had tried once at one of Robert's rehearsals to be moved by the music. It had been so long since she had even tried to really listen to music that she wondered if she was even able to feel anything the way she used to. Way at the back of the hall she stood with her eyes closed. It had nearly killed her to let her guard down like that and she instantly regretted it. Cold sweat, dry mouth, a racing heart. Singing would not redeem her in the eyes of the world. She was compelled to do something that would make some difference to people. Something that would make up for the evil her past represented. But even though she spoke the soothing words, and held the ailing hands, she never felt anything more than pity. There was no well from which to coax more complex emotions. Beauty was lost to Heinz. The war had robbed him of the ability to see it. And because of him Johanna suffered the same loss.

• • • •

Albert had already made coffee for her and was fussing over a pot of peppermint tea when Johanna got to the kitchen. "What do you normally have for breakfast?" he asked. There was a half-eaten toasted bagel on the counter.

"Usually I make my breakfast in the blender," she said with an uncertain smile, wondering if she was supposed to mention his singing. "I'll just have toast. My appetite isn't what it should be. That was nice, your singing."

He shrugged. "Just trying to stay in shape. I hope it didn't bother you." Albert came over to where she stood and squeezed her shoulders for longer than she felt comfortable. She spilled some of the coffee she was pouring. "It'll be a tough day but we'll get through it. I was going to go for a massage this morning. I can make an appointment for you too."

"No, I think I'll stay here. Maybe I'll go through some boxes. I have to call Robert. It's his birthday today. I was going to make him a ham." She paused. "How many people do you think will come after the service?"

"I don't know. The ladies from the church will be here to set up."

"They will be here when we are out?"

"Yes, that's how they do it. They set up while the service is going on so that things are prepared and ready when guests arrive."

"I don't know if I want them in here unsupervised."

Albert suppressed a smile. "They are church ladies, Johanna. The most they will do is peek under the teacups."

"Well, I don't like that much either."

After Albert left, she sat at the table and gazed out the kitchen window through the bright orange curtains she'd helped Barbara hang the last time she was here. They were a bit wild for her taste with big carrots and yellow peppers on them, but Barbara insisted that the kitchen be a cheery room and she had grown tired of the limes and lemons that preceded these. Johanna didn't understand how a person could constantly change things around them. She was thankful for the stability in her life and the muted colours in her apartment. There was an even tone there. It calmed her.

She moved to the living room and set to work. There was no point in sorting though a big box of fabric ends. It all could all be thrown away. She picked up the phone and called Robert. "Happy birthday. I'll make you a ham when I get back. How are you?"

"Oh fine. Rehearsal went well last night."

"The service is this afternoon. I'm trying to get the place ready before the church ladies get here."

"The church ladies?"

"Oh, Albert's arranged it all. They come while the service is on and prepare the food and coffee." She sighed. "It's all a bit much, but I'm sure Barbara would have wanted something like this."

"Will there be a lot of people?"

"Oh, it's hard to say. People come out of the woodwork for these things. I won't know any of them, but that's all right. They can mingle with each other. I'd rather see that nothing goes missing." There was a flutter of nerves in her chest when she thought about the service. She and Albert would be the main attraction and all the others would be there to gawk at the sister Barbara used to talk about. She wondered what Barbara might have said about her.

"How are you holding up?" he asked, knowing already what she would say.

"As good as can be expected." She tried to make her voice sound cheery, before Robert asked her too many questions. "There are so many things to do. Boxes to sort through and such. Then I suppose we'll call a realtor and sell the house. Albert knows someone. I won't have to stay too much longer. How is Felix?"

"He misses you but he's okay."

"Good. Let him out of the cage once in awhile. He needs his exercise. I'll see you soon." Johanna hung up the phone and felt a pang. She wished she were at home. This couch was too soft. It hurt her back. Robert wouldn't let the bird out. He was probably just teaching it silly things to say. It felt strange to be here without Barbara and with Albert whom she hardly knew. At home there was the comfort of her routine, her conversations with Frank and his effusive appreciation of her sandwiches. And, Pearl. She wished she could knock on Pearl's door and drink instant coffee and watch the shopping channel with her. She longed for the predictable right now. All of her joints felt loose. At any moment she could collapse, literally, like a shaky table. Just collapse onto the floor into fifty useless pieces.

"How's it going?"

Johanna spun around, her heart in her throat. Her knee bumped the table and bits of coloured fabric spilled onto the floor. "Oh! Albert. You startled me. I am thoroughly absorbed here. I've lost track of the time. How was your massage?"

"Excellent. I feel much better. My back was getting stiff and I can't sing if the muscles aren't relaxed."

"Of course." Johanna got to her feet. "Oh, I got up too fast." The walls went black and she clung to the wall a moment until it passed. "I'll fix some lunch and then I'll vacuum through."

The doorbell rang. There was a delivery of flowers that Johanna placed on the buffet with the others. None of the names on the cards meant anything to her. She did her best to arrange all the flowers nicely and have the cards on display for when the people came after the service. They would want to see that their condolences had been received. Then she rearranged everything in the fridge to make room for all the food the church ladies were bringing over and laid out fresh tea towels and a few good cutting knives. She was not sure what else to do to make things easier for them.

CHAPTER 8

Johanna returned from Calgary wan and tired, a transparency to her skin that had not been apparent when she left. Robert picked up her suitcase from where she left it by the elevator. Frank, thankfully, was somewhere making his rounds when they arrived, so Robert was able to shepherd Johanna upstairs without a stirring overture from the doorman. Pearl's door popped open as soon as they stepped off the elevator. The television blared from her living room. She wore a worn pink sweat suit and untied runners with no socks. "Johanna, you're back!"

She stumbled from the support of the doorframe, her jagged hips propelling her with outstretched arms. Johanna turned and smiled. She steadied Pearl with her forearm. "Yes, I'm back, Pearl."

"Come have a coffee with me when you're unpacked." Pearl had returned to the doorframe and clutched at it with pink painted fingernails. A puzzled look crossed her face as though she was trying to recall why she had opened the door. "And you too, Robert. There's always enough."

Robert wondered if she had that southern drawl in her voice when she was sober. Coffee indeed. She could do with a cup once in awhile just to change it up. He smiled and tipped an imaginary Panama hat at Pearl and followed Johanna inside. The invitation – an immediate task – would suit Johanna.

"Mother, you look thin." Robert said, following her gaze around the apartment.

"I haven't had any exercise in a week and a half. I didn't exactly want to walk outside in a strange neighbourhood. And it was hard to eat there. Barbara had everything in the freezer, you don't know where it comes from or how long it's been there." Felix recognized her voice and performed a song and dance across his perch.

"There's no food in his dish." She frowned and reached into the cage where Felix pecked affectionately at her hand. "Say JoJo, Felix. Come on. Aren't you happy to see me? JoJo."

He perched on her finger as she carried him over to the bookshelf where he hopped up onto the top shelf and waddled back and forth, chirping with uncontrollable mirth.

"He's been fed. I think he ate himself sick without you here. Look how frisky he is now that you're back. Come to think of it, Pearl seemed kind of frisky too."

"Be nice. I'm going to unpack. Keep an eye on Felix for me."

Robert sat down. He wished his mother had a stereo. Anything other than the cheap plastic radio she kept on the kitchen counter to listen to call-in shows and the news. He had offered many times to give her his old one as an excuse for him to upgrade to something better, but she always refused, claiming not to have time to sit and listen to music. It completely baffled him how something as universally essential as music could be deemed superfluous. It was like one of those vague allergies some people had to the sun or the wind. Not a day went by that he did not listen to music. Impossible.

Johanna opened the suitcase on her bed. There was one photograph of herself and Barbara that Johanna had helped herself to. It had been taken when they were last together, in Barbara's back yard. They each held a wine glass, raised up in a toast. Barbara was laughing at Johanna and Johanna was locked in a gaze with the lens because she wanted to see when the timer went off. They had balanced the camera on the deck railing and had taken three of the same photo.

There had been hundreds of old black and white photos, all arranged in albums with the years written in felt pen on little stickers stuck to the spines. Johanna remembered putting them all in a box before they left Germany and handing them over to Barbara once they got to Canada without looking through them. When she came across them again in Barbara's closet, she did the same thing for Albert. The past didn't interest her the way it did most people. Nostalgia was for the soft-hearted – for those who found fulfillment in their yearning and sought solace from the dead. Even without the photos Johanna's mind was a whir with vivid, disjointed scenes and images, like a silent newsreel.

The church had been about three-quarters full. Everyone smiled at Johanna as though they knew her. Albert did his best to introduce her to the people he knew. Others approached and introduced themselves with downcast eyes. Many people came from the salon where Barbara worked, some may have been clients. Then there were others from the church. When Johanna turned her back she knew they whispered, but she could not make out what they were saying. Her purse was filled with tissue but she knew she would not tear up in front of all those strangers. She and Albert sat in the front pew and Johanna had to endure the strain of being the focus of everyone's attention. She had never been comfortable in a church: a place to be judged. All the people in the pews – God's filters.

There were sniffles and sobs behind her and Johanna thought everyone was watching to see when she too might shed a tear. Albert dabbed at his eyes. He looked down at her and smiled. Not sure what he meant, she reached out and squeezed his arm in an attempt to keep the peace. They had never talked of her singing again and Johanna had it in her mind that it was the only thing he thought about now. Every time he opened his mouth she was afraid he would bring it up.

Albert stood beside Johanna after the service as the mourners filed by. They all spoke fondly of Barbara and wept when they thought about her and squeezed Johanna's hand. When they saw no tears welling in Johanna's eyes, they blinked their wet lashes and tore themselves away to be with someone else who shared their sorrow. Whispers and hushed conversations buzzed around her and Johanna tried to ignore them. At the cemetery, Johanna braced herself as the coffin was lowered into the ground. She wrapped her arms around herself in an effort to hold herself together. All of a sudden she stopped breathing. She was very aware of this and tried not to panic. Her fingers and toes moved on command. She was able to bite her lip. But her lungs had seized completely. Her fingers clutched spasmodically at her arms. She shook her head back and forth. Alfred cast a worried look her way and she turned her back to him and indicated for him to hit her on the back. Three times he thumped on her back. People must have seen. Finally, she hacked out a breath and took another in. Without a word she reassumed her place before Barbara's grave.

• • • •

Johanna's mind eased with the growing pile of dirty clothes beside her, a well-defined task. Some order to her day. She carried the empty suitcase back to the front closet. Robert had the doors open and she could hear the seagulls. The fresh air blowing in was a soothing presence. Johanna checked through the mail and took a few sips of wine. She slipped her shoes off and discovered a hole in the toe of her stockings. "I'll have to have a shower later. All that airplane air is seeping into my pores. I've got to scrub it off before I feel toxic. Lord knows what it does to your lungs up there."

Robert had prepared a tray with cheese and crackers and he bit into a wedge of Camembert. Johanna scanned the tray and then took a rice cracker and nibbled around the edges. "Oh, Albert is coming on Wednesday. He's got rehearsals and performances at The Grand."

"What do you mean coming? Coming here?"

"Yes, he's coming here. Staying here, with me. I hope you'll have some time to spend with him. Heat up some soup if you're hungry. I'll have a bowl when I finish cleaning up."

"For how long?" It felt just like all the other times he and Albert were forced into one another's company. Robert emptied his drink and reached for the bottle.

"Three weeks or so. You might like to get to know him now. He wants to get to know his family. People do change. He sings all over North America."

Three weeks of incessant humming and ice-cube crunching. Robert slumped down in his chair. Johanna simply stared at him from the bathroom door. "You always used to get along. Why should it be so different now?"

Why indeed? He and Albert hardly knew one another. How could they when their interests were diametrically opposed, antagonistic even? Wagner and Gilbert and Sullivan shared no common ground. Albert was married with twin boys. Robert, an avowed bachelor with a few finicky African violets, dusty wineglasses and a bottle of fine scotch that was always on the verge of being empty.

Robert tried to think of the last time he and Albert had seen one another. It had to have been on one of their summer vacations. After his father died, he and his mother made the trip out west a few summers in a row. They would drive up into the mountains and stay in motels with swimming pools. Without fail, Albert would cannonball into the water off the diving board and then challenge Robert to do the same. Robert, with his fear of heights, would paddle around the shallow end and jeer at Albert about his weight and pasty skin. And Albert would call Robert a pansy and try to dive under the water and pull Robert under. He swore one time that Albert was really going to drown him. He would heave himself up onto Robert and push down on his head and hold it under the water. The rule of this kind of horseplay was to let the other person up when they really start to thrash around. Albert gave no sign of letting Robert up until Robert finally decided to try going limp and he hung lifelessly in the water and let his arms and legs float to the top.

"You asshole," he screamed when finally Albert let go and swam away.

"Pussy," Albert screeched back. The screech in his voice wavered and Robert knew he had scared Albert a little.

This was how they used to get along. It gave Robert the jitters to think how they would manage now.

• • • •

Her first shift back at the hospital and Johanna's arms itched. She sniffed the sleeve of her smock but couldn't tell if they'd switched the detergent or not. The dream that woke her in the early hours of the morning coursed around her brain: she is on the plane, sitting next to the same old man from her flight to Calgary. He asks if she wants to see photos of his grandchildren. When he opens his wallet, there is a shadowy black and white photo of two bodies, emaciated and naked with wide, garish eyes and skeletal arms and legs. The man in the photo holds his hand out towards the camera. They have no teeth and the skin over their bellies lies in loose folds. The man laughs a little and apologizes. Sorry, those are my parents. When he flips to the next photo, it is the same thing. Photo after photo he shows her of prisoners. Finally she grabs his hand and shakes it. Is this some kind of a joke? Where are your grandchildren? She demands. Spit flies from her mouth. She screams at him and he cowers, pulling his wallet away. Somewhere. They're here somewhere…

A terrible dream. She still felt numb as she wheeled her cart past Karen's office. A voice yodelled after her. "Jo? Come on in here a minute."

Johanna stopped the cart and peered inside.

"How are you? We were all so sorry to hear..." Karen looked up briefly from her computer. "Just a sec. Have a seat."

Johanna saw that both chairs in Karen's office were draped with children's clothing. "Thank you. I got the flowers and the card." Johanna rested one foot on the bottom of the cart and rolled it back and forth.

Karen rose from her desk and approached the door. Her hand reached for Johanna. Copper fingernails, expertly painted, clasped her arm. "Are you sure you're all right to be back? It's awfully soon."

"I'm fine," Johanna said. "I'd rather keep busy." She made a slight motion with her arm and Karen let go. Johanna took a step back. "I better get upstairs."

Johanna noticed more toys and clothing than usual stacked in Karen's office. "Things from Brenda's neighbour," Karen explained. "We're thinking of opening a store on eBay."

"I didn't know that was possible," Johanna replied. For some reason this made Karen laugh.

"Oh, Jo! Anything's possible." And it was, according to the posters Karen hung in the volunteer lounge to inspire them.

One time Karen had exclaimed to Johanna, "I just love your accent. It's so dignified." She had said the word dignified as though she were bestowing a blessing on Johanna. For years Johanna had tried to lose her accent. Ever since Karen had drawn attention to it, she didn't like to say much around her. It made her self-conscious. She knew what Karen thought of her. Maybe right now she felt sorry for her because her sister had died, but on a normal day they thought of her as a person who had been through the war. The war: the one where six million Jews were killed. Where the German people let a madman come to power and then stood naively by while he tried to exterminate an entire people. They might have thought she had something to do with it. Six million was not a number that anyone could be expected to comprehend. It was unfathomable. When she imagined those ghostly prisoners, huddled together, all their dreams diminished to a base instinct, and then to view the piles of corpses – it was staggering. Johanna could only allow thin slivers of those images through at a time. To Karen and others, there was no Germany other than the one that existed between 1933 and 1945. That was the legacy of all German people who lived through it and those that followed. Johanna was among those who suffered such guilt: guilt by association. This was how the Nazis had ruled and the fear still resonated down generations. Some, like Barbara, could ignore it and others, like Johanna, shaped their lives around it.

• • • •

At the end of her shift when Johanna removed her smock, her arms were covered in a rash.

"Did they switch the detergent?" she asked Angela.

"I have no idea." Angela checked her arms. "Nothing here. Maybe it's stress. You have been through a lot lately."

Johanna scowled. She felt fine. "I'll just take it home and wash it there. I'm fine. The stressful part is over."

"Oh, Jo. Don't try to be so tough." Angela came over and put her arm around Johanna's shoulders. There was affection there, in those hands. Johanna stood still and let Angela squeeze her arm.

"I have to be tough, Angela. How else do you get through these things?"

"You let your friends help you." She stood in front of her now with her hands on Johanna's shoulders and looked seriously into her eyes. "There's no shame in mourning someone you've lost, Johanna. We've all been through it by now. We're seniors after all."

Johanna smiled. "I'll be fine."

"I'll be watching." Angela let go and stood by while Johanna pulled on her sweater. She was the second person to cast doubt on Johanna's fitness for work. It wasn't in Johanna to pull the curtains and sit in the dark until the sadness passed. It never would if that's how she went about it. It reminded her of the time when Jim died and nobody could understand why she wanted to continue working when there was a sizeable settlement from the workers compensation board and the hospital she could comfortably retire on. She used to feel the eyes boring into her as she counted the meds for her patients – waiting for her to make a mistake, certain the stress of it all would catch up with her.

"I'll walk out with you." Angela said and hooked her arm through Johanna's.

"Sure." Johanna made sure to put a spring in her step as she led Angela along. On the way out Angela chattered to Johanna about her day. Everyday Karen told them what time the flowers were coming and to make sure the deliveries were done *asap*. "She loves saying that – *asap*. She never spells it out like normal people but says it like a word. Say, Robert's orchestra sounded really good last week. Was that his girlfriend with him?"

"His what?" Johanna wasn't paying attention.

"He had a girl with him. She listened from the balcony. He smiled up at her every time he turned around." Angela grinned expectantly at Johanna.

"I don't know. What did she look like?"

"She looked nice enough. I couldn't really see her from where I was." Angela tugged at Johanna's arm. "What do you mean what does she look like? How many girlfriends does he have?"

"I don't know."

Bewildered, Johanna drove slowly home. Angela could have been mistaken. It could have been a student, or no one in particular. If Robert had a girlfriend, surely she would have noticed.

• • • •

"How's your mother doing?" Leonard liked to call right after he'd eaten and before any good programs came on television. Robert stretched his legs out under his desk. A stack of essays on philosophy and music lay untouched before him. A pot of coffee perked in the kitchen. He was settling in for a late night.

"Oh, she's fine. Albert is coming to do a show at The Grand."

"Ah, the celebrated tenor."

"Baritone, actually. I haven't seen or heard from him since we were kids. I'm not all that eager to re-establish our old rivalry. He was never my favourite company."

"Why not?"

"Oh, he was just a bit weird. Kind of wimpy. You know how kids are. He's married now. Has twins."

"Twins? They didn't go in-vitro did they?"

"I have no idea."

"They're lucky they only had two if they did. I've had it with these people screeching about their miracle babies, having five at a time. It's not a miracle. It's a bloody travesty. Everyone's up in arms about genetically modified tomatoes and we're breeding babies like Dachshunds." Leonard paused to cough. "Are you going see him?"

"See him? I've got no choice. I've been recruited as head chauffeur and social co-ordinator, besides which I will have to attend a performance of the bloody *Mikado*. Have mercy!"

"You poor shmuck," Leonard said. "Led to the gallows."

Robert groaned. "I may have to call on you to help me out. Would you come to dinner once?"

"Of course. Can I bring a date?"

"I'll bring one for you."

"Sounds good."

Good? It was a stroke of genius. He would ask Marcelline. At least then there would be two more people to steer the conversation away from Albert's theatre chatter. Leonard's dates never seemed to work out anyway. After he hung up Robert turned the oven on and pulled a frozen chicken pie from the freezer. It clunked onto the cookie sheet, a desolate sound. The frozen food clunk – across the city tonight countless people were experiencing the loneliness brought on by a frozen entrée.

Leonard was probably doing the same thing. Twice divorced and one son living in Ottawa. Ever since he and his second wife split up, Robert heard from him a lot more. His first marriage had segued into the second by way of an affair he'd been having. But now he was alone for the first time in years and relied on Robert for company. Although Robert spent a lot of his time alone, he did not always feel lonely the way Leonard did. Solitude was a necessity for Robert. Too much time spent in the company of others and his stomach became dyspeptic.

CHAPTER 9

With all her preparations for Albert's visit Johanna had forgotten she had a meeting first thing in the morning. Karen, Brenda and Judy sat at the head of the table in the volunteer lounge. Their collective perfumes were overpowering. Brenda passed out agendas to the handful of volunteers who were scheduled to work. A box of muffins was passed around the table. The box paused in front of Johanna who declined.

"Have one," Marg implored. "You need your strength."

Johanna suppressed a frown. She was tired of them all waiting for her to fall apart. This brief persistence with the muffins, the constant rueful looks they cast upon her; she'd had enough. "I'm fine. I had a big breakfast, I promise."

Once everyone was settled with a coffee and a muffin, Karen brought the meeting to order. A sheaf of agendas was passed around and each of them dutifully slid one onto the table in front of them and studied it. Such officious behaviour for a meeting with three volunteers. It was laughable the way some people wore their authority like a gold cape. Karen might as well have a gold cape – all available body parts dangled with gold. When Karen clapped her hand on the table to start the meeting Angela nudged Johanna's foot under the table and pretended to puzzle over the agenda as though she didn't understand it. Johanna bit her lip and let Karen prattle on about the inventory that needed to be completed by next week.

You had to really listen to what Karen was saying because she smiled no matter what was coming out of her mouth. There was a new volunteer starting at the end of the week. Johanna would do the orientation. After the meeting Marg and Angela helped Johanna try to find a smock, but there were none. Karen didn't know where there would be a smock if the usual places didn't produce one. "Just wear a lab coat for today, Jo. You don't want anything spilled on your pretty blouse." When she said this she brushed her fingertips along Johanna's sleeve.

Johanna kicked herself for forgetting. The patients were used to the pink smocks and had there been one she would have had it on before the meeting. The lab coat was too big and Johanna rolled up the sleeves to just below her elbow so that she could see her watch.

"So, did you find out what Robert's girlfriend looks like?" Angela was at Johanna's side.

"She's not his girlfriend. It's a girl who lives down the hall from him." Johanna had called Robert and asked him outright. Her suspicion was confirmed the moment he told her it had been that silly girl, Marcelline. "He's teaching her piano."

"I didn't know he taught at home."

"Neither did I," Johanna shrugged. "He's doing her a favour."

Johanna had everything on her cart ready. She rolled it to the elevator. The people made room for her as she expertly backed on with the cart. On the sixth floor she got off and began her route through the north wing. A nurse smiled at her and said good morning although, like her colleagues, she was busy. Johanna tried to stay out of their way. There were a few patients in the lounge that had their money ready and bought newspapers to read. She peeked into a few rooms where the patients were eating their breakfast. Often they asked her to open some of the packages for them. "Gladly," she said. "People don't come here for the food, do they?"

Johanna peeked into the next room. A frail old man lay in the bed with both feet stuck between the railings and the sheets twisted around his body like a cocoon from which he wrestled to escape. He writhed around in the blanket trying to get out of bed but the sheets twisted tighter around him and his feet were completely jammed in the bedrails. It was terrible to watch him and Johanna approached the bed and asked if she could help. The man started to mutter and kick at the sheets but his feet wouldn't move. His hair was matted and there was food crusted on his chin. The moaning grew louder as he panicked and thrashed around. Whenever he moved his left leg he yelped.

"Come now, let me help you. Just stop for a second." Johanna pulled his legs back through the railing and unwound him from the sheets and told him to get straightened up in the bed. His eyes focussed for a moment, taking Johanna in. She smiled at him and reached over for his arm. His face froze, his steely grey eyes locked on hers. Something was wrong. Suddenly he screamed and lashed out at Johanna. She ducked out of the way. Awful animal-like sounds came from his throat, as if his leg had been caught in a trap. It was a nauseating sound – snarling and grunting. She tried again to get near but he thrashed and screamed, getting completely stuck and entangled in the sheets. Johanna sensed his panic. He yelled, "No, no, no." Over and over and then "Get away from me!" He had no strength for more words. He lurched around on the bed trying with no hope of getting free. Johanna worried that someone would hear and think she was hurting him. He screamed again and clawed at Johanna. It was unclear whether he was pulling her close or pushing her away. The smell of urine seeped into the air. He grabbed at the bedclothes and tried to climb over the rail and away from her. His legs were bone and sinew. Johanna got hold of his arm and pulled him back into bed, afraid it would break in her grip and then she saw it – a faded blue tattoo on the fleshy part of his arm. Her heart stopped. She held his arm a moment too long. He wrenched it free and his thick, orange fingernails dug deep into Johanna's forearm. It wasn't a quick jab, but a fiery force, like she was being branded.

"Come now." She did not know his name. With her other hand she tried to stroke his hair but when his grip didn't loosen she had to pry his fingers off her arm. For such a feeble and frail man, he possessed a lot of strength. The pain was exquisite and the intensity made its way to her head and she felt as though she might faint. A nurse came to the door. "What's going on here?"

"He's got my arm," Johanna gasped. The nurse deftly clamped her hand over the man's wrist in such a way that his fingers let go. Blood rushed into Johanna's arm and it immediately began to throb. "Thank you. He really had me there. I don't know what set him off. I was trying to help get him back into bed. He was all twisted in the sheets." Johanna prattled on to the nurse, adrenaline rushing in all directions, her heart pounding and mouth dry. The nurse straightened the patient up and covered him loosely with a sheet.

"It's that white coat. Somebody should have told you. The same thing happened to Dr. Saunders this morning but she didn't get as close as you. He's supposed to be in restraints but that really sets him off. Poor thing." She stroked his hair to calm him. "It's all right now, Harold."

"What do you mean the coat? There were no more pink smocks."

"He's a Holocaust survivor. Dachau or Auschwitz. One of those. Seeing a white lab coat must give him flashbacks. He's got Alzheimer's but some things will still trigger the switch. Let me look at your arm. I might have to fill out a report." She looked at Harold. "And he'll need a sedative. His eyes are still wild."

"A report? But I didn't do anything. I was trying to help."

The nurse laughed and guided Johanna from the room. "Not that kind of report. I have to see if you need to go to Occupational Health. Are you bleeding?"

"No." Johanna held out her arm. Deep moon shaped gouges started to turn a sinister, deep purple. There were a few flecks of blood coming from two of them. The nurse scrutinized the cuts, unable to decide if they were bad enough to go to all the trouble of reporting the incident.

"I can take care of these. I used to be a nurse here, you know."

The nurse smiled at Johanna, relieved that the reports would be avoided. "You were? When?"

"I've been retired eight years now. But, as you can see I just can't stay away." Her arm throbbed all the way into her hand. "If you have some Polysporin and gauze up here I'll wrap it and be on my way."

"Are you sure?"

"Of course! They're just little cuts. They'll be healed up in no time. Better to spend your time with Harold than with me."

"Well, it will save me a lot of trouble. Just don't let anyone from Occupational Health know. It'll be weeks before you're cleared to work if they get involved."

"I will."

The nurse disappeared to find some supplies for Johanna. She reached for a tissue and pressed it to her wounds. It was unbelievable how much the cuts stung. The man had survived Dachau. Just the name sent shivers through her. And he mistook her for one of the doctors from the camp. The nurse had said he had Alzheimer's. She wanted to feel sorry for him but worried that there was something more than the white coat that had set him off. Was it her accent, her "dignified" accent? She cursed herself for leaving her smock at home. Everything would have been fine if she'd been wearing a pink smock.

Johanna wrestled the cart back to the volunteer lounge. At the sink she picked at the tissue that had become stuck to her wounds as she ran cool water over her arm. The gouges were red. She applied a good amount of the

Polysporin and then wound the gauze over it. Angela arrived just in time to help with the tape. "What happened?"

With as little embellishment as possible Johanna recounted the story.

"I've heard that about the Holocaust survivors. You have to be careful around them. They freak out." She paused. "With good reason I guess."

Johanna nodded. Her knees wobbled. "I better sit," she said.

Angela brought her some water. "So, why don't you want Robert to have a girlfriend?"

The question took Johanna by surprise. This girlfriend really had piqued Angela's curiosity. She often asked about Robert and now it seemed something interesting might be happening to him. Most of the time Johanna didn't have that much to say about Robert. Angela wanted him to have a girlfriend. She thought it would be something that would make Johanna happy.

"I'm not sure," Johanna said. It felt strange to admit it, but Angela already knew.

"Well, mothers are naturally protective of their sons. They don't want them to be taken advantage of."

"I guess that's it." Johanna was relieved there was an explanation. She was protective of Robert. She didn't know how not to be.

Then with her usual uncanny sense of timing, Karen poked her head in the door. "There you are, Jo. I just got a call from the nurse up on six. Is everything all right?"

Johanna waved her bandaged arm at her. "Nancy," she said. It was just like Karen not to know anybody's name. "I'm just fine. All fixed up."

"You look pale."

"The guy thought she was from the concentration camp." Angela said, happy to have some details to add. "He freaked out and attacked her."

"It wasn't exactly as bad as that. I was trying to help him and he became confused and combative. I'll be fine." It irked her that Nancy had called. Now Karen might insist on a report. These managers all had the same agenda – to gather information and keep things in thick files. She did not want a report on file that said she was attacked by a Holocaust survivor.

"She's a bit shaken up," Angela said and patted Johanna on the back. "I'll take care of her."

"Go on home for today, Jo," Karen said. "And if you need some time off, just let me know. You've been through so much lately. It's amazing that you're even here. I'll run up to the ward and talk to the nurse."

She made it sound serious. Like lives had been lost. Johanna was tired of everyone waiting for her to fall apart.

"I was trying to prevent a patient from falling out of bed. That's all. I didn't hurt him." Johanna wasn't sure now what Nancy would say. Sometimes people changed their stories. Karen would go up there and make a big deal of everything and make Nancy unsure of what had happened.

"I'll let her know of your intention." Completely insincere, standing with all her weight on one leg, hip protruding, hand on jutted hip, her head aflame with newly-dyed orange hair. Why did she talk like that? Using words like intention?

Johanna rose to go. "I'll be in tomorrow," Johanna said, her voice acid. Her head spun as the events of the morning reeled incessantly before her. Angela saw her to her car.

"You can report back to Karen that you've escorted me off the premises."

"You know she'll be asking." Angela leaned in through the open window. "See you tomorrow. Don't forget your smock."

"Never again."

Once safely in her car, Johanna's arm really started to burn, all the way down to her hand and up past her elbow. She glanced up at the building and thought she saw Karen watching from her office window. Johanna felt the car pull forward; felt her hands on the wheel. Past all the cars, different colours but muted grey with dust. The streets weren't busy that time of day, late morning. The car glided along, nearly floating as Johanna steered for home. She wished she knew what Karen was up to. What to expect the next time she rounded a corner and came face to face with her.

At least the extra time would give her a chance to make sure everything was set for when Robert and Albert arrived. Her arm throbbed with deep pulsing beats. Those fingernails had seared through her. Had he hung on any longer she might have needed stitches. For the old man, the incident was probably already forgotten, but all the nurses would know about it by now. And whenever the story was told it would be the part about the Holocaust victim that would be the salient detail. People would savour that. She knew how people's minds worked. Then word would spread to the volunteers. The whispers were already hissing in her ears.

• • • •

Frank let Johanna in when he saw her coming. "No sign of them yet," he said. He'd been on the lookout for Albert and Robert. The bandage on her arm caught his attention.

"It's just a scratch. Nothing really. It's this rash that's really getting on my nerves."

"What happened?"

"They switched the laundry detergent at the hospital and I broke out in a rash. Look, it's all the way up to my neck."

"No, I mean to your arm." He pressed the elevator button for her and waited with her while she explained about the confused patient.

"I got bitten by a dog once and had to take two sets of antibiotics because I thought I was better and the infection came right back after a day. But they say it's the human bite that's worst of all."

"Humans are toxic to one another, Frank. I could have told you that. We are constantly infesting one another with poison."

"Well, I don't think it's as bad as all that," he mustered. "I don't think you're injecting me with poison right now, Mrs. Turner."

"I hope not, Frank. I hope not…" her voice trailed off. A delivery van pulled through to the front door and Frank had to buzz the driver in.

Just as she stepped off the elevator Pearl opened her door. The smell of onion and bacon wafted into the hallway. At least Johanna could count on Pearl not to notice her bandaged arm. "Making lunch, Pearl?"

"Oh, yeah, frying up some perogies. Have you eaten?" She was not aware of the spatula she held in her hand and waved about.

"I've got a salad I have to finish. But thanks." Johanna tried to get Pearl to eat healthier things, but perogies and tinned soup were all she could manage on her own. "And I've got my nephew coming to stay for awhile. He's a performer."

"Oh? What kind?"

"A singer. He's going to be in *The Mikado*. My sister's son."

It took a moment for this to sink in and a sorrowful look spread across Pearl's face. "Oh," she said again. "It's so sad. I don't know what I would do if I lost my sister."

"It's all right." Johanna's voice was curt. The sympathy was wearing on her. And what did Pearl know of it anyway? Her sister existed only in a pile of brief handwritten notes accompanied by Bible verses. "It will be nice to have him here. Maybe you can come and meet him one day."

"Oh, that would be nice." Her voice drawled as she seemed to think of something else. "Will you still be able to take me to the doctor on Monday? They need to check me for sugar diabetes."

"Of course. Albert will be busy with rehearsals, I expect." Johanna's legs were starting to feel heavy. She opened her door. "I've got to get a move on here. The boys will be back from the airport soon."

"Right." The spatula cracked against the doorframe and startled Pearl. "Darn thing."

• • • •

Johanna debated about taking a pill for the pain in her arm. She usually only took a pill if she had a bad headache. Felix hopped around on the bookshelf, chirruping contentedly. She eyed the bird intently and tried to sound encouraging. "JoJo. Come on. Say something for me. Say JoJo."

There was no sound from the bird, just a cocked head and amused glint in his eye. "Fine. Don't say anything."

The emptiness of the apartment pressed on her. What right did she have to mourn a sister she'd hardly known? Angrily she swiped the tears away. They had moved miles apart and Johanna had done nothing to close that gap. The tears wouldn't stop. Too bad there wasn't an audience here now to witness them. Everyone would be so pleased.

• • • •

Robert pulled the car into the short-term lot and made his way to the arrivals terminal. The airport wasn't busy and Robert quickly found the gate and got situated close to the doors. A few passengers trickled through. Robert clutched the copy of *Opera News* that he had grabbed at the last moment to bring along in case there was a long wait. He expected a big man in a cape and beret, like the posters by Toulouse-Lautrec. When he appeared, Albert wore a simple beige turtleneck sweater and light well-tailored jacket and a silk scarf around his neck, something that made Robert laugh inwardly. He knew there would be a scarf! The hair startled Robert. It was entirely grey and clipped short. In his mind's eye he had expected a Japanese topknot, the way Albert would wear it on stage. Robert waved and Albert beamed and came over, hand extended.

"Behold, the Lord High Everything Else," Robert said, trying not to wince at the crushing pain of the giant's grip. Albert towered over the other passengers and Robert marvelled at the cut of Albert's suit, how normal it looked on such a large man. He laughed at Robert's joke. People turned and stared when they heard the sound of his laughter. This was something Robert had noticed about professional singers. Their laughter was innately musical. Sweet and smooth, like water rippling over thousand year old stones.

"I'm surprised you know my official title. I thought Gilbert and Sullivan were anathema to Wagner."

"That they are." Two seconds into their reunion and already Albert was needling him. "It's part of a well-rounded education to be able to distinguish the good from the terrible."

"Ha, ha." Albert thought he was kidding. He slapped Robert on the back. "It was Wagner who got me interested in singing. Remember?"

"I remember you sitting on my chest and telling me to prepare to die."

"Ha!" Albert clasped his hands behind him. They walked to the luggage carousel. People noticed Albert even when he wasn't laughing. Probably because they weren't used to seeing a man who wore a silk scarf and flounced. Robert waited with the luggage cart while Albert loaded it up with three garment bags, two suitcases and the two satchels he had for carry on – all this for a man who would spend the next three weeks in a costume.

"Robert, how long has it been now?" They walked towards the exit, Albert pushing the cart and Robert toting his briefcase.

"I was trying to remember that myself. At least ten years." Robert took a step back rather than crane his neck. "I'm sorry for your loss. Your mother. Very sorry."

"Yes, it was sudden. Pretty awful." Albert's face turned grave for a moment. "She had a stroke in the mall you know. Collapsed right there surrounded by strangers."

Robert recoiled at the thought – Aunt Barbara on the tile floor in front of the lottery kiosk, causing great panic among the gamblers as they clutched their dollars and put any thoughts of fate out of their minds.

"Is everything settled now?" Robert didn't know how to carry on the conversation.

"Oh well, those tangible things that can be settled after someone dies. Life goes on. It must." The sun shone and both of them removed sunglasses from inner jacket pockets at the same time. Albert grinned at Robert, who didn't notice or pretended not to.

They drove along the QEW. Traffic was stop and go, typical of rush hour. Albert didn't seem to mind and gazed out the window. Every once in awhile he fiddled with the fan and redirected the airflow inside the car. "I'm susceptible to any kind of draft or breeze," he explained and clutched the scarf around his neck.

"Understandable," Robert said.

"The timing of this show is perfect. I know your mother puts up a strong front, but I think we both can use the company and solace of family right now. How is Johanna doing?"

"Oh, you know. She's right back into things." Solace of family – Robert pondered this. Here was his long lost cousin and he was supposed to feel great peace rather than a nerve biting at his temples. Maybe once they'd opened the champagne the solace would kick in. "The day after she got back she had the neighbour over for coffee and drove her to the supermarket. And she's back volunteering at the hospital. She likes to keep busy."

"Yes, I noticed that in Calgary. She had that house cleaned out in no time."

A Brahms violin concerto played on the radio and much to Robert's surprise, Albert hummed along. They drove past an accident along the oncoming lanes at a snail's pace as people slowed to gawk. Albert turned to see out Robert's window.

"Does she talk much of the past? The war?" Albert asked.

"Unless it was last week, the past stays in the past. She hardly ever talks about it. It's amazing how deft she is at avoiding questions and changing the subject. She's like an illusionist that way. A wave of her magic wand and the questions disappear."

"I wonder why that is?"

Robert laughed. "You've got me there. I've learned not to ask."

They lapsed into silence.

"What about Barbara, did she tell you anything?"

"Oh, here and there. Nothing earth-shattering. I told you the few things she told me. It's strange isn't it? That you and I don't know more. It's all so matter-of-fact to them. Like living through a war is nothing at all."

"It was enough to make them want to come here."

"That was your mother's idea. I got the impression that my mother didn't have much choice. My guess is it has something to do with Heinz."

Robert was quiet. It was one of those obvious statements that had gone unsaid for years. She was ashamed. "If that's it, then it makes perfect sense to me that she wouldn't want to talk about it."

He didn't like Albert talking as if he knew Johanna better than Robert did. Barbara wasn't here anymore to fill Albert's head with speculation about his mother's motivations.

• • • •

While they waited for Albert to freshen up, Johanna told Robert about her arm. "The poor man was confused. I think he thought I was trying to hurt him. It must be awful to be disorientated and in strange surroundings." Johanna regarded her arm. It was remarkable how sore it felt, the skin pulled tight where the gouges were and the stinging had not subsided. It could be her imagination but it looked a bit swollen around the cuts. She didn't want to say anything about the Holocaust flashbacks. That part she wanted to forget.

"Will you work your shifts at the hospital?"

"Of course I will. I'm not an invalid. You sound just like those people at work, insisting I am stressed and exhausted. I feel perfectly fine." To underline this, Johanna stood by Felix's cage and tried to coax him onto her finger. He was wary of the bandaged arm and scuttled to the corner. She snapped the cage shut again.

"What's taking him so long?" Robert checked his watch. Albert's idea of freshening up took a long time. On the dining room table a tray with champagne flutes waited, the champagne chilled in the fridge and Robert desperate for a bit of numbing pleasure.

"For Pete's sake, Robert. Stop pacing. He'll be out shortly." Johanna stood by the bird's cage once more and this time tried the other hand. The bird trod cautiously towards her and hopped onto her finger. "There. That's better." She guided him to his perch on the bookshelves.

Albert appeared from the guest room, changed and smelling of cologne. "Ah," he said with satisfaction. "That's much better."

The champagne was poured and they drank a toast to Albert's arrival.

"Dinner will be another half hour," said Johanna.

The chicken was warming in the oven, the salad was ready in the fridge. Johanna returned to the dining room to set the table. Her arm burned under the gauze, a constant reminder. She tried to put it from her mind but the face of the old man plagued her, contorted with fear at the sight of her.

Albert and Robert were outside on the balcony, leaning over the railing, enjoying the view, talking. The screen door was open but she could not hear them. Albert was laughing at something Robert had said. Their glasses were empty. With the bottle in hand she slid open the screen door and offered more champagne. "You two must have a lot to talk about."

"Yes, it's good to be here," Albert said and held his glass out. Johanna scanned their faces for clues but both seemed relaxed and content. When she got back in she heard the rice boiling over on the stove, Felix spilled birdseed onto the floor, the champagne bottle dripped onto the fresh tablecloth, Robert and Albert laughed and Johanna froze. Thoughts would not sequence themselves. The rice, the bird, the bottle. She stood rooted in the middle of the living room and did not know which way to turn. A feather fluttered to the floor and she snapped out of it. "Goodness," she thought. "I'm losing my marbles."

She gave Felix a bit of cheese, carried the bottle to the kitchen where she poured herself the last sip and turned down the rice.

CHAPTER 10

In the morning Johanna dressed her arm again. The gouges were weepy. A few of them had crusted over with yellow pus, but the deepest ones remained open and raw. Her hand felt stiff. She flexed and stretched her fingers a few times to loosen up. When she held her arms side by side she saw that the left one was a bit swollen, something that would settle once she got moving.

When she got to the volunteer lounge Angela and Marg were there, poring over the latest *People* magazine before it hit the shelves of the gift shop. There was coffee enough for Johanna to have some. It was nine-twenty. Nine o'clock was the start of shift. It would be noted that she was late.

"Sorry I'm late. I caught a train."

They asked about her arm and Johanna assured them it was healing. She pulled her pink smock from her bag and held it up for them to see.

"A patient went crazy in the gift shop one day," Angela said. "Started rolling her wheelchair into the stuffed animals so they fell off the shelf and them she started running them over screaming about road kill. It was creepy. I had to call security to get her out of there. They should really forget about day passes for some of those people."

"Well, this man wasn't going anywhere on a day pass."

"Except in his head," said Marg and tapped the side of her head with her finger.

Their efforts made Johanna feel a bit better, but it didn't erase the horror on the man's face, and the hatred. He had branded her, almost like the way that he had been branded years ago. The image of Heinz's cold eyes and haggard face flashed through Johanna's thoughts. That patient could have come face to face with Heinz. Frozen before Johanna was Heinz, in the black uniform of the SS, pointing his pistol at the man and prodding him along to where the doctor in the white coat waited.

• • • •

Johanna sniffed the milk before she poured it in her coffee. Then sniffed the coffee before she drank it. Karen entered the room trailed by a thin, sallow woman.

"Girls," she announced. "This is Giselle. She's here for orientation this morning."

"Hello, how are you?" The woman spoke with a marked German accent. It immediately set Johanna on edge. Giselle had been the name of Johanna's best friend all through school. A tremor swept through Johanna as she warily eyed Karen. When she came to introduce Johanna she said her name the German way, with the J sounding like a Y. Johanna's eyes flashed on Giselle to see her reaction. The woman nodded. Barbara had been the last person to pronounce Johanna properly and here was Karen, out of the blue, pretending that she had been speaking fluent German her whole life and bringing another German woman on for Johanna to befriend. She couldn't imagine what it all meant.

"We're going to mix things up today. I'll have Giselle start with the cart on the units with Angela and then she will deliver Giselle to me for policies and procedures." Karen paused and smiled at everyone. That smile. Johanna should have seen it coming. When her face turned to Johanna, the smile faded and then returned. "Johanna, you and I will do some things together."

Together? Johanna envisioned herself leashed to Karen with a baby harness, being dragged from one tedious errand to the next. Something was brewing this morning. Marg and Angela shepherded Giselle out into the corridor and left Karen with Johanna. As they were leaving Angela whispered to Johanna, "Karen loves German volunteers. You're so efficient." She nudged Johanna and gave her a mischievous wink. Angela always seemed to know when Johanna was uncomfortable. She tried to forget about Giselle.

"Jo, I know it's normally you who trains the new volunteers, but Giselle wants to practise her English. She's only been here a year. I offered to have you train her but she is afraid she will lapse into German. Besides, we weren't sure given that injury to your arm that you would even be here today." Karen reached up to tuck her hair behind her ear, but with her new-wave hairdo there was no hair to tuck. She wore a tight leather skirt and a blouse that gaped to reveal a black lace bra. "I guess I should have known better than to think you would miss a shift. How is your arm?"

"Healing up nicely." Johanna kept her answers short. "I haven't spoken German in years." There was relief in being separated from Giselle, yet on the other hand suspicion that she had been pulled from her usual duties of training the new volunteers. There was probably a typewritten incident report on file. She knew what those reports looked like. There was a section that required a statement on how such an incident could be prevented in the future. *Bar the volunteer from patient contact. Don't leave her alone.*

"And there are lots of pink smocks today. The laundry finally was delivered." Karen's attempt to smooth things over with Johanna was fascinating. Johanna found the transparent performance riveting.

"I brought my own."

"Right. The rash."

All morning Johanna followed Karen around and tried to remain pleasant. Outside in the gusting wind Johanna stood with the clear frame of the sign flapping against her and handed Karen letters that spelled Craft and Bake Sale, Saturday, October 5. That was in two weeks. That meant all the volunteers would spend the next two weeks baking and knitting. Johanna would bake five dozen almond tarts and five dozen peach turnovers. On the day of the sale all the volunteers would be serving coffee and banana bread. Karen and her team would set up a table with all the baby goods they didn't sell over the Internet and then write up a charitable donation receipt.

At ten-thirty Karen needed a coffee break. She bought Johanna a coffee and led her to a table by the window. "If you need to talk to someone, Jo, we can arrange an appointment for you."

"What kind of an appointment?"

"You have been through a lot. And that patient attacking you didn't help."

"He didn't attack me." Johanna's nostrils flared. She clenched her hand around her coffee. "Is that what it says in the report?"

"I think so." Karen said. "What else would it say?"

"That I was helping him."

"It says that. Why are you so worried about a report, Jo? It will go in your file and be forgotten. You know how these things are." There was a large deep purple lip print on Karen's cup. She was not to be trusted. Nobody in management would make light of a hospital policy and procedure. Johanna didn't feel well. Her coffee sat up high in her esophagus. Her in stinct told her to flee, but her head told her to stay. This was not a time to show signs of weakness.

• • • •

Robert's hands shook even after he'd secured all the locks. What a night. He had rallied Marcelline and Leonard and had taken them all along with Albert to dinner.

"She's the date you mentioned?" Leonard looked skeptical.

"Yes, she's the date." Robert tried to smile. "This is for me, remember? Just don't get Albert talking about the New York scene. I'll end up with heartburn."

Robert had ended up seated right by the fireplace and got overheated. Marcelline had been enthralled by Albert who spent the entire evening softly singing songs she didn't know into her good ear while Robert tried to chew his gnocchi. She chirped at Albert about her piano lessons, of which there had now been two. Robert wished he had never introduced them. Now Marcelline was all star-struck by that buffoon. Even Leonard had not provided him with much support as he prattled on about the food chain, vying with Marcelline for Albert's attention. But the bill was paid, Marcelline delivered safely home and Robert was finally at ease back in his apartment.

His desk was piled with folders and books filled with paper slips marking numerous references for an article Robert was preparing on the *Festspielhaus* at Bayreuth. He regarded the desk with pride: the little glass pot of ink and the mahogany pen, inlaid with ivory that he used only for his compositions. Sheets of heavy manuscript paper covered in tiny sixteenth and thirty-second notes – his arrangements of early renaissance motets for eight mallets. The parts would be doubled but overlapping so that the notes would sustain. Four registers. He could hear it in his head so clearly. Those arrangements came to him easily, and yet to compose his own music was tortuous. The harp and timpani that had come into his mind at dinner would work well in a scene of his opera. A scene of enlightenment, where his protagonist realizes that his insanity has saved him from a fruitless life.

The manuscript lay at the bottom of his desk in an envelope. Nobody had ever heard it, not even Leonard. Nobody knew it existed. Too many years had passed for him to take it seriously anymore. Once in a while he leafed through it and tinkered away at parts. Some sections were quite melodic. But, only about a quarter of the opera was complete and none of it in any sequence. There was a lot of incidental music and a few choruses and duets. That ordeal of a meal he'd just endured – there had to be something here to reward him. He pulled the envelope out from under four years of tax returns and plopped it on the desk. It was an opera about the tenor, Emile Scaria, who went crazy in the streets of London after singing the role of Wotan night after night in 1882. He was going to simply call it Scaria. It fit – rhymed with aria. An unfinished trio lay on top. There were pages of half-finished motifs, a few lines of phrases he'd tried out and then abandoned.

Wagner dodged debtors, juggled women and duped a king and still managed to write his operas. Wagner was sixty-three by the time the *Festspielhaus* was complete – a long time to wait for a dream to be realized. *Parsifal* was written with the specific theatre acoustics in mind and was the only opera Wagner wrote after the theatre was complete and he had a notion of the acoustics. This was the subject of the paper Robert was preparing. Part of its legacy was that for years no other opera company was granted the rights to perform it until it came out of copyright thirty years later. Cosima, Richard Wagner's devoted wife, fought in vain to prevent performances from taking place elsewhere. She wanted *Parsifal* to remain in its rightful home but her request was not granted. Wagner had capped his career with *Parsifal*; Robert would leave a thousand dangling phrases.

Robert drained the rest of his brandy and reached for the bottle. To finish the project would take him at least fifteen years. For a while he sat at the piano and played through his opera, making a few notations here and there. Fuelled by the brandy, he set a fresh piece of manuscript paper in front of him and began. Rolling F major arpeggios, a rumble of A's beneath. The sound faded and a lone oboe took up a plaintive tune. It wasn't half bad. Robert leaned back and rubbed his eyes. In an effort to eradicate the image of Marcelline beaming at Albert, he sat at the piano until three in the morning. His head filled with harps and basses, layer upon layer of texture and grace. Texture, balance and melody – those were the elements to blend in order to create a sublime suspension of sound. Mahler and Wagner did it best, and Richard Strauss.

When he finally crawled into bed, Robert had written a reasonable aria. He drifted off with the lush sound of the cellos and viola, two parts, an octave apart, playing major fourths along the E minor scale. In perfect cadence before the horns take over, mutes on, a bass triad, and then trombone takes the high E. Trombone! Above the horns! In his mind, the fog from the dry ice rolled ominously across the stage, the lights dim and a single streetlight illuminates the scene. A bridge, two lovers and a madman. Robert shivered with delight and curled into the sheets. The full moon shone down on him and bathed him in blue light. He felt euphoric. This opera was his alone. It had nothing to do with anybody else and that was reason enough to get back to it.

• • • •

It was Albert's fault. It had not been her intention that morning to let Albert see her arm. She had taken the bandages off in order to let the air at it. The shower in the guest bathroom was running. She was sure of it, but there he was fussing over a pot of boiled eggs just as Johanna came in to make her coffee.

"Your arm looks terrible. Maybe you should see a doctor."

"And what's a doctor going to tell me?" She snapped, seeing three eggs in the pot. "How many eggs are you going to eat?"

"I'm making one for you. Four minutes?"

"It doesn't matter. Coffee?"

"You might need antibiotics. It looks infected."

"Infected? Don't you think I would know if it was infected or not? I'm a nurse, you know."

She left the apartment without making coffee and without replacing the bandages, thinking she could do it in the volunteer lounge. There would be plenty of time to have her coffee there. But, just as Albert had headed her off in the kitchen, Karen was inexplicably checking the cupboards in the volunteer lounge.

"Hi, Jo. I sent a memo to clear out all perishables. How long have those crackers been there?"

"I don't know." She held her hands behind her back. "I can do that. There are a lot of cream and ketchup packets in the fridge too. I'm early. Let me do it."

"Let me see your arm." Johanna clenched her fist to get some blood circulating to her hand. "It's fine." Johanna took a step back as Karen's copper fingernails reached for her arm.

One look and there was no stopping Karen. There was no chance to argue as she steered Johanna towards the Occupational Health office. The feeling that came over her was beyond anxiety. As she followed Karen all sensation drained out of her. She could hear her shoes on the floor, she could see the corridor stretch before her, and yet, those senses weren't her own. She was only aware of them in that she understood these kinds of feelings to be possible. Her feet must be in contact with the floor and propelling her forwards if the corridor was passing by her. An unseen current swept her along. Johanna was only vaguely aware of her arm being held over a basin while a nurse slopped saline over the cuts. She dabbed them with swabs and then cleaned them with another solution. There were distorted voices swirling around her. Johanna sat rigid, not speaking and not flinching. A force field around her deflected the stares and words. She could not respond to anything they said. Something gripped and was shaking her. Karen's face was inches from hers and Johanna snapped to attention.

"Jo, are you all right?"

"Yes, of course." It did not sound convincing. But Johanna quickly realized that they had to be convinced or they would keep her here. Already the nurse had brought a pillow for the treatment bed. "I'm fine."

"Can't you see this arm is infected?" The occupational health nurse scolded Johanna.

"No, I can't. It doesn't look infected to me."

"I thought you used to be a nurse."

Johanna bit her lip. They were talking an awful lot amongst themselves and not a lot to her. The walls wavered and Johanna stared at the floor. A young female doctor arrived wearing a long lab coat with all the pockets stuffed with papers, a stethoscope around her neck and a large Styrofoam cup of coffee in her hand. She glanced cursorily at Johanna and joined the huddle in the far corner of the room.

After five minutes of secret chatter the group descended upon Johanna. The doctor pulled her hand and held it under a lamp. She turned Johanna's arm over and made funny noises at the back of her throat. "You should have started on antibiotics right away with this kind of thing. You never know what those patients are carrying. I'm giving you ten days worth of Erythromycin and if that doesn't clear it we'll have to go to something stronger."

"Like what?"

"IV."

"Intravenous? It can't possibly be as bad as all that."

"Well, so far it's not. But a few more days and you could have quite a mess on your hands."

The doctor left and Karen told Johanna to go home early. "You don't look well. Get some rest and start those pills. Take a few days off and come back on Thursday for the nurse to assess your arm."

Johanna nodded, eager to escape. There was something fishy about the pills. She had seen them spilled onto the counter. The doctor had been back there with them and Johanna heard one of them mention sedatives. The pills they had given her didn't look like any antibiotics she had ever seen. They were too small and the dosage was wrong. Antibiotics were normally taken twice a day and this prescription said to take them four times a day.

When they were finished with her, Johanna grabbed her purse and dashed out the door. Karen said something but she didn't hear. Johanna walked down the corridor at a brisk, steady pace and got on the elevator. It was difficult not to let everything around her blur. She had to blink constantly to stay focussed. All she had to do was get out of the building and into her car. The blood flowed back into her legs and she regained control. As she made her way to her car she noticed the throbbing coming from her hand. The nurse had wound the gauze quite tight, tighter than was necessary. Johanna undid the bandage and threw it on the floor of the car. She stuck the key in the ignition and pulled the car into gear. A deep breath in. She did not want to race out of the parking lot and draw attention to herself. Once she was past the perimeter and on the road home, she let out a long, slow breath. The panic subsided the farther she got from the hospital. Never before had she felt an out-of-body sensation like that.

• • • •

It wasn't often that Robert got to be host. He took the potato salad from his mother and guided her and Albert into his apartment. It had taken all afternoon to achieve the non-meticulous appearance he was after. Music was strewn around the piano. He had rested a stack of manuscript papers on the desk marked with turquoise ink and his fountain pen askew beside it. An air of productivity mixed with absent-minded genius.

Albert sauntered around and plinked a few notes on the piano. Johanna followed Robert into the kitchen. "That needs to go in the fridge after I put the eggs in." She dropped her purse onto the counter and the bottle of pills rolled towards the sink.

"What are these?" Robert picked them up and read the label.

"I got them from Occupational Health. I didn't have a chance to tell you.

They like to interfere in everything. Even when people are feeling fine they get after them for things. Well, they gave me these antibiotics – gave them to me – I didn't have to pay. I'm a bit suspicious of that."

"Maybe they're expired." Robert turned the bottle in his hand and watched the pills tumble.

"They're not expired. I'm sure they're the freshest batch of whatever they are."

"Erythromycin."

"Sure, that's what it says. Look at them. Do those look like antibiotics to you?"

"I don't know."

"Antibiotics are big horse pills. Those are tiny. They can't possibly fight infection."

"Maybe the styles have changed."

"What styles?"

"Pill styles. Everything is getting smaller these days. Phones, cars, computers. Why not pills?"

"Don't be silly." Johanna opened the packages of sausages and arranged them on a plate. "There, now they're ready when you want to cook them."

"I'll get them started."

"Well, fine. But let Albert help." Albert had made himself comfortable at Robert's piano and Johanna didn't want to hear it right now. The door swung shut behind Robert. Johanna set the pills on the counter and gave them a stern look. Whatever was in them was not going to fix her arm. She picked up a hard-boiled egg and cracked it against the counter.

Out on the balcony Albert whispered to Robert. "Have you seen your mother's arm?"

"No, I haven't." The barbecue billowed smoke when Robert lifted the lid. He reared back and the lid dropped shut with a bang.

Albert lifted the lid and took the plate from Robert. "I do this all the time."

"So do I." Robert sat down, thankful that Albert was cooking. The last time he'd used the barbecue was when Leonard had come over and cooked marinated shrimp skewers. He sipped a beer. "So, what about her arm?"

"It's in pretty bad shape. I saw it this morning,"

"She's got antibiotics in her purse."

"Oh, good. That's what it needs." Flames shot up from the barbecue and the fat sizzled and spattered.

Robert went back in to check on his mother. She was wiping down the space between the wall and the refrigerator. "How is your arm?"

"Fine."

"Albert says it looks bad."

"Albert doesn't know everything." She shook out the cloth and draped it over the tap. "You don't have to worry about me, Robert. I have enough people on the lookout already."

• • • •

After dinner Albert and Johanna settled down to a game of checkers while Robert sat at the piano. He played aimlessly whatever notes fell under his fingers and gazed out at the night sky. The sound of the piano startled Johanna. Albert smiled. "Isn't it lovely to sit and be serenaded?"

There was an odd look on Johanna's face. Her eyes stared at Robert, transfixed.

"Johanna?" Albert laid a hand on her arm. "Are you all right?"

Robert stopped playing and turned around. "Mother? What is it?" She seemed not to have heard. Suddenly, she jumped to her feet and bumped the table with her knee. The checkers skewed across the board.

Albert jumped to his feet. "What's wrong?"

"I just got a chill, that's all. I'll make some tea."

Robert followed her into the kitchen and took the kettle from her. "I'll make it. Don't forget your pill," Robert said.

"I took it already." Johanna made her way to the bathroom. Without warning the floor rose up under her feet and the walls wowed in. Her arm shot out to brace herself and pain pierced through to her chest. The floor settled back to flat and the walls retreated. She saw her face in the bathroom mirror, sunken and pale with dark circles under her eyes. "I look like I've lived a thousand years," she whispered. Those notes. That music. She thought she must have imagined it. It simply couldn't be that Robert sat there playing music Heinz had written so long ago. And when she dared look over, it wasn't Robert at all who sat there, but Heinz. The sight of him terrified her. She could smell his unwashed clothes and hair, the dank room in which he slept without ever opening a window.

Albert rinsed the last of the glasses and left the pans to soak. "I don't mean to interfere, but I don't think your mother is taking those pills."

"Hmm?" Robert poured boiling water into the teapot.

"I've been checking the bottle and I don't think she's taken any."

"Why are you checking the bottle?"

"Because her arm isn't getting any better. She can't even cut her own food. Did you notice that?"

"Yes, I noticed that. I cut her sausage for her." He bristled at Albert's insinuation that he wouldn't see if his mother were unwell. Who did he think he was anyway coming here and checking up on Johanna? "She's a nurse," Robert reminded him. "She knows how to take care of herself. I've never known her to be sick for more than two hours."

"Don't you think she's acting a bit strange?"

"Kind of spaced out, you mean?"

"Well, yes. And she doesn't look well."

"But she told me she was taking them. Why would she lie?" He made a show of checking the bottle for listed side effects.

"Let's just give her a few extra." Albert crushed two pills and stirred them into one of the mugs. "There. At least we'll know she's taken one dose."

"Do you really think this is necessary? I hate to deceive her like this."

"It won't hurt."

"All right." For the sake of peace with his cousin, Robert carried the tray out to the living room. "Ready for some tea?"

Johanna's face was pale and her lips drawn. The whites of her eyes had a spongy unhealthy look to them and Robert wondered if Albert was right about the pills. "Please drink some tea. It will do you good."

CHAPTER 11

Robert pulled up the collar of his jacket as he hurried to the parking lot. It was ten past five. He removed his watch from his wrist and dropped it into his pocket. The band irritated his wrist during the course of the day.

The wind was bracing. Students spilled in vast numbers over the sidewalks and roads. His mother had drilled into him the merit of a brisk walk and so his car was parked in the farthest spot on the farthest lot from the Faculty of Music building. A group of rough-looking characters crossed over the far side of the parking lot. One of them carried a baseball bat and they did not look the type to be in search of a ball field. He paused mid-stride and looked around for the hood of his car. He usually backed the car in so the Mercedes hood ornament would make it easy to find among the sea of silver and gray cars. It wouldn't be the first time he had ambled down the wrong aisle while distracted by thoughts humming around his head, especially now with the renewed productivity on his opera. In his mind he hummed a short passage and debated whether it would sound better on bassoon or bass clarinet. He scanned the parking lot to get his bearings. The sun hung low and red; a hush perceptible beneath the din, and beneath that a quivering sense of foreboding. It unnerved Robert to be lost in the parking lot. As he approached his car he pulled the keys from his pocket and didn't even notice the shattered glass at his feet until he had the key in the lock. The inside of his car was a mess. Wires stuck out where the stereo had been, his CDs had been taken, the glove compartment emptied onto the passenger seat and sticky cola sprayed throughout the interior.

He spun around to see where the trio of skinheads had gone but they were out of sight. Robert's hands trembled. There was no parking lot attendant, just a receiver he waved a transponder at to get in and out of the lot. There were a few cameras but his car in its remote spot was out of range. A feeling of utter helplessness came over him. He felt like a small woodland creature returned home to find its nest destroyed. Not so much devastated as confused and bewildered. Unable to determine where such an act fit into the flow of his life.

Robert made his way to the nearest building where he called campus security. Two thick-necked young men appeared about ten minutes later and called the police. While he waited, Robert accepted a cup of coffee from one of the security officers. The first sip scalded his tongue. He felt foolish for wanting to call his mother. His heart was sick over his CDs. The one in the disk player had been an imported recording of the second symphony of Sibelius. He could hardly imagine those cretins collapsing in a rapturous seizure at the start of the fourth movement. And if they did, then he would believe that he had done one small thing to advance humanity. Had he only been a minute sooner he would have caught them in the act. And then what? Wrestled them to the ground and shoved dirt in their mouths? He was lucky he had missed them or his head could have been smashed in.

It took over two hours for the police to come. They politely took notes while Robert rambled, fully aware of their lack of interest. They told him frankly that these kinds of crimes were rarely solved and admitted his insurance company would be able to do more for him than they could.

After the police officers left Robert stood and gripped the antitheft device that had been fastened to the steering wheel. The tow truck hitched up the shattered car and a taxi came for him. In the back seat Robert opened the window and held his face into the cold air. The taxi dropped him at his front door. The meter read eighteen dollars and eighty-five cents. Robert was magnanimous in handing over a twenty. Once inside Marcelline cornered him with her laundry basket.

"Did your car break down?" She nodded at the Club in Robert's hand.

"No, it was vandalized." He smacked the Club into his hand like a gangster wielding a bat. "By a trio of skinheads."

"Did you chase them with that?"

"No, I had to remove it so the tow truck driver could take it to the mechanic." Robert sighed. A hero he would never be.

"Well it's a good thing you didn't. That's just asking for it." Marcelline wanted to hear the whole story and Robert found himself once again seated across from the orange beanbag chair with a glass of sweet white wine in his hand. Adrenaline surged through him. He felt like he had survived a natural disaster. Marcelline's angelfish swam ellipses in its tank. It could not see its food and there were no visible rivals. No invisible threats to its home. No wonder it got its eye poked out. That fish was utterly unprepared for the hardships of life.

Marcelline laughed. "I can just picture you chasing them down, armed with that club. Vigilante justice."

"Well, I can see why people take the law into their own hands. It's infuriating how helpless one feels. It would feel so good to land just one solid blow against one of their soft skulls."

So, she was laughing. She was probably right. In his mind he thought himself perfectly capable of scaring them off, or even hurting them in some way. Turning the tables and making them scared of him. Frothing at the mouth, arteries bulging, eyes whirling, unfocussed, fists clenched, gibberish spewing from his mouth. That would do it. Like his poor Scaria. He would write a scene for him just like it. Insanity was a good defence. A hard resonant rap on a wood block. Metal on hollow wood had a certain menace to it. Crack! People would jump out of their seats.

"They sprayed pop inside your car?" A full laundry basket sat at her feet – bright t-shirts and striped socks. Happy colours. No grey or navy blue.

"They knew how to dismantle the stereo pretty quickly. These were seasoned thieves."

"Are the police on the lookout for a pimped up vehicle pumping out Wagner?"

"They better be." Robert's mind was now on his opera. Strange how he had not worked on it for years and now ideas flooded his brain.

Marcelline perched on the edge of the beanbag chair and folded her laundry. Small piles of clothing grew on the floor. There was a neat stack of rolled socks and underwear folded in four. Boxers, Robert noticed and didn't know quite what to make of it. She did not seem at all embarrassed to be shaking and folding her underwear in front of him.

"I want to get this place shipshape before my girlfriend comes to visit." Marcelline giggled. "Shipshape – whatever that means."

"Oh. Where is she from?"

"Sarnia. I think I've finally convinced her to move here."

Robert sneezed, only half listening to her and reached for his handkerchief. "I think I'm getting bronchitis again."

"Sounds serious." Marcelline piled everything back into the basket and carried it down the hallway to her bedroom. Robert had not seen in her bedroom. He imagined black walls and an evil eye mural. Some things were best left to the imagination.

"Do you think the head controls the body or the body controls the head?" She asked him when she returned. "You know, like when you're sick. Do you think it's possible to make yourself sick just by thinking about it?"

"I used to do it all the time to get a day home from school. I lay in my bed moaning and clutching my stomach and before long my stomach really did start to hurt."

Marcelline laughed. "You little brat."

"It wasn't funny. I really got sick. Once I even threw up after I had woken up feeling perfectly fine."

"Have you done it lately?"

"Made myself sick? I don't know the difference any more. My mind and body have melded into a blissful symbiotic relationship. Neither one knows what the other is doing. They duke it out and I suffer." He blew his nose. Ever since he had been teaching Marcelline piano he felt more relaxed around her.

"Well, goody for you." Her cheeks were flushed with the wine and she had sat herself down right next to Robert on the couch. The thread of the conversation drifted out of range. Marcelline tucked her feet up underneath her and rested her arm on the back of the couch.

"My head is pounding," he said. "It's telling my body to go home and take a shower and an aspirin."

"All right," she said ever so lightly as she aimed the clicker at the television. She pulled a blanket from the back of the couch and covered up her feet. "Drink some hot lemon for that cold."

The lights in the hallway shimmered and made everything wavy. His muscles trembled and his knees felt light. For sure he had a fever. The antidote rested on the piano in his apartment. He settled in with a snifter of brandy, a fresh sheet of manuscript paper and a crack on the woodblock followed by pianissimo tremolo on the high F sharp in the upper registers of the violins.

• • • •

Johanna caught her breath as they sat in the waiting room of the hospital. Unexpectedly, panic had seized her in the front lobby. Around every corner she expected somebody to see her. What they would want with her she could not fathom but a feeling of dread clung to her nevertheless. Karen and Giselle had been in the gift shop with their backs turned but Johanna made sure to slip onto the elevator when it came to make sure they didn't see her. That scene in Occupational Health was still fresh in Johanna's mind, the pills still untouched on the kitchen counter.

Pearl fidgeted with her purse. In the night she had tripped over a throw rug and had turned her ankle. Before they left Johanna had wrapped it in a tensor. She was sure it wasn't broken. The last thing she wanted was a long wait in the emergency department. She had Pearl try walking on it and convinced her she would be fine. Pearl's one shoe remained untied and it made her unsteady on her feet.

As much as Johanna didn't want to be in the hospital today, she felt she had to take Pearl to her doctor's appointment. Pearl needed to hear a physician tell her to start eating better. Diabetes sounded so common people forgot that it was a serious disease. "I don't like hospitals," Pearl whispered. "I don't know how you can work in this place."

"What don't you like about it?" Johanna wondered since she was beginning not to like it so much either.

"All these sick people. A person could catch something and never make it out of here." She looked at her watch. They both sat and waited. Pearl cleared her throat several times and Johanna feared she knew what was coming.

"Gosh, I could really use a coffee. It's so dry in here." She coughed again and dug through her purse. "I'll give you money. Get one for yourself too."

Johanna remained rooted to her seat. "I'm not thirsty. There's a cooler right there, with paper cups."

"I'd rather have a coffee. We might be here awhile. If it's not too much trouble."

Nothing was ever too much trouble. With a firm grip on her purse and as much poise as she could manage with her wounded arm supported sling-like in her sweater, Johanna trod cautiously towards the door. She stood in the hallway before venturing any further to see if the walls were going to close in on her. Nothing happened so she walked slowly towards the elevators. The cafeteria was abuzz and Johanna's eyes darted quickly from one person to the next. Nobody she recognized was there. She poured cream and sweetener into Pearl's coffee and stood in line to pay with all the interns who fuelled up on giant bottles of cola and bags of chips.

The wait for the elevator was interminable. Johanna heard a familiar sound coming down the corridor. Somebody called. "Hold the elevator please."

Johanna whirled around. The wheels were coming closer. Her feet froze. From the corner of her eye she saw Marg approach around the corner. The elevator doors opened and Johanna leapt aboard. Quickly, she pushed the button for the doors to close but Marg had wheeled the cart ahead of her in a calculated manoeuvre to keep them open and the doors banged against the metal cart and slid open.

"Jo. I thought that was you. What are you doing here?" She wheeled the cart onto the elevator and had Johanna cornered. "Jesus, Jo, you're bleeding."

The doors closed and the elevator paused. Suspended there, at the mercy of unseen mechanisms, Johanna shrunk into the corner.

"Your nose. Here." Marg handed her a tissue. "What are you doing here on your day off?"

"I'm here with a friend. She needed a ride to an appointment." Johanna set the coffee on the cart and held the tissue to her nose. When she brought it away from her face it was covered in bright blood.

Marg saw how Johanna supported her arm in her sweater and alarm crossed her face. "What's wrong with your arm? Isn't it getting better?"

"Oh, it's fine. It just feels heavy sometimes." Marg was the type to overreact. Johanna needed to get away from her as fast as possible.

"Johanna, you should stop by Occupational Health while you're here. They might want to check up on you. I'll go with you."

"It's fine. I'll check in tomorrow when I'm officially here for my shift. I have an appointment," she added as she watched the elevator lights.

Marg got off on the fourth floor.

"See you tomorrow," Johanna made her voice sing. "And don't worry about this nosebleed. I get them all the time."

Johanna ducked into a bathroom to assess the state of her face. Blood was beginning to dry around her nostrils and the flow was slowing. It was really the oddest thing. She never got nosebleeds. She tugged at a tissue from the dispenser and ran the cold water. There was no place to sit and her legs shook from the elevator ride. She steadied herself with her sore arm on the side of the sink and dabbed at her face. The water splashed up and soaked the bandage on her arm. Without thinking Johanna unwound the wet gauze and ran the cool water over the sores. The soothing effect made her feel euphoric. The back of her neck tingled with pleasure at the sensation and warmth flooded her body. She wished she could stand there and let the water run over her wounded skin forever. Her hand was twice its usual size and the tightness of the skin made it glow deep red. Her arm was covered in weepy pustules. She couldn't possibly go out into the corridor with it exposed like that. She pulled at the tissue dispenser and wrapped her arm as best as she could with the scratchy brown paper and then secured it in the sleeve of her sweater.

• • • •

The receptionist stared at Johanna who burrowed her face deep in a magazine. To Johanna's horror, blood dripped onto the pages and she had to get up and take a tissue from the receptionist's counter.

"Are you all right ma'am?"

Johanna nodded with the tissue pressed up to her face. "It's just a nosebleed. It's awfully dry in here."

Pearl was in with the doctor, which was just as well since Johanna had left her coffee on Marg's cart. Heels clicked past the door and each time Johanna held her breath and watched the door. She was sure any time it would swing open and Karen would stride in. Most likely Marg had made a beeline for the volunteer lounge to tell everyone she had seen Johanna with a bloody nose and lame arm.

A woman sat across from her and tried to soothe her crying baby. The child grew frantic, hiccupping for air. Finally its mother rose and bounced the baby on her shoulder and sang a lullaby. In an instant the child calmed down. The woman circled and sang – her only focus the state of her child.

Johanna turned the page of the magazine. "Mediterranean casserole." She pretended to read, all the while listening to the overhead intercom. There was a constant buzz in the air: doctors being paged, patients asked to return to their rooms. And then she heard her name. *Johanna Turner*. At least she thought she heard it. She tilted her head to listen. They didn't repeat it. The airwaves were suddenly silent.

Johanna looked at the receptionist. Should she ask her? Her fingers stuck to the magazine pages. A cold sweat formed on her brow. Now she knew for sure that Marg had told Karen. She twisted the magazine in her hands. Pearl emerged from the examination room. Johanna didn't give her a chance to sit down. She grabbed her arm and steered her towards the door. "We have to go. Now!"

"Your face. There's blood." Pearl pointed.

"It stopped. It's okay. Let's go now."

"But I have to make another appointment. I'm supposed to see the dietician." Pearl hobbled along beside Johanna. "I'm a borderline diabetic."

"I could have told you that." Johanna grabbed Pearl by the arm and hurried her along in the direction of the stairs. The lights swirled overhead. Pearl's shoes clomped on the floor. "I can tell you the same thing the dietician can. Come on. We're going out the back."

"Down the stairs?" Pearl pointed at her foot. "I can't."

"There's a railing and it's only three flights. It's faster to the car. They paged me. Didn't you hear? They're looking for me."

"It's the fifth floor. Why do we need to take the stairs?" They were at the stairwell and Pearl hesitated at the sight of the descent.

"Hold the railing and take my arm." Johanna commanded.

Pearl leaned heavily on the railing and on Johanna's arm. In her other arm Johanna carried Pearl's purse and with the weight of her own purse added to it, the arm burned fiercely. There were more pages overhead, but Johanna couldn't make out any of the names. The hospital had recently installed cameras at all the exits, that much Johanna knew. But how quick would they be to recognize her?

Pearl needed to rest at each landing. The elevator would get them out quicker, but they would have to walk through the front lobby to get out. They were in a back stairwell, one Johanna knew well. Last week they had been painting here but now only the smell of fresh paint remained and the stairwell was deserted. It led to the rear doors, far from the parking lot and therefore rarely used. She had to be swift, but Pearl could only go so fast.

"Give me your scarf." Pearl had no breath with which to reply and simply pointed to her purse. Johanna fished it out and tied it around her head. "All right. Let's get going now. The next two flights all at once."

There was no time to pay attention to the whimpers coming from Pearl. Johanna maintained a firm grip and propelled her down the stairs and out the back door. Nobody tried to stop them. They hustled past the helicopter pad and into the parking lot. The wind whipped at the scarf on Johanna's head. The weight of two purses on her arm made her gasp in pain. Once in the car, Johanna peeled out of the spot and lurched to a stop at the exit booth. The mechanical arm swung up and the car zoomed away. When Pearl caught her breath, she exclaimed, "I'm going to go straight to bed after lunch and won't be able to get up for a week. Why are you in such a hurry?"

When Frank saw Johanna come in with Pearl he raced to the door to meet them.

"Should I call the police? Who did this to you?" He took Johanna's arm from Pearl and led her to the lobby with one arm around her.

"It's nothing, Frank, just a nosebleed. I'm feeling a little weak." He helped her to sit down in one of the lobby chairs and hardly noticed Pearl sink into the other one with a long sigh of relief. "I don't think I'll ever walk again," she moaned. "She took me down five flights of stairs."

Frank hovered nearby, not sure what to do next. Pearl got to her feet and pressed the elevator button. "Come Johanna. We better get upstairs while we still can walk."

Her knees wavered, the backs of her calves thick and tight. Frank insisted on going with them. Johanna unwound Pearl's scarf from around her head and handed it to her. "Thank you, Pearl. I'll call when I'm feeling better."

Albert was there, heating up some soup. Frank's face fell when he saw that someone was home and he wouldn't have a chance to stay with Johanna.

"What happened to you?" Albert asked.

"Oh, I got a nosebleed in the hospital. I always knew the air in there was too dry."

"I'll help her from here, Frank. Thanks for bringing her up."

Frank reluctantly let go of Johanna's arm. The answering machine light was flashing and gave Johanna a diversion. It was Robert explaining about his car and asking if they could drive to Albert's opening night in hers. Vandals attacking her son's car. It was sickening what went on in this world. She picked up the phone and called her son.

He assured her that he was unharmed. "Just a bunch of dopey skinheads."

"Skinheads? Like Neo-Nazis?"

It sounded so harsh the way she said it. Robert chuckled. "No, I doubt that. More like punks."

"I don't like the sound of this."

"Mother, I was not targeted in a Neo-Nazi attack. It was entirely random. Besides, aren't I part German? They would look rather foolish don't you think?" His mother's over-reaction helped him to gain some perspective. People were victims of far more deliberate crimes.

"How would they know you are German?"

"They don't. They saw a nice car and smashed it up. These are not thoughtful criminals." His voice reached her over a deep void. It sounded to her like he was speaking to her from under the sea. Albert sang in the kitchen and Felix chirped from his cage.

"I'm working on the opera again."

"What? What opera is that?" Her mind snapped to attention. Unwanted images formed in her head.

"The one I started years ago. My muse has returned."

"I thought you had given up on that." The manuscript in the basement! Her heart shuddered. Opening night. Perhaps she could exaggerate this flu. Albert would be out and Robert could go with Leonard. She had to retrieve it while there was still time.

"Given up? It has merely been lying fallow. The soil is fertile now and ready for sowing."

"Stop talking like that." It annoyed her to have these thoughts continuously resurfacing. Neo-Nazis now entering the picture. "You can use my car but I won't be going. I'm sick. But you have to bring it back tonight. There are cameras here."

"Sick with what?"

"I have the flu." She hung up and pulled her sweater around her. Albert brought her a bowl of vegetable soup with buttered toast and a cup of black tea.

"I don't think I'll make it tonight, Albert. I hope you don't mind." She sighed. Maybe Robert would want to bring that silly girl.

Albert sat beside her and patted her. "I'll make sure there are tickets for you on closing night."

She nodded and tried the soup. It scalded her tongue. The toast was difficult to chew and made her jaw ache. Out of nowhere a melody filled her head and she was led to a piano by unseen hands. A soldier sat with his back to her and rested his hands on the keys. Thankfully she recognized the first bars because she was expected to sing. Ordered to sing. But when she came to her entrance, there were no words that came to her. She only recognized the accompaniment. The soldier turned and gave her a hard look. Fear gripped her. He was at her piano, in her study. Yet she did not know where she was.

• • • •

Johanna soaked a cloth with some water and soap and dabbed at her face to clean the blood from her nose. Albert leaned against the bathroom doorframe and watched. She had fallen asleep in her chair over her lunch and Albert had awakened her. Johanna took the bottle of Aspirin from the medicine cabinet. At least she knew what was in that bottle and it would help ease the pain. She picked bits of paper out of the sores in her arm and flicked them into the garbage. It didn't even feel like her arm anymore. When she looked at it, it could have been anyone's arm. She wiggled her fingers but didn't quite believe those fingers belonged to her.

"Good Lord, Johanna. You need to see a doctor about that arm."

"Hmm."

"It's a complete mess." Albert reached over and held her arm up as if he were examining a ham. "You have to keep up with your antibiotics."

"I have been."

"Johanna. There are hardly any pills out of the bottle. Why aren't you taking them?"

"Why are you spying on me? I know what I'm doing." She pulled her arm away and applied some ointment to the sores. "It has to go through a healing process."

"It's been nearly a week. Do you really think it would look like that if it was healing?"

"Albert," she could not keep the irritation out of her voice. "I know what's best for my arm, okay? Now I'm going to have a bath and some tea and lie down. It's been a busy morning. You have no idea."

Johanna sat on the edge of the tub while the water ran. Albert left. Then she eased her aching body into the warm water. Her arm felt better submerged. There was music coming from somewhere. With the whir of the bathroom fan Johanna couldn't be sure. It sounded like a choir singing in a church. The sound disappeared for a moment and then resumed. A large choir, maybe a hundred or more voices. Johanna tried to make out the words but couldn`t identify them. It could be Latin, if they were in a church. Then she recognized it – Heinz's opera. It wasn't just in her head now. She heard it everywhere. She lay back on the bath pillow and closed her eyes. The music filled the room with gentle waves. The chorus repeated over and over and a soft light appeared behind her eyes. Her body swayed gently, back and forth, a tender lullaby sung for her by a choir of angels who knew the tranquility she craved could only be found in those sweet notes.

She woke with a start. It was one of her fears to fall asleep in the tub. This was how tragedy befell people. The water was nearly cold and she dried herself vigorously with a towel before pulling on a fleece suit. Felix chirped in his cage. On the bottom of the cage were many half-eaten bits of fruit and vegetables. Johanna opened the cage and reached inside to clear them out. Felix pecked at her hand to be let out. She lifted him up onto the bookshelf and went back to cleaning the cage. When she was done she tried to coax him down from the shelf. "Come on now, Felix. I have to lie down." The bird would not come to her. He marched along the spines of books. *Nazi Schwein, Nazi Schwein* he squawked. Johanna stopped short. "What did you say?"

The bird looked at her with menace in its eye "What's that?" Not sure what she had heard, Johanna cocked her head. Felix scuttled back and forth.

Nazi Schwein, Nazi Schwein. Aghast, Johanna shouted at him. "Felix. Bad boy! Who taught you that?"

But the bird, oblivious to her chiding, busied itself preening. Feathers floated down to the floor. Then he flapped his wings triumphantly and squawked: Nazi Schwein, Nazi Schwein, Nazi Schwein.

The bookcase rocked under the marching bird. Johanna steadied it with her hand. "Such a filthy mouth. You stop that now or I'll wring your neck."

She craned to see where he'd gone but Felix was back against the wall. "You get down here you filthy animal," she growled. Johanna got the broom out of the closet and with one arm, jabbed at where she thought he was sitting. "Bad bird. Bad boy."

Felix, not used to these attacks, didn't know if it was a new game. The bird screeched, not sure what was happening.

"I'll fix you, you little devil. Now, get back down here. You're going back in your cage.'

Felix fled to the very back of the shelf to escape the thrusts of the broom. Johanna's voice was sinister and unfamiliar to him and the broom kept getting closer and closer with each poke.

Clumps of dust and bird droppings rained from above. The bird was finally silent and Johanna took a step back to see it. A terrible feeling came over her. Winded and perspiring, she leaned against the sofa. Blood trickled from her nose again and she licked at it with her tongue, not wanting to let the bird out of her sight.

"You stop talking nonsense. I'll do you in, I will. I don't need a bird telling me off. You keep your trap shut!"

She sat on the couch across from the bird. It huddled in the corner and clucked nervously. He tried to bob his ruffled head up and down when he saw she was looking but she quickly looked away. She reached for some tissue and blew her nose. A thick clot of blood came out.

Seeing the broom gone, Felix flew down from on high and sat on the arm of the couch and picked at the pills on the fabric, the same way Johanna did when she was nervous. Like lightening, Johanna's arm shot out and she grabbed Felix tight and squeezed his warm and beating body. She looked at the cage and looked at the balcony door. "I should throw you right out the door."

But she strode over to the cage, threw him in and slammed the door shut. The bird shook it off and huddled at the bottom of its cage. Johanna took the cover and drew it hard over the cage, leaving the bird in darkness.

• • • •

When Robert came by for the car he found his mother on the sofa with a cold cloth over her head, the droppings and dust from the top of the bookshelf scattered all over the floor and the cover over the birdcage long before it was night. "What happened here?"

Johanna removed the cloth from her head. "I don't know why you think it's so funny to teach that bird those awful things."

"What awful things? I haven't taught him awful things. He teaches himself."

He regarded her a moment. Something about her didn't look right. Her hair was damp, the bandage on her arm hung loose and needed to be taped up. And it wasn't like her to let dirt stay on the floor. "Would you like me to sweep that up?"

"You're all dressed up already. I'll do it later."

"Did you take your pill tonight?" Already the tone of the conversation made him less worried, although she did seem to be shooing him out the door.

"What do you think?" She got the keys for him even though he was closer. "Have a good time."

After he left, Johanna stared awhile at the dirty floor. It would have to wait. The task at hand beckoned.

• • • •

Robert sat with Leonard in the second row of the first balcony. Albert had wanted him to ask Marcelline to come but Robert didn't want to give Albert any more opportunities to make a fool of himself. So Leonard had been called upon with the promise of a champagne reception that Robert would apologize for later when it did not materialise. He scanned the crowd with a pair of opera glasses. The theatre was a typical modern-day abomination: grey concrete risers and orange upholstered seats. Robert had never attended a performance here and he winced in anticipation of the throbbing that would set into his molars once the music started.

Leonard read the program. They were both mellow after drinking a pre-performance scotch. Musicians filed into the pit. Wagner had been first to build a pit for the orchestra when he constructed the *Festspielhaus* in Bayreuth. To his credit, the acoustics turned out to be quite good. For the first time in history the lights had been dimmed during the performance and the orchestra was hidden. The stage itself was constructed with a double proscenium – the unused portion of foreground stage gave the audience the illusion that the drama was taking place somewhere in the distance. This coupled with the music mysteriously emanating from the pit made for a fantastical theatre experience. The mystic abyss, Wagner called it – the space through which the audience and performers connect. Robert looked around at this new auditorium. No danger of a mystical abyss engulfing them here.

• • • •

The curtain rose to reveal the courtyard of the high officials of Titipu. Robert and Leonard settled back in the darkened theatre and focused on the glow from the orchestra pit. The overture began. A few members of the audience gasped in astonishment as the stage filled with Japanese noblemen, all marching around and wielding swords. Then the women came, opening and closing their fans in an elaborate choreographic display. Robert turned to Leonard and raised his eyebrows, in mock amazement. Albert was in the first scene, standing among the noblemen while Ko-Ko sang the first number, a troubadour-esque song about a wandering minstrel. The actor playing the part mugged for the audience in a shameless fashion which drew the expected laughs and the orchestra had to *rubato* for a half measure each time he batted his eyes or pretended to break a string on his lute.

The story line moved quickly. Wagner it was not, the themes of each song introduced in turn to remind the audience of their favourites and what was to come. Albert took centre stage for his first number. He did strike a foreboding presence on the stage. He sang "Young Man Despair" in a sure and penetrating baritone. There was enthusiastic applause when he finished and again the action was interrupted for a quick bow of acknowledgement to the audience. Such liberties would never be condoned in Wagner. Soloists were not encouraged to embellish and showboat. Such behaviour was thought to diminish the rest of the work. And certainly no bows before the final curtain. What a way to spoil the mood. However, this was not the opera, Robert reminded himself. Not even close.

• • • •

The back of her neck was slick. The pain in her arm didn't register and she hauled all the boxes down and onto the floor. Her legs felt shaky and weak and she sat on the concrete floor against the chain link that divided the cubicles. It was cold in the basement storage room. She opened one after another. After a few minutes she took off her sweater. Her blouse was soaked through with sweat. The boxes were filled with clothes and recipes and gifts and things Johanna hadn't thought about in years. It had to be in one of them. She accelerated her search and let things pile up around her until soon she was dwarfed by a mountain of her belongings. She got up on her knees only to crash back into the chain link. Where was it? All the boxes were open and empty. She rummaged through the piles, using her arms as sweepers, pushing everything around randomly in a frantic effort to find it. Then, at last, in between some of Robert's old comic books, she found what she had come for. She could feel the leather binding. The shape and thickness were familiar to her, as was the smell of the old leather. Here it was, finally in her hands. She dug into the box again and hauled out the manuscript. She barely had the strength to lift it and let it fall to the floor beside her. When she tried to stand, she fell over onto her elbow and had to crawl, clutching the journal and the manuscript in one hand. She crawled with great effort but didn't know where the door was. No direction held any meaning. The room spun. Her head weighed her down. But she clutched the book and kept crawling. For what seemed like hours Johanna crawled and tried to find her way out until eventually she came upon a dusty road. It had to be the right way. She recognized the low stone fence and beyond it the swing where Heinz would push her when his friends weren't around. Finally, she was able to stand. It felt good to stretch her legs. She scanned the horizon. Tall grasses swayed in the wind and the air smelled comfortingly of sand and sun. The swing set was deserted. She could have it all to herself. The swings were made of broad planks and Johanna sat on one and waited for him to come. Any day now, she was sure he would be home.

• • • •

On the swing next to her she placed the manuscript and weighed it down carefully with the journal so the pages wouldn't blow away. She hoped he would let her keep it. It was the most beautiful music. Slowly she pumped her legs and the swing moved. Her hands gripped the ropes with sure strength. It wasn't as fun as being pushed but it was boring sitting on a swing and not moving. Where was he? She pumped her legs harder and soon she could see the road over the fence and the brick chimneys and gabled rooftops all around. There were four stork nests in all but only one stork to be seen today. The others must be off hunting. They returned each year to the same nests and this brought good luck.

Far off in the distance a figure walked towards her. Her heart leapt. It was him! He scuffed his feet along the ground, kicking up more dust than was necessary as he pushed a bicycle along beside him. She wondered why he wasn't riding it. It would have been faster. Johanna swung higher and higher and shouted his name but he was too far away and didn't hear. Her heart swelled with joy and the swing took her up until she was even with the top bar. The swing took her so high she could make out the distant ribbon of water between the sky and land.

He was getting closer. When she saw his face, her heart sank. His eyes were set on her and his mouth firm. He was cross. His clothes were too big and he looked like a rag doll, all skinny and dusty with big worn-out boots on his feet. He didn't see Johanna. She slowed the swing down with her feet. "Heinz, are you coming to push me?"

But he didn't stop. As he got closer, she saw his mouth set in a firm line. He stared at the ground as he walked. For a moment she wasn't at all sure. "Heinz, come and give me a push. Do you hear me?"

The swing undulated with her weight. To her delight Heinz laid the bicycle down and came over from the road and stood behind her. He gently pushed the swing. Back and forth, higher each time. His hands on her back felt strong and warm. Johanna twisted her head around so she could see him, but he pushed harder so she had to sit still. Soon, the swing was as high as it could go. The air rushed past her bare legs and gave her goosebumps. Her ears ached with the rush of wind. Each push sent her higher off the ground. Each time the swing returned she anticipated with great joy the hands that met her and pushed her back into the air. With her hands tight on the ropes, her stomach in her throat, Johanna never wanted the swing to stop. It arced back and forth in long, thrilling swoops.

But then the hands suddenly weren't there any more. Once, twice, three times the swing went back and there were no hands to meet her. The muscles in her back tensed in anticipation of his touch. She couldn't see where Heinz had gone. She scraped her feet on the ground but the swing kept going on its own. She started to panic and then scream because the swing would not stop. Finally, she threw herself off and braced for a rough landing. She fell from way up in the air. She kept falling and falling and when she landed, it didn't hurt at all. She rolled onto her back and lay on the ground staring up at the sky. The swing jumped around on the ropes as it came to a stop. The wind had scattered the pages of the manuscript and they blew in swirls all around her. She jumped to her feet and ran crazily around, grabbing at the dancing pages. She had to put the manuscript together again. There were sheets of music everywhere and Johanna ran in circles, tripping over her feet in an effort to gather them all together.

When she had all she could find, she dusted herself off and stood on the road, tears stinging her eyes. "I have it, Heinz. It's all right here! I'll keep it for you." She shouted. "Heinz!" But, there was nobody in sight, no matter which direction she looked. Nobody to hear her call. The swing stopped. She climbed back on and started again. She had to get high enough to see where Heinz had gone. The air was so still that it was hard to imagine he had been there at all.

Act 2

Magdeburg, Germany, 1945

CHAPTER 12

The train trip back to Dachau took all day. Wind blew through the tiny window and Heinz breathed in the last of the fresh air. Paul's satchel was wedged between his body and the armrest. There hadn't been time to read everything but the journal did reveal more than enough for any officer to have killed Paul. As he'd expected, there was mention of BBC broadcasts; it was against the law to listen to them. And the journal was full of ideas that went against the Fatherland. The manuscript was rightfully his anyway. Most of the ideas were his. The pages Paul had written were skeletal allusions to structure. Nothing dynamic had been written. Now Heinz knew why Paul never told him about the libretto. His entire opera was based on the presumption that Germany would lose the war. Had Heinz known this he would have shot Paul through his glass of beer the first night. He got what he deserved. Heinz was duty-bound to punish people like Paul. One more dead body in a war didn't amount to anything at all.

• • • •

Eight months later, it was over. The enemy was within ten kilometres of the camp. Heinz made his escape when he was escorting a group of starving inmates to a neighbouring compound where mass graves had been prepared. He had with him his satchel and some bread he'd taken from the kitchen. The group was large and there were only a few boy-soldiers left to guard them. It would be some time before anyone noticed he was gone. Had he been caught, any remaining SS men would have shot him as a deserter. For years now he had not had to make any decisions and, though his survival instinct was strong, the panic he felt as he hid motionless in the forest awaiting an uncertain freedom made his bowels seize.

He travelled by night on a stolen bicycle. He hid during the day in forests or barns. Those long hungry days were interminable and his mind drifted in and out of sleep. He wanted to keep moving, to reach Magdeburg in the north where he would rest in the familiar comfort of his home. He dreamt of sitting in the study at the piano, Johanna standing behind him with her hand on the edge of the piano, nodding in time to the intro and then her voice, out of nowhere, floating, undulating, stopping his heart. How she could sing! His mother and Barbara on the settee, listening and clapping wildly after each piece. The world was so quiet now, no bombs, no planes, no screaming, no music. He had to stop himself from humming as he waited for night to fall.

When one day he came upon clothes fluttering on a clothesline, he stole a pair of pants and a shirt and left his uniform in a ditch. The clothes were too big and he secured the pants with a length of rope he found tied to a fence post. He kept his pistol with him. If he were caught with it he would be arrested. But he didn't want to risk being caught without it. The Allies, especially the Russians, would be looking for him. He travelled by day now in his civilian disguise. It was liberating to be rid of that uniform. To think he had been so proud to wear it. How pointless it now seemed. He was too far removed from his fellow Germans to know how they felt about the outcome of the war. There would be people like him who would be disappointed in the way things turned out. Not his family. They had been displeased with his decision to join the SS. But he had been young, defiant – the very age at which a young man will do the opposite of what his parents want just to exercise his independence.

It took ten days to reach home. Most buildings in the town stood in ruins. People lined the streets in front of the few shops that had any food for sale. He slowed down and stared at them, his fellow countrymen breathing the dust of defeat. Left downtrodden and restless, they shuffled and stared at the ground, the will to move forward lost. Many of the streets were impassable for the rubble that lay everywhere in heaps. Old men and women with wheelbarrows worked to clear the debris. Everything was covered with fine dust. The air was still. Nobody looked twice at him as he wheeled his bicycle in the direction of his home. The devastation around him did not upset him; he was numb. He saw the same senselessness in the people around him as they regarded the gaping holes and piles of garbage, resigned to a state of ruin.

• • • •

He imagined the taste of nougat, sweet between his teeth, a gooseberry cake, hot from the oven served with whipped cream, the taste of strong coffee and the sound of women's laughter. His mother's breast pressed at his cheek. The harder she squeezed the more she loved him.

His heart quickened as he walked along the fence towards the garden gate. It had been four years since he had last seen his mother and his sisters. He knew his father would be gone. He had been killed early in the war. The Party flag on the front of his house had been taken down. He wondered how long ago. His mother would have taken it down at the first opportunity. The gate had grown rusty and made a loud grinding noise when he opened it. It alerted his sister who was hanging laundry in the garden. Johanna stared at him and he tried to gauge her reaction. There was alarm in her eyes. Fear. It disturbed him to see this from his sister when he had witnessed the same in a thousand subhuman faces at Dachau. He set the bicycle down without taking his eyes off her and held his hands up. "Johanna, it's me."

She hesitated with a wet towel in her hands, her fingers knotted on a twist of fabric. He dared to take one step, his heavy boots grating on the gravel. His eyes shifted to the door, expecting his mother to come rushing out at any moment, wiping her hands on her apron, tears flowing from her eyes, her outstretched hands trembling with relief.

"I guess you didn't get the letter." She knew what he was thinking. "She died nine months ago. I sent a letter."

There was no comfort in her voice, no solace, only bitterness. He leaned over and picked up the satchel.

"Get inside," she ordered. "The neighbours might see you."

He slouched up the stairs behind her, wary of a new battle line. Her eyes flared with anger. "So, the brave soldier has returned from battle. News of your heroics precedes you."

His legs shook with fatigue and his eyes stung. His mouth was dry, his stomach empty. He brushed past her. "Don't listen to all that anti-German propaganda."

"Take those boots off."

The house smelled of dust and soot. Beneath that he thought he could smell lemon polish and fresh, hot cake – memories of how his home used to smell. He entered the hallway and slowly walked through to the living room. He stopped at the sofa, pulled off his boots and left them in a heap where they fell. He was tired of obeying orders. The war was finished, his work done.

The house was bare. All the paintings that had hung on the walls, the china and crystal in the cabinets, the books that lined an entire wall of the living room had all been packed away, sold or covered in sheets. Preparations made in case they had to flee. The back of the house had been damaged by mortar-fire. The living room windows were shattered and the debris that had filled the room had been painstakingly shovelled and thrown outside by his sisters.

"We've had to burn some of the old kitchen chairs. There hasn't been heat in months." She followed behind him. That morning she and Barbara had finished the last flour and butter rations. There wouldn't be more for a week and there was no way to get ration cards for Heinz. They were near starvation. It was dangerous for him to be here – dangerous for all of them.

She followed him to the kitchen where he stood before the pantry. It was empty except for a bowl of tiny green pears and a basket of brown apples. His stomach twisted at the message that there was no food. "I am very tired," he said finally. "Is there a bed for me?"

Her mouth tensed and she nodded. "We'll have to bring it from upstairs. The roof caved in. We've been living on the main floor. There's room in the study. Our beds are in the dining room."

He trod up the stairs behind her. Lath and plaster from the damaged roof was heaped in the corner. They had tried to patch the hole with old shingles but the summer sky still peeked through.

"The neighbours were ordered to take in two families of refugees. Because of this," she indicated the roof, "we don't have to. Lucky for you it's only us here."

Together they carried a tattered mattress down the stairs. Tufts of stuffing fell from where rats had pulled fibres out for their nests. They dropped it in the middle of the study floor. In the corner stood the piano, lid closed, the dark finish scratched and dusty, but otherwise unharmed. Heinz's eyes fixed on it while he straightened the mattress with his foot.

"We had to burn the bench," Johanna stated.

"It's all right." His fingers tingled with anticipation as he pulled up a metal garden chair. He felt the smooth, cool ivory, the gentle, precise action of his fingers on the keys. He reached out and played a few notes she would recognize.

"It's out of tune."

"I want to hear you sing." He hadn't intended it to sound like an order, but there the words hovered between them and he was unable to snap them back.

"What is there to sing about?" she hissed.

Heinz pulled a chair over to the piano and tried to tell her softly, "Johanna, I sang at Bayreuth! Can you believe it? *Die Meistersinger*."

She looked puzzled. "How did you come to do that?"

"They called us up. They needed extra singers for the chorus. How have you practised with the piano so out of tune?"

Her hands clenched into white-knuckled fists. He used to spend hours in here listening to Wagner, singing along and now the only thing he had to say for himself was that the war made all his dreams come true.

"We have been through a war while you were gone. Singing! Maybe the outcome would have been different if you had actually fought rather than murdering innocent Germans. And opera, well, I'll never understand what good was meant to come of that in the middle of a war."

He played the introduction to a Mozart aria that she used to sing, but her face grew ashen and she shook her head.

"Stop it! You're lucky you didn't come here and find a hole in the ground. People are starving in the streets, fighting over rotten potatoes, the roof of our home is caved in, our parents are dead and this zone is in the hands of the Russians. And you did nothing to stop it. You and that imbecile Adolf Hitler have led us straight into hell. Singing! What good is singing at a time like this? You have lost your mind."

Heinz's eyes blazed. "I've been through the same war as you," he shouted. "What kind of a welcome is this for your brother? There are people who will never see their brothers again."

"Ha!" She scoffed. "When were you ever in any danger during this war? Did you see the state of the roof? We had to barricade ourselves in the cellar for nearly two days while the Americans dropped bombs on us. The firestorm burned down half the buildings in the city. The bombs fell endlessly. We had to huddle with wet rags over our faces and when it was over, we could not get the door open and thought we had survived the worst only to die after all. The same war! You are dreaming if you think you suffered as we did. Completely mad. All you did was kill innocent Jews. It's despicable!"

"They were enemies of the state. We had orders." He loomed over her, impossible to keep the menace out of his voice. People could speak freely now without fear. He was not used to it.

"Women and children! What threat did they pose?"

"The threat of procreation!"

"How could you ever have believed that nonsense? You and your blind faith. It's a good thing Mother is gone. To see you here after what you have done would surely have killed her."

He slouched back onto the chair and plinked at the keys, his face stony and cold.

She felt faint. The absurdity of his conviction was staggering. She wanted to slam the piano lid down onto his stubborn fingers. Their mother would not believe the terrible rumours about the camps. She could not imagine her son had anything to do with it. It was too horrible to imagine. Other mothers mourned sons lost in battle. All she could do was keep quiet and hope nobody asked.

"I need a bath. A hot bath."

"There's no firewood. I could burn the piano, if you really want hot water."

Heinz stared at the piano while Johanna threw pillows and blankets onto the mattress in a heap. "You can make your own bed." She turned and left the room. Her words clung to him like barbs, but where there should have been pain there was no emotion at all. He rested his head back on the hard chair and stared at the swirls in the ceiling plaster. She couldn't stand the sight of him, didn't look at him unless it was to spit out some contemptible words. But she would learn. The past cannot be recaptured like a bird that has escaped from its cage.

• • • •

Heinz stood before the mirror and filled the sink with cold water. The razor in his hand was dull and he scraped it against his skin with no effect. He stared at his reflection: empty eyes, hollow cheeks, a brittle beard, stained teeth, sagging shoulders. He had aged a thousand years.

When he'd left home he'd been so confident, his purpose clear. He couldn't understand why nobody in his family shared his conviction. When he came home at Christmas in his uniform he deflected the look of disappointment on his mother's face with an air of bravado. His heart had developed a sturdy shield. The deeds could not be undone but his intention was true. A good son will do anything to please his mother. But she failed to see that what he was doing, he was doing for her. As he stared into the mirror, a melody from the opera came into his head and he began to hum.

• • • •

Johanna sat on the sofa and could not breathe. She would never do it – burn the piano. She would have done it by now and the reason she hadn't was because she had been waiting for him to come home. She wanted so much to feel happy to see him. She had imagined it throughout the war. He would return, alive and grateful to her for keeping their home ready. More than anything she'd wanted to give him a hero's welcome. When he had first left she had no idea what that black uniform meant, other than that he showed less interest in his music and spent a lot of time at meetings. Although only a year older than Johanna, he acted as though he was ten years older. The change that came over him when he wore that uniform took her by surprise. She was used to different things from her brother. They had always been close but in those days of Heinz's early enthusiasm, they hardly ever spoke unless it was about Hitler and the new Germany. "There's going to be a war and father and I will be called to fight," he announced as though this was news to her. Every day they waited for the orders. As it turned out, her father was called up early and sent to Poland where he died early in the campaign when his bunker was hit. Heinz was still at home when they received the news.

Then he received his orders. Her mother was torn when he announced that he would be stationed at Dachau. At least he wouldn't see any fighting there. Both she and Johanna knew Heinz was not cut out for war. But there were rumours about the camps, the things that went on there.

The false airs of bluster that he put on didn't fool her. How could he one minute be crying over a broken butterfly net and the next be standing at attention, ready to fight. He had the notion that what he would be doing was terribly important. "You are Germany," he told Johanna with his hand resting on her shoulder. This was before he left and she had helped him carry his heavy duffel bag down the stairs. "You are the future. It is for you that I will fight. So that you and your children can live in a pure and strong country."

At sixteen she was old enough to know he was reciting ideas that were not his own. It almost made her laugh but he was quick to anger those days. Perhaps it was the inherent belligerence of his youth. She had no idea then what he meant then by a pure and strong country.

• • • •

Barbara found Johanna hunched over a pillow in the living room, crying.

"What is it?"

"Listen."

The sound of Heinz's voice reached them. "Heinz?" Barbara's face flushed with excitement. "He's back?"

"Yes," Johanna whispered. "Nobody knows."

Barbara didn't understand.

"I should have turned him away at the gate." What she was doing was not just illegal but dangerous. Those stupid Nazis. Now when their time was up, they expected people to turn a blind eye. And he stood in the bathroom singing.

"But that's wonderful he is home," Barbara exclaimed. "Isn't it?"

Johanna paused. She wasn't sure how much Barbara knew.

"He deserted. Others are in prison and facing death. He wasn't just a soldier – he was at Dachau. Now he is hiding here. It's not safe."

"But it was war. Everybody was killing people. Not just Heinz." Barbara's face was serious. "All that stuff about the camps – it's just propaganda. To make us feel bad."

Johanna felt sick. "It's over, Barbara. We cannot hide anymore. The Allies may have destroyed our cities but we have destroyed Germany. The world will never look upon us in a kind way."

"Well, I don't believe it. Heinz would never do those things."

"Believe it. He's guilty of terrible crimes. Do you have any idea how many people he may have killed?"

"Do you?"

Johanna shook her head. The shock of his return still stung. It was going to be difficult to convince Barbara of his guilt. She was young. The conclusions she reached in her mind were innocent. But Johanna knew he could not stay here. This was the most immediate concern. Someone would find out and then they would all be punished. She wanted him out. Each note he sang slashed through her with an unexpected violence. Her heart disintegrated into a thousand ragged pieces and the beauty that once lived there fled in disgrace.

• • • •

It had happened insidiously. Johanna was young when it started and could not remember when she first heard the name Adolf Hitler. Then, she couldn't remember a time of not hearing it. Suddenly Germany was flooded with images of *der Führer* and anticipation quivered in the air. There was a new energy in the streets. The sidewalks and shops buzzed with charged conversations. She could feel it in the stores, everywhere people gathered. At school, there was a new sense of purpose – an undercurrent of industry and order. The injustices dealt them by the Treaty of Versailles were finally going to be erased. Germany was on the move. Hitler's voice was on the radio every day. Without him they would not even have had a radio in their living room. It was a wondrous invention and Hitler kept everyone abreast of Germany's growing importance on the world stage.

Her mother, usually one to make a point of listening to the news, now sighed and left the room when these broadcasts came on. Hitler's screeching voice made Johanna giggle. It reminded her of the ogres in fairy tales, the ones who were all huff and puff and tried to scare everybody but really didn't fool anybody.

"He reminds me of the big bad wolf," she said and grinned at her father.

"That man will lead us all straight to hell. I can't trust someone who yells like that all the time."

"I can't even understand what he's saying. He's crazy."

Her father smiled and stroked her hair. "That is Germany's only hope. That there are more people like you who don't understand what he's saying and think he's crazy."

Johanna could see the worry in his eyes and the looks of concern that passed between him and her mother. They didn't mind that Johanna listened to the radio but they did not discuss the war in front of her. It was because of Heinz.

At first her parents had told the children not to say anything at school concerning familial minor infractions to the new rules. Like eating roast on the one Sunday of the month that everyone was supposed to eat soup and give the extra money to the poor. Or listening to the BBC. But when Heinz started to embrace Nazi ideals they had to be careful in their own home. If he knew what his parents really thought there was a chance he might turn them in. It was happening every day, people being turned in by informants. So they got a Party flag and hung it outside on certain days – Hitler's birthday and the first of May – Labour Day. And when Johanna and Barbara wanted to go to the meetings of the League of German Girls, their parents no longer expressed concern for their enthusiasm but pretended that they wanted them to go. All German children were being raised in this atmosphere. It was not unusual or uncomfortable. As far as Johanna knew, nobody ever disobeyed.

• • • •

Heinz returned to the study and made up the bed. A gramophone stood in the corner where it always had. The records were still stacked neatly in the dresser beside it. Some things had no value on the black market. His hands trembled as he placed the recording of *Tristan and Isolde* on the turntable. It had been so long since he'd heard such a heavenly sound. As the opening chords filled the room, he stumbled to the bed and pulled the sheets over his weary body. The music replenished his soul. As he sank exhausted into the cushions he was vaguely aware of the smell of fresh air and pine trees on the sheets. Later, when he awoke, it was dark. The needle skipped against the end of the record. He dressed in the clothes Johanna had placed on the chair next to the bed. They thought he would not be back and had packed his clothes away. They smelled dank, relics from another era. He followed the smell of food to the kitchen. Johanna was by the sink.

"We've eaten." She stated without turning around. Barbara leapt from the stool and nearly threw him to the ground with an enthusiastic embrace. Johanna kept her back to them. It didn't surprise her that the first thing he would do was to turn the gramophone on. This was how she remembered him – his ear glued to his beloved Wagner. She recognized the opening of *Tristan and Isolde* immediately. Heinz used to pull her over to the speaker and implore her to listen to the parts he found particularly moving or ingenious. She remembered him explaining the unresolved chord to her. In Wagner's words they were meant to convey the endless yearning, longing, rapture and misery of love. To hear it again now made her feel sick.

Barbara led Heinz to a place at the table. She set a bowl of thin bean soup in front of him with an end of dry bread and a cup of dark, strong tea. She sat down across from him, her eyes eager with anticipation. Heinz stared into his soup. Out on the kitchen balcony, Johanna snapped the towels on the railing to dry. Heinz hunched over the table and lifted the spoon to his lips. He ate quickly, keeping his mouth full. Anything to prevent a conversation with his little sister.

• • • •

The manuscript captivated him. The neat precise notes, the melodies he had once played. And the libretto that Paul had kept from him. Paul had never told Heinz what the opera was about. And now Heinz knew why. With the libretto before him, Heinz read what he had all along suspected. Long before the defeat of Germany, here was a citizen apologizing to the world via a half-crazed saint. How sickeningly prophetic that the ideas within the opera were now to come true. Heinz needed only to see Johanna glare at him to know what lay in store for the people of Germany. It was people like Johanna who would have to endure the icy waters and hot ovens and bear the burden of having covered the earth with the stench of human sin. If his character Christina was symbolic of Germany then she was also symbolic of Johanna. He would unite their voices in the opera. The power of this revelation made him clutch his head. It all had to be rewritten. Paul had a tendency to favour the higher registers and Johanna's range reached E-flat. There was a lot of work still to be done

The manuscript was unfinished. The libretto was complete but the music stopped halfway through the second act. It burned him to think Paul had been right about the war. Had he thought Heinz a fool the entire time he was asking for his help? 'Poor buggers.' That's what he had written in his journal about anyone who believed the war could be won. Smug bastard. But now Heinz had the manuscript and could make it his own. He leafed through the pages until he came upon an aria for Christina and hummed the notes to himself. It would sound better with flute accompaniment rather than the violins. Perhaps flute and violins in unison. That would work. And then a section with inverted triads singing through the wind section. He imagined how it would sound with Johanna singing. The notes held with effortless tension, each a fragile bubble that floated along and never touched the ground.

• • • •

The following days were strained. Heinz stayed in the study and avoided Johanna's icy glare. He tried to forget Paul and all the nonsense in the journal. His own name was in there, as he'd suspected. The time he threatened to shoot Paul. It had made Paul angry. But Paul had forgotten his place and Heinz had had to remind him. Even in Bayreuth there had to be order. The apple cake on his birthday – how that brief moment of happiness soured him. This was the nature of happiness – fleeting. But that was the maddening thing about Paul. He was happy most of the time. They were in the middle of a war and yet he could laugh and work. Such was his luck that he and his friend spent a day in the woods and met two pretty girls. Not once had there been a pretty girl for Heinz to talk to during the entire war. The only girls he encountered were the ones he shepherded to their death at the camp. *Move along! Quiet!* That was the extent of his words to them. And that stupid comment about choosing evil – he didn't recall being given a choice. All he had been given was a uniform, a gun, some training and then orders. He was made to feel like an adult. And that is all a boy of seventeen wants.

It was so easy for Paul. There was work for him in the orchestra. There was time for him to compose. There was no reason for anyone not to like him. It was as though in Paul's world there was no war at all. Whether Germany won or lost, his life would have remained the idyllic existence it already was. This was why he had so little respect for Heinz. The difficult but necessary work the Nazi Party was doing made no difference to him. His journal was filled with objections to the regime and questions about the war and yet it had no impact at all on his life.

Heinz knew his parents had felt the same way. They had considered Hitler a nuisance at best. He saw the looks they gave one another when the radio came on. There had been a boy at school who had turned his parents in, something Heinz had been to afraid to do, even though he knew he should. They were all under pressure to inform on enemies of the regime. It was a relief when they finally hung a Nazi Party flag outside. Then he could pretend that all was well under his roof.

The piano needed to be tuned. Barbara sat on a chair beside him while he worked with a pair of pliers to tune it. Just the sound of the repeating notes lifted his spirits. He knew Johanna would sing with him once he got the opera underway. The manuscript was hidden. He didn't want them to know he had it. Not until he had something to show Johanna. She would help him the way he had helped Paul. Music was in her the way it was in him. The first duet, sung by Christina and the priest, where he tries to coax her down from the rafters, telling her not to be afraid, that would be the first piece he would work on and then they would sing it together. Their voices united once again, washing atop one another like gentle waves. It was the only conceivable way to bring her back to him. Like Paul had said, the music will prevail. She may turn her back on him but she would never turn away from this. It would be like losing a limb.

He waited until the house was empty to open the piano and play an aria that Paul had written. It was in C minor, for the role of Christina. Heinz sang the aria as he remembered it – a haunting lyric of a woman who fears humanity and yet has been called to save them. The sound rang through the empty house and quenched the thirsty walls. Heinz played the score through from the beginning. He remembered most of it. There were sketched in parts that Paul had written but had not asked Heinz to play. Instinctively he found himself filling in the parts in his head. He could hear the instruments. It was all there. Six hours he stayed at the piano and played and played.

• • • •

There were days Johanna never saw Heinz. They drifted around the big house, pushed in opposite directions by an invisible wind. He sat at the piano much of the time behind closed doors. Johanna could never make out what he was playing but was thankful he had withdrawn into his own world and left her and Barbara to themselves. He didn't ask her again to sing. The times she poked her head into the room, he would be at the keyboard, his head resting on his arm and his other hand playing random notes, nothing coherent at all. Sometimes he would hum meaningless notes and at other times sing brief phrases she couldn't place. There were papers strewn all around the study and his shirts were stained with ink and food. Thankfully he had smoked the last of his cigarettes, though the air in the piano room still smelled stale from the lack of circulation. The doors were rarely opened and he rarely left. He took his meals in his room, whatever he found in the pantry. He didn't care what sustained him: a slice of ham, a hard pear from the tree in the garden, a crust of bread. He grew ever thinner and wouldn't wash for days on end, allowing his beard to grow and dirt to gather under his nails. Johanna watched his transformation and could not bring herself to care.

"Do you know what he's doing in there?" she asked Barbara one day.

"On the piano?" Barbara shook her head. "It's good he's playing, don't you think? Maybe if you asked him he would sing with you again. It's been so long since we've had any music in the house."

At this Johanna scoffed as if to make light of it. "I doubt I could sing a note anymore. Those days are gone. There's too much to be done."

"He asks about Mother. He misses her, I think."

Johanna shrugged. She had sent the letters about her death. There was no other way to contact him. The mail was unreliable.

And now, at the end of the war, if Heinz were discovered under their roof, they would all be punished equally. The only way for Heinz to save them was to turn himself in. Barbara sensed this. She was afraid that Johanna would betray him. "What do you know of betrayal?" Johanna spit out the words. "Don't you know what he has done? Those SS brutes are responsible for bringing the hatred of the whole world on Germany. It will never end. We won't be able to move freely. Our children and their children will forever carry this burden."

But Barbara would not hear it. When she saw his bleary, bloodshot eyes and heard his moans at night, she thought it was remorse. But Johanna knew better. Remorse was foreign to him. It had been stamped out years ago.

• • • •

Work on the opera sustained him. He could hear the music in his head, the cellos scrubbing up and down a D minor scale and then the horn, plaintive and howling with the bassoon underneath, the wind through the dark trees. Christina's Leitmotif – a soft, low B-flat major arpeggio, two octaves, uttered unevenly, not quite a true syncopation, descending and then slowly ascending the scale until she appears, determined to fight her battle to its end.

Paul had described the stage set to him – an old brick church with part of the wall crumbling so that the outside and inside could be seen at the same time. The entire set would be on a turntable so that when it revolved, it revealed the outside while the inside of the church remained visible. There was a haunting motif for Christina played in the lower registers on the flute. For a scene with her sisters, there was to be a flute off stage playing the theme while the sisters tried to coax Christina from a freezing river to return to the life she once knew. They would hide behind some rocks and observe the priest as he ministered to Christina in the cold waters of the river. Once he left, Christina would sing an aria praising the priest and the Lord for her good fortune of being called upon to serve. The sisters, dismayed to overhear that Christina had embraced her insanity as a divine calling, would sing a duet. Reaching out over an impregnable void, their song of yearning would speak of how things used to be when life's simple tasks led them from one day to the next. Behind the rocks they would have a sheep, with which they would hope to remind Christina of her life before her death, in the hope that she would come out of the water and join them again in the world of mortals. At the summation of the scene, they would all realize there is no turning back once immortality has been ordained and Christina would immerse herself in the waters again. For Christina it would be too late. She could not go with them; she would know she had to be fearless before God and trust no harm would come to her. The sisters would turn to go, knowing Christina had been lost to them. They would implore the priest to convince Christina to return to them. They wanted their old sister back, the way she was before her enlightenment caused her to go insane.

Heinz worked feverishly. Every waking hour he spent behind closed doors with the piano and his thoughts. He wanted to believe in Germany too, like Paul. He was a fugitive here in this house; without some purpose he would go mad. Johanna could barely stand the sight of him.

He forgot that it was Paul's idea to have Christina sing off stage, in a muted, airy voice. Her lines were the Count's thoughts. She sings what he wants to hear. She sings that she loves him, will give up her life for him and he sings that he will never let harm come to her again. It is a tender and bittersweet scene because when Christina does appear she is half-crazed, running barefoot across the stage with twigs in her hair, her clothing torn. She doesn't recognize him and flees when he reaches for her. The beauty of the music is gripping. A section in the winds, made to sound like the whooshing wind and the sound of birds twittering and chirping and then from out of the branches, Christina sings. The whole time she has been singing but in harmony with the birds and so there is no way to discern her voice from theirs until she becomes visible. And then she sings her aria. It is towards the end of the second act. There is a bird she sings to. The entire scene is fairytale-like with just Christina on the stage alone in the woods. Here she is at peace with the animals, the sun and the flowers. If she doesn't go to heaven, she will come here.

Heinz was possessed with the sound he was creating. He wished he were back in Bayreuth. He wished he could sing again with the powerful chorus and hear the sound reverberate and rattle his spine. He wrote fanfares for the brass, triple fortissimo, the blazing sound, an unearthly inferno, a mythical beast unleashed from the back row of the orchestra – a sound that would pin people to the backs of their seats. He dropped into bed at the end of each day, utterly limp with fatigue. Yet, he could not sleep. All night long he imagined the opera. Music looped through his mind, unending themes and phrases all yet to be written. As he neared completion he knew the music had kept him alive, as surely as it would mark his end.

The day he led Johanna into the study, blood thrummed at his temples. It could be contained no longer. He had to hear it, their duet. "Come with me."

She balked. "What for? Do you need clean sheets? You know where to find them."

"I don't need clean sheets. Come. I have something for you."

"I can't imagine what."

He propelled her towards the piano and placed her beside his chair. The manuscript was laid out all across the entire length of the keyboard. His palms were slick. He wiped them on his trousers. "Can you see?"

"What?" Her voice trembled.

"The notes. Your part is here." He pointed to the turquoise ink. "It's not too hard. Don't worry about the trill in the fourth measure for now."

"What have you done?" A hoarse whisper.

"It is an opera. There's a part for you. The lead. Christina – she is a saint. I will play it through and then we'll try it. I have been waiting to hear you sing again. For us to sing. Please, just listen."

"An opera?" She was stunned. "That's what you have been doing in here? Do you have any idea what is going on?" She waved her hand towards the window. "They have divided the country into zones. There are mass graves being uncovered. Dachau was one of the worst! You have no right to be sitting here enjoying yourself."

He turned away from her, faced the piano and played the piece through, humming her part for her, anticipating the sound of her voice. The final chord sounded and he prepared to begin again.

"I can't sing!" she said, breathless. "What are you thinking? This is madness."

He reached for her hand but she was quick to pull it away. "Stay away from me. I can't stand the sight of you. You should be shot like the rest of them."

She turned and stormed out of the room, slamming the door so that the small panes of glass rattled. He winced as he waited for one of them to shatter. When the crash didn't come, he stared at the keys on the piano where a normal man's tears should fall.

• • • •

Johanna fled the room. Her hands trembled with rage. It incensed her that he had no notion of the gravity of their situation. For him to sit in there and compose some stupid opera and think anyone cared about such things at such a time. And to expect her to sing while she waited for the Russians to storm their house and take them all away. Writing a part for her, as though the war, all this madness, had been a holiday. It was proof that he had lost his mind. He and the rest of them who thought it made sense to stage an opera festival with the Allies storming the borders. One would think someone would have come to their senses and declared Hitler incompetent. Up until the very end they tried to fool the nation into believing they were winning the war. The Reichstag had to be captured room by room. No surrender – the German people abandoned to their fate. Hitler lay dead in his bunker; the country in ruins and thousands of children named Adolf left shaking at the hatred their name suddenly invoked.

"While he sits there playing we stand in line for eggs, or dig hard roots up in the garden so those few seeds can be planted from last year's peas. Look at my hands." She held them out for Barbara to see the rash from the stinging nettles she'd cut down for tea.

"He said he wants to sing with you again."

"I can't imagine why."

Barbara watched Johanna cut up onions from a sack. Meticulously she separated the rotten parts and threw the good parts into a pan of fat. "You sing so beautifully. Remember when you won the second prize at the music festival? We were all so proud of you."

"It's crazy, what he's doing. Thoughtless bastard. He should turn himself in if he truly cares anything about us."

"But he might be killed."

"He needs to stand up and take responsibility." Johanna threw some rancid oil onto the pan and it sizzled and spit so that she had to stand back. "The last thing I feel like doing is singing."

She rested her hands against the edge of the table. Her breathing was heavy and her stomach heaved. Barbara came over and laid a hand on her shoulder. "Not singing won't change anything," she said. "It will only make you unhappy. You'll sing again, Johanna. It is in you to sing."

Johanna turned back to the stove, bit back the tears and said something about the strong onions. Barbara left her alone. The sound of the piano seeped out through the study door and filled the air like a noxious gas.

• • • •

In his dream, Heinz shoots and shoots but Paul does not die. All the bullets go astray and Paul laughs at him. "Poor bugger," he says. "What are you going to do with that? Mount your own production of an unfinished opera. You think you can turn your life around after taking part in this mess?" Paul lurches forward and shoots at Heinz with his fingers pointed like pistols. It makes Heinz flinch. "You're such a sucker, Beckmesser. A coward. Shoot me then. Kill me for an opera that you'll never hear. If you can make sense of that then you might as well kill yourself too."

Then before Heinz raises his gun, Paul falls dead to the ground.

Heinz awoke shaking at the image of himself in that dream. But some of the dream was very real. The opera sat on his lap. Notes filled the pages. This was the man he wanted to be – the one who writes the opera. Not the other one. But he could not be both the hero and the villain.

The house closed in. The confines of the study stifled him. The opera was complete. This was the drug that had extended his life. It had given him five weeks and now it was finished. There would never be a performance of the work, but that didn't matter. It would remain unknown, written anonymously and left to disintegrate back to the earth. What mattered to him was that he had done the one thing that might redeem what had become of his life. He took a leather cord and tied it around the manuscript. The title page read: *From the Rafters – The Life of Christina the Astonishing. An opera in three acts by Heinz Friedrich.*

He was finished. The enveloping silence drove him outdoors. It was not safe and Johanna had warned him countless times to stay out of sight. But he needed to see the sky and feel the sun on his face. It didn't matter anymore. He stepped into the garden and shaded his eyes shut against the bright, unfamiliar sun. He breathed deeply the scent of roses and listened to the chirping birds and humming flies. Scenes from his childhood swirled around him. Coffee parties in the garden, the hose spraying ice cold water on him when the sun sweltered, butterflies dancing among the leafy shadows, his mother cutting a small bouquet for the table. He walked the perimeter of the property, his hand trailing along the rough wall that surrounded it. The sand box where he used to play had been converted into a vegetable garden. All his old toys sat on shelves in the cold and musty shed – trucks with sand still stuck in the wheels, shovels and pails that they would load into the car and take with them to the sea for their summer holidays. He picked up an old fire truck and pushed it along the edge of a shelf. Children had no idea that one day those languorous, golden holidays by the sea would visit their imagination as distant memories – places and events never to be relived. Those blissful moments that go unnamed because they come so frequently. Children were blessed with a sense of the immediate. If only that feeling could be strengthened throughout one's life.

He sat near the back of the garden on a stone bench. A bench that had always been there but that he had never sat on. One of many corners and unclaimed spaces he took for granted. He gazed over the garden and viewed the back of the house, the sun porch, the small kitchen balcony under which they kept their bicycles. Barbara's was there now and Johanna had taken hers to the store. This place, every inch of which he knew, made him feel strange, as though he had never seen it before. As though he had no right to claim any of it as his own.

• • • •

Frau Schultz met Johanna at the end of the sidewalk. "Someone was in your garden today."

"What?" Johanna's face paled. "Are you sure?" She shifted the bag of rations she was carrying from one hand to the other. There was cauliflower today and she had managed to buy three heads. They were getting heavy but there would be enough soup for a week.

"Yes. I was in my guest room on the second floor and saw a man coming out of your shed. You better make sure there's nothing missing."

Her tone was baiting. Johanna tensed. Had she heard the piano? Had she noticed the extra sheets that hung with the laundry? Maybe she already knew about Heinz and wanted to see if Johanna would confess. Frau Schultz had been their neighbour since Johanna was a young girl. Sometimes she gave them potatoes from her garden and ham from the farmer she traded with. But today she sounded different, without concern in her voice. Johanna was certain she had seen Heinz.

"You better call the police," her voice commanded. "He might have been stealing from you."

"Thanks. I'll go home and check." Johanna walked with deliberate steps. The house was silent. No music came from the study and the door was shut. She left the food in the kitchen and stepped outside. Something in the garden caught her eye. An old toy fire truck had fallen into the beans. Johanna stared at the red toy. Her heart raced. For fear that Frau Schultz was watching she left the fire truck where it was and stepped quickly back to the house. She veered towards the study. As her hand rested on the cool handle of the French door she had a fleeting thought that it was good Barbara wasn't home.

He lay on the mattress. Blood pooled around his head. The gun had fallen out of his hand. Johanna stared at the body on the bed. The pillow was saturated in blood. Transfixed, she stared at the brain matter spattered against the wall and wondered what final thoughts of his it contained. She took one step towards him and dropped to her knees. Her stomach heaved and she retched violently. Her stomach twisted so that it was painful to stand. She staggered over to the piano. It had been closed, his papers all tidied and left in a neat pile on top. There was no suicide note. Taking a deep breath, she lifted the lid and rested her hand on the keys. One finger pressed down onto E flat and held there until the tone faded away.

To call the police or the doctor – somebody had to come and take him away before Barbara came home. A dreadful feeling came over her. There was no one to call. Even dead, he posed a threat. They would come, shove a boot into the side of his body and then take her away, and Barbara. The gun – she would have to bury it in the garden, hide it somehow. Her hands twitched uncontrollably. Where they once had all lived as a family, in this room where the piano used to draw them together and the sounds that they created here made them all so happy. It was finished, that part of her life. She stood alone, on the precipitous floe that would now transport her.

• • • •

"Where is he?" Barbara demanded when Johanna told her Heinz was gone. The study was empty. "Where's his bed? What have you done?" She was hysterical, gasping. She glared at Johanna. "You turned him in, didn't you? How could you?"

"He's dead. It's a good thing you weren't here." She held her arms around herself. "He shot himself."

"Where's the note? I don't believe you."

"There was no note."

Barbara ran from the room, sobbing. Johanna's arms and legs ached with fatigue. She had pulled the body through the house on a sheet, and then the mattress. The cellar door faced north, where the prying eyes of Frau Schultz could not reach. Johanna had not been down there since the night of the bombing. She wrapped and rewrapped the body tight in some canvas and then rolled an old carpet around it. It was exhausting, back-breaking work. The cellar door fell shut with a thud and she padlocked the latch and threw the key with all her might into the garden. The war was over. They would not need the shelter again.

Act 3

Toronto, Canada, Present Day

CHAPTER 13

The second act began same as the first. A fluffy overture and the curtain rose to a lovely garden scene where Yum-Yum was having her hair braided by her friends before her wedding. The lights were bright, the mood always the same. Robert wished a sphere of red would appear shimmering in the middle of a darkened stage for just a few seconds. Something abstract for the audience to ponder. But no, there was no emotion here other than delight. Any momentary tension always lightened by a prat-fall or sly grin directed at the audience. Every song sung at the same volume – brash. The audience would later file out of the theatre unchanged – no richer than they had been when they entered.

The entire premise that Ko-Ko would decapitate someone was never to be realized. So the audience laughed and clapped at every turn, no matter what was going on. Robert grew restless until Albert made another entrance halfway through the act to sing "The Criminal Cried As He Dropped Him Down." Albert sang with Ko-Ko and Pitti-Sing and all of them sang different lines at the same time so nothing could be understood. The entire audience hooted with laughter. Only Robert clenched his teeth. Through his opera glasses Robert saw the thick make-up plastered to Albert's face. Remarkably he didn't look much different without it, but he did know how to act. Or overact as this particular work required. His sword never saw any action, Robert noticed, whereas the women were kept busy with their fans. The fans were a key part of the show. There was a flurry of wrist snapping as the fans came to life in each number.

Robert handed the opera glasses to Leonard, who scanned the faces of the bored musicians in the orchestra pit. The second act dragged as all the intricacies of the plot were cleverly and light-heartedly worked out. The show came to a rousing conclusion with a song and dance.

"Well, do you want to come backstage and meet the great Pooh Bah? We can fight off the crowd together," Robert said to Leonard as they filed out to the lobby. Leonard declined.

"I don't blame you. I'll probably just stay a minute and congratulate Albert. He was quite good, I thought."

"Were you surprised?"

"No, not really. He's like that all the time." Actors mystified Robert. How could they be trusted with that ability to transform themselves? Disassociation. This was what they practised. They practised putting themselves into a clinically certifiable state of mind. It couldn't be healthy.

They stood in the lobby among the surge of exiting patrons. Leonard shook Robert's hand. "You owe me for this. I was expecting champagne and caviar."

The lobby was nearly empty. Robert made his way over to the stage door. His name was on a list and the person checking names let him through. He could see through the wings the expanse of the stage and the rows of seats for the audience. A few ushers swept along the rows picking up dropped programs and ticket stubs. This view from stage left caused a mild panic in Robert. It always did. He didn't know how people did it. To get up under the blaze of lights in front of an audience. For Robert it was like a fear of heights – innate and irreversible. He had a new respect for Albert.

Albert waved Robert over. He was at the food table, still in full costume. He clapped a cell phone shut. "No answer. Do you have time to stop by the apartment and check on your mother?"

"She's probably in bed. Why are you calling her so late?"

"There was no answer earlier. I called during intermission."

Robert ran his hand through his hair. He supposed a good son would have called during intermission rather than stand in line at the bar in order to gulp down a double scotch.

"I have to return her car anyway. I'll run up and check on her. But I tell you, she's sleeping."

"Why don't you wait for me there and we'll have a nightcap? I won't be much longer here. Just some press to do, you know how it is." Albert munched on a cracker. There were beads of sweat pearling between the creases of his make-up.

Robert made his way to the exit through the costumed cast. He glanced back once more before leaving and saw Albert surrounded by the women who had played the three little maids from school. They were laughing at something he'd just said. Albert looked like the happiest man on earth.

• • • •

Frank was still on duty when Robert arrived at the front door. He leapt to his feet as soon as he saw Robert.

"She's not dead. They put the oxygen on her right away, so I know that. I tried to call the hospital but they don't give out any information on the phone. Not to the doorman anyway."

Automatically Robert pressed the button on the elevator and stepped inside. Nothing Frank had said registered.

"Robert, she's not there. She's at the hospital."

Frank stood with his arm blocking the door from sliding shut. "You have to go to the hospital. She collapsed in the basement. She's in the hospital."

Finally he let Frank coax him out of the elevator and sit him in one of the lobby chairs. Frank brought a coffee from his thermos. The unexpected always had a way of bowling Robert over. He listened again as Frank explained.

"When she didn't come back after an hour I went to look for her and found her passed out on the floor. I feel terrible. I offered to help her earlier but she didn't want any help."

"Which hospital did they take her to?"

"St. Mary's. I've called over there but they won't give out any information." Frank wrung his hands. "I'm so sorry. Terribly sorry. After they took her I went upstairs to make sure the apartment was all right. Everything was locked and the bird was in its cage."

Robert fished the keys out of his pocket and stood up. Frank stopped him.

"Wait a minute."

Frank handed Robert a thick manuscript and a journal. "She was holding onto these when I found her. I guess that's what she went down there to find."

Robert took the papers from Frank and glanced at them. They meant nothing to him. He had to get to the hospital. He carried the package out to the car, tossed it onto the passenger seat and sped off for downtown.

• • • •

At the hospital he was alarmed to be directed to intensive care. The nurse on duty ushered him to Johanna's bed and tried to explain her condition. "We've got her sedated and on high dosage IV antibiotics. She was septic when she came in. I'll page the doctor and he'll fill you in on her prognosis."

Even the word prognosis filled him with doom. Johanna lay motionless on her back in a blue hospital gown. Fresh bulky dressings had been wound around her arm and two ominous IV lines fed into each arm. Monitors flashed lights and meaningless numbers at uncertain intervals. Oxygen flowed through a valve in the wall and into a mask on her face. Her chest moved with each shallow breath and Robert deduced from the lack of a ventilator that she was at least breathing on her own. He was afraid to touch her. The nurse brought him a chair and assured him she was comfortable. "One of the drips is morphine. The pain in her arm must have been unbearable."

The nurse sensed his distress. She said in a calm voice, "Tell her about your day. Anything. Just talk to her."

The nurse walked away and left Robert standing. He pulled the chair closer to the bed and sat down. He wished Albert were with him. Albert would take her hand and say something. Robert just sat and stared at her and wished she would open her eyes and tell him she was fine, in that stern voice she used when people fussed over her. "Albert's performance was shrill flummery," he said, louder than he'd intended. Nobody appeared to have heard him and Johanna's face did not move. Albert would be back at the apartment any time and would wonder where everyone had gone.

He asked the nurse for a telephone, and called to leave a message on the machine for Albert. The doctor came in and checked the chart at the foot of the bed. He flipped some pages.

"She's stable," he told Robert. "But her condition is guarded. She's lucky someone found her when they did."

Robert nodded. Stable meant she would survive. "How long before she's safe?"

"We have to wait and see how these antibiotics work. The fever should come down in the next twenty-four to forty-eight hours. We're doing blood work to isolate the bacteria that's causing the infection. At least it's obvious where the primary site is, so that part's easy, and once we have that information we can administer a more specific antibiotic. When she's stable and her fever is normal we can switch her to pills and she can go home. For her to be free of the infection, if she rallies, will take another four to six weeks of medication. We'll keep her sedated and once the fever is down try to bring her around. There is a chance of brain damage, depending on how long her temperature was elevated. Your mother is very sick. It was very close to being too late."

• • • •

The doctor looked up from his paperwork. "Did she show any signs of confusion or delirium? How long has she been this sick?"

"Maybe a day or two. She never complained. It was hard to tell."

"She must have a pretty high pain threshold," the doctor said, his nose back in the chart.

"I guess she does."

The doctor left Robert sitting at the bedside, wondering what Albert would have to say. Brain damage? The nurse came over and told Robert to go home. "There won't be much change tonight. She's stable. Come back tomorrow and hopefully her fever will be down."

CHAPTER 14

The night was still, the streets wet from a late rain. Robert rolled down the window and breathed in the cool, damp air. He drove down deserted streets. If he followed the lakeshore the road would turn into a highway. And the highway stretched on and on. The driving calmed him, to be in motion, not going anywhere really, between points. Alone. The windshield wipers swiped away random drops. He couldn't help but think that this was somehow deliberate. His mother did not allow herself to get sick. All the supplements and healthy food she ate. That bread she ate looked as though, with sun and water, it would sprout. It was unfathomable that she wouldn't notice when her body was breaking down. She was in denial for some reason and now she lay near death in the intensive care unit.

• • • •

Albert leapt to his feet as soon as the lock turned.

"I got your message. I didn't want our paths to cross so I stayed here. How is she?"

"Stable, they say, though she looks like death." A tremor caught in Robert's throat. He swallowed hard and let Albert take his arm and lead him into the living room. He dropped the documents from the car onto the hallstand. "I don't know how this happened. Frank found her in the basement and called an ambulance. She said she was fine. You heard her."

Robert glanced into the cage at Felix who knew something was afoot. The bird bit at the bars of its cage. "You knew this was going to happen, didn't you?

Albert sat beside Robert on the arm of the sofa, sipping from a snifter of brandy. He handed another to Robert. "What did they say was wrong with her?"

"Septic. That's the word they used. Septic. Those tiny scratches infected her whole body." All he could think of was of a septic tank filled with sewage. If that was what was wrong with Johanna then things were quite grave. "They couldn't believe she didn't complain of pain."

"It's hard to tell with someone like that. She doesn't exactly share her feelings very freely. I think she convinced herself that she was in no pain. She'll be taken care of. Stable means she'll live."

"Well, she's not in pain now. She's in a coma. I should have listened to you." Robert gulped his brandy. "Why do you think she let it get so bad? She's a nurse for God's sake."

"That doesn't mean she would look after herself."

Was that an accusation? Robert got to his feet. "I need some air," he muttered.

On the balcony Robert forced the damp air into his lungs. The lake was smooth and calm. Stars twinkled in the sky. The same stars every night. Shifting imperceptibly across the universe, long journeys with predictable paths. Catastrophes were required to divert them and up there catastrophes were rare. Among the human race, they were all too common.

"You should come look at this," Albert called from inside. He had picked up the journal and the manuscript where Robert had dropped them and was flipping through them. "Where did it come from?"

Robert stepped back into the room. "Frank said she was holding onto that stuff when he found her. I haven't looked at it yet."

"Maybe you should." Albert held the book out towards Robert, turned to the first page. The words leapt out at Robert – Bayreuth, May 14, 1944 – the last year of the war festivals. His heart lurched.

"What the hell is this?" He took the journal from Albert. The ink had faded. Robert tried to make out the text but it was written in German. He gingerly turned the pages. The entries went through the summer of 1944. His German was shaky but he recognized a few words. *Die Meistersinger* – a memoir of the festival? During the war it was the only opera performed there. Perhaps someone who had attended? There was mention of the performers, names familiar to him – Jaro Prohaska, Maria Müller, Beckmesser, the lead role – and something about the SS. The name of Steeger, the chorus master too. Robert sank into the sofa, still holding the journal. Steeger? The audience would have been soldiers and munitions workers. It was odd a person would mention the chorus master in their memoirs, unless they knew him. His heart sped up. Maybe the writer was involved in the production!

Albert was leafing through the manuscript pages, humming. "This is a manuscript for an opera. *The story of Christina the Astonishing; Written by Heinz Friedrich.*"

"What? Heinz? Our Uncle Heinz wrote an opera?" It was just the kind of stupid joke Albert would have played when they were kids.

"That's what it says."

"Give it here." Robert grabbed the thick stack of pages from Albert. It was true. The notation looked eerily like his own. Robert sank onto the sofa. He felt dreadful, the way he did after a frightening dream.

"We'll figure it out," Albert said in an effort to calm Robert. "My German's not too bad. I try to speak it to my kids. Is there a German/ English dictionary?"

Robert pointed at the bookshelf.

Albert settled in beside Robert with the journal on his lap. Robert held the dictionary and looked up words as they came up. Side by side on the sofa, the way they sat when they were boys and told to be quiet while the adults napped. It took them most of the night as they painstakingly read and translated the entire journal. Every so often they stared at one another, each of them perplexed and astonished at this discovery. When he finished, Albert placed the journal on the coffee table. "Remarkable," he said.

"I'm speechless," Robert replied. "Who wrote it? It wasn't Heinz."

Albert shook his head. "There's no name anywhere. One of the orchestra musicians I guess. I wonder how Heinz got it?"

"Mother hates Wagner," Robert mused aloud. "And now she comes up with these documents. You think she would have mentioned Heinz writing an opera to me. I mean it's my passion, my career. You'd think it would have come up."

"She must have meant to give them to you, but just didn't make it back upstairs. It's the only thing that makes sense."

"If she had this all along then why didn't she give it to me sooner? She knows what it would mean to me."

Albert shrugged. "I doubt she would have forgotten about it. Maybe my mother's death triggered something in her. Maybe she wants us to get to know her brother before she's gone too."

"Oh God," Robert cried. "What if she dies? I won't be able to survive that."

"Don't worry, Rob. Frank found her in time. She'll rally. You know her." Albert indicated the documents they'd just found. "She's a fighter and if she went downstairs to retrieve these things, then she had some plan for them. It wouldn't be like her to leave it unfinished."

They sat in silence. Robert's mind whirred as he flipped through pages of the journal.

"Beckmesser," he said. "Do you think he means Heinz?"

"He was SS."

"Yeah, I know. That's all she ever told me. Did your mother know about this?"

"My mother told me that Heinz and Johanna used to sing together. Quite beautifully, according to her. When Heinz came home after the war she refused to sing with him again. Never sang at all after that. I wonder if this is why." Albert picked up the opera. "There must be a connection. I asked Johanna about it in Calgary and she wouldn't say. Pretended that giving up singing was no big deal. But Mom said she could have made a career of it."

"My mother could have had a singing career?"

"So the story goes."

Robert was stunned. "I've only heard her sing once, when she didn't know I was there."

"This has to be it." Albert patted the manuscript. "If she and Heinz sang together then it would be painful for her to remember those days. She's kept this to herself as a way of keeping those memories of Heinz to herself. No wonder she never talks about it."

Robert nodded but his mind was elsewhere. That distant melody came to him as he stared at the pages of manuscript. His face blanched. He gathered up the manuscript and made for the door. The car keys were still on the side table and he swept them up and twisted the deadbolt. "I've got to go. I need to check on something."

When he arrived at his apartment, Robert immediately sat at the piano. The lamp cast a golden orb of light across the keys. Robert caught his breath, sat unmoving before the yellowed paper across which the music was strewn like so many seeds. His fingers trembled atop the keyboard. The first notes resounded in his ears before a key was struck. The sound was deafening and exhilarating. The music gave way under his fingers – form and motion undulating effortlessly. And suddenly, there it was – the melody that had been with him since he was a boy. Written for soprano and strings, the first section in unison sung in A major, low in the register. Robert shivered. The sound of the soprano would be imperceptible among the strings. It would blend in until the twelfth measure where the strings departed, one by one and left the voice to carry the melody. His mother's voice. The revelation left him trembling. For a long time he sat and stared at the notes, unable or unwilling to unravel the mystery and paralyzed by the thought of asking his mother to reveal it to him.

• • • •

For two days Johanna lay in the hospital, heavily sedated. Robert sat by her bed and waited. By now he had scoured the opera. Parts were written in precise black script but the bulk of it looked like it had been filled in hastily in turquoise ink. Two composers – the orchestra violinist and Heinz. He needed his mother to wake up and explain to him why she had never told him that his uncle had sung at Bayreuth and had composed the better part of an opera. It was driving him crazy. He wanted to know why she had closed her heart to music and stopped singing. Why she couldn't even hear music without wincing.

Visiting hours were from four until eight and Robert sat and waited and tried telepathically to pull thoughts from his mother's mind while she slept. All the while he thought of the opera. Over and over scenes played through his head while he stared at his mother's closed eyes and wondered what she saw behind them. Christina the Astonishing – such a compelling subject for an opera. A saint – a shattered soul who is given the chance to make a difference. Her life is full of tests and torment but she serves a higher purpose. She lives for God alone. The first scene, a church full of people who have gathered at Christina's funeral. All is silent. Until suddenly there is movement in the casket and Christina rises up from the dead and stares at all those around her. The first thing she notices is the stench. None of the others notice. Only Christina. It is the smell of human sin. It overwhelms her and she flees to the rafters in fear. By this time the church has emptied out because all the people are terrified to have witnessed a body rising from the dead. The fear of God is in them. Only the priest remains to try to coax her down from the rafters. But Christina hovers there. She doesn't know why this has happened to her. What is expected of her here? She was dead and was looking forward to her reunion with God and entrance into heaven and instead she is sent back and not only that, the smell horrifies her. It is hopeless, what has been asked of her.

There is a touching duet between the priest and Christina. He explains to her that her resurrection had to have been preordained. That God has work for her to do and she must overlook the flaws of humanity and help them to see the light. He sings to her, almost a lullaby, that all will be well, she has a purpose here – that humans are not to be feared but understood as merely weak. Robert loved that part.

But it was the aria that he'd heard his mother sing that held him spellbound. Christina has accepted God's will for her. She understands that her earthbound duty must prevail before she will be united with God. It is a bittersweet moment; Christina alone on the stage, surrounded by the trees and animals to remind her that God is present even here. Robert imagined his mother's voice singing it, sweet, lilting, without effort – a stirring effect. He'd finally seen what Heinz had done. It was a variation of the Tristan Chord. The notes were different and the phrasing different, but the intervals were the same: an augmented fourth, an augmented sixth and the augmented second. It started in the cellos with the woodwinds underneath – an obvious homage to Wagner who had used the same orchestration but with the woodwinds leading and the cellos to float the sound. Those notes of profound longing, specifically written for Johanna. It was confounding why all this was such a secret. His mother would never have recognized the significance. He stared at her impassive face and waited.

• • • •

A day at the beach. They are all there: Johanna, Barbara, Heinz. Johanna and Barbara are wearing matching sundresses and gather seashells and driftwood to make walkways for the town they are building in the sand. Heinz is by himself on the shore building a castle. Their parents are farther up the beach, sunning themselves. They are always sunning themselves, but once the sand-town is complete they will come and see and take a picture. Heinz comes over and kicks sand on their town. The waves have washed his castle away and it is easier to destroy than to rebuild. The girls cry in dismay and throw pebbles at him but Heinz runs into the water and dives under the waves to escape. The girls look at what is left of his sand castle and help themselves to the seashells that remain. Slowly, ignoring their splashing brother, they pull all their sticks and shells from the rubble and start to rebuild.

Johanna takes a break and rocks back on her heels. Heinz is still in the water and motions for her to come in. But the town is nearly finished. The sun overhead is hot, a white globe in the sky. Johanna stares right into it.

Her eyes can't take it and yet when she tries to turn her head, she can't. The backs of her eyelids are blood red and the light even through that thin skin is too bright. She reaches up with her hand to cover her eyes and hits something hard. Suddenly, there is another hand on top of hers, pulling it away.

"Mrs. Turner? Are you awake?" A woman's voice. One she does not recognize. *Mrs. Turner? Am I not Fraulein Friedrich?* The names sounded familiar. She opened her eyes and immediately shut them again. The glare was blinding. A hand squeezed hers and called her name again. "Mrs. Turner. Try to squeeze my hand. Don't open your eyes. It's too bright."

Confused, she squeezed, as she was told, but the voice asked her to squeeze again. "There, that's better. I'm going to page the doctor."

A doctor? Still afraid of the light, Johanna moved her feet. There was a sheet covering her and she was lying down. She became aware of the smell – an antiseptic smell and beneath that a faint odour of human waste. Something was beeping very close to her. She tried to feel with her hands but her left arm would not move. She tried to wiggle her fingers but nothing happened. Her right arm moved but she could feel tape stuck to the back of her hand and needles stuck there. She felt the weight of the IV tubes when she tried to lift it.

Johanna opened her eyes long enough to see a brown-haired nurse. She tried to speak but the mask was in the way and her lips wouldn't move. The nurse left her bedside and Johanna closed her eyes. They would not stay open. She tried to determine what had happened. There was no pain she could distinguish. Each limb, ten fingers, ten toes, accounted for. She drifted off with the effort of thinking. Soon there was another voice and a hand holding hers. The doctor had come. A flash of light blinded her as he pushed up her eyelid and shone a flashlight directly into her eyes. Something scraped the bottom of her foot. She pulled her leg up.

"Good, Mrs. Turner. Just checking your reflexes."

She tried to speak and this time a croak came out. They removed the oxygen mask and encouraged her to try again but Johanna could think of nothing to say.

"You're in St. Mary's hospital, Mrs. Turner. Squeeze my fingers if you understand." She squeezed. "Good."

It was her they meant when they said Mrs. Turner. It was her name. "You passed out at home. The infection in your arm spread and we have you on some strong medication. You've been here three days."

The doctor would be back later. There was more activity around her now. The nurse put the head of the bed up. It made Johanna's head spin. Her eyes were slits through which she allowed a little light at a time. Soon, she could take in the intensive care unit. About six beds, four of them occupied. She was the only one awake. There was a plastic clip on her big toe. She managed to turn her head. IV poles all around her held bags of clear fluid. Her left arm was heavily bandaged. She regarded this a moment, feeling it was significant but made no connection. It did not come to her why she was there, or even to wonder. It only registered that she was. She had already forgotten all the doctor had said. Music played and she had no choice but to hear it. On the psych ward where she worked they used to play classical music for the patients to keep them calm. Johanna had learned to block it out because it caused her to become agitated and short-tempered. Now they were playing it for her with the idea that it would be soothing. Maybe she was too tired or too weak to become twitchy but the music did not have its usual effect. It sounded like one of the Brandenburg Concertos. Nice inoffensive chamber music. Her eyes fell shut and she slept.

When she awoke, Robert was there. He had been sitting beside her for nearly an hour. "Robert," she said, her voice a hoarse whisper.

"Yes, it's me. It's okay. How are you feeling?"

"Robert." It was her son. She knew him, she understood with some relief. His presence alerted her that something had happened to bring her here. His face gave it away. Something bad.

"What happened to me?"

"Frank found you in the basement. The infection spread and made you very sick." He touched her bandaged arm so she would know.

"My arm?" What basement? The cellar? The only cellar that came to mind was where she had left Heinz. "The storm cellar?"

"No, the storage lockers in the basement. You've never had a storm cellar."

It made no sense, what Robert was saying, and Johanna remained silent.

"Remember? Your arm has been bandaged up for awhile. You were taking care of it but it got infected anyway."

"Hmm." She tried to process this but couldn't remember anything.

"I'm only supposed to visit for ten minutes," he said. He felt jumpy, not used to his mother's helpless state. She could hardly keep her eyes open and it unnerved him to see her so weak and confused. It took all his willpower not to bring up the journal and the manuscript. Albert had thought it best to wait until she had her strength back. "Albert wants to come see you too."

"Albert?"

"Yes, Albert. Barbara's son." She didn't understand and Robert didn't know how better to explain it. His hands rested on the bedrail. "Do you know your name?"

She pursed her lips but did not speak. What an odd question. She stared at Robert. Her eyes dropped shut. Robert waited a few minutes and then the nurse signalled him. He rose to go, pulling his jacket from the back of the chair. Johanna's arm reached for him, her eyes imploring.

"It's okay if you don't remember right now. I'll come back later. You need to sleep. Your body needs to heal."

Weakly, she raised her hand for him to come close. He leaned over.

"Heinz is dead."

Robert straightened up, his lips drawn in, not sure what to say. "Do you know where you are? What year is it?"

The questions stumped her. He could see her mind working them over. At least she knew that she didn't know the answer. The nurse pulled back the curtains and fussed with the covers. "She needs to rest. She can't get overtired." And then to Johanna: "You're not out of the woods yet. Your son has to go now."

Robert took her hand. "Barbara is dead. Three weeks ago. She was seventy-one years old. Do you remember?" The nurse scowled at him but he couldn't leave his mother like this.

"Barbara."

"Yes, your sister. Very suddenly in Calgary. Heinz died after the war. A long time ago in Germany when he was a young man. But you still have me and Albert to look after you. You live in Toronto in a beautiful apartment that overlooks the lake. Do you remember?"

She smiled weakly, too tired to talk anymore. Her confusion had frightened him and now he was talking too much, but she had remembered something. She remembered Barbara and Albert. He was at the apartment. She lay her head back down on the pillow. When Robert glanced back at her, he saw her eyes closed, her cheeks drawn. There was something else. No worry. Those tiny ever-present lines around her eyes and mouth were not there. The IV bags dripped steadily into her blood. It must be the sedatives, he decided.

Though the sedatives calmed her and made her drowsy, Johanna fought to try to remember everything. She still wasn't clear on how she had come to the hospital. Something to do with her arm. An infection. But what did that have to do with Barbara and how did she get such a bad infection in her arm that she had to be hospitalized?

The nurse changed the IV bag. "Just another bag of fluid. Once you start eating and drinking more we'll be able to take all those needles out. Your blood work came back so you only need one antibiotic now. The doctor will switch you over to pills and you can probably go home in two days."

"How did my arm get so bad?"

The nurse shook her head and lightly held Johanna's hand. "My dear, this is what happens when you don't take your medicine."

"Who brought me here?"

"You came in an ambulance. The record says you collapsed in the basement and the door man found you."

"I didn't take my medicine?"

"Well, somebody must have prescribed some antibiotics for you. With an infection that bad."

Another piece to the puzzle. She remembered pale blue pills, in a plastic bottle. Erythromycin. She was supposed to take them but didn't.

"I took some of them. They made me sick and I thought they would kill me."

"Well, you're here now. That's the main thing. I've ordered up some soup for you. We have to build up your strength so you can go home."

Frank found her. In the basement? The only thing down there was the storage locker. Suddenly everything came flooding back. She remembered sitting on the cold floor of the basement and dragging all those bags and boxes out of the storage locker. She had gone down for the journal and the opera so that she could burn them in the sink. That had been her plan. A pang of unease sliced through her. She couldn't remember if she'd found them. The only thing she remembered was the pain in her arm.

CHAPTER 15

Robert tinkered with the opera. He found it hard to concentrate. He was eager to get back to the hospital and talk to his mother. Robert knew this was going to be a big project, one that would surely earn him a sabbatical. There were gaps that he could fill with some of the work he'd done on his own opera. Finally, a use for some of his pretty phrases.

He decided since he too liked to work with turquoise ink that it was predestined that he and his uncle collaborate. Not wanting to disturb the original he started by buying a pot of turquoise ink and recopying. That way he could edit it the way he wanted and clean up the messy parts. The notes were sometimes illegible but he quickly got into Heinz's head and learned his tendencies and nuances. There were parts that were over-orchestrated that Robert stripped down. Given the story, it didn't need a Wagnerian thunder. It must have been the influence of being at Bayreuth while he was composing. The work was dizzying. Robert couldn't believe it had fallen into his lap. He chose to overlook the reasons for its existence. What mattered to him was that his mother had finally decided to give it to him. The explanation would come eventually, when she was better.

Albert had tried to dissuade him. "You don't know for sure what she wanted with it, Robert. She did keep it a secret for a long time."

But Robert was not receptive to that logic. "Wait until you hear it. You will be convinced that it was something she was proud of. Parts of it are absolutely sublime."

"How do you propose we will ever hear it?"

"Come on. I conduct an orchestra, you sing. We'll give a performance. I can't wait to see the look on her face."

"Careful, Rob," Albert said. "You might not like the look on her face."

He had been right about the pills and that was all the credit Robert was willing to give him. There was no way this opera was not rightfully his.

Absolutely impossible. He forged ahead with his plans. As soon as possible he would hear it from Johanna and then he would have news for Albert.

• • • •

Johanna sensed a presence beside the bed and opened her eyes. Nurses didn't take pulses anymore. Or put the back of their hands on your forehead. They stood beside the bed and wrote down the numbers from the monitors. It was hard to tell when someone was there.

"You're doing so much better, Mrs. Turner. For awhile there we weren't sure if you were with us or not."

Johanna managed a smile and was rewarded with a pat on the arm. "Did you have a nice visit with your son? He's been in every day, sitting right in that chair."

"Yes, it was a good visit. He was happy I recognized him, I think. Relieved."

"Good thing you did. Most people are afraid of that. Not being recognized. And sometimes it happens." She flicked her finger on the tube to get it dripping. "The doctor will be around later. He'll probably let you go the day after tomorrow. Your son will be pleased." The nurse straightened up the sheets, then smiled. "I remember you."

"What?" Johanna eyed the nurse and wondered what she was talking about. "Me?"

"Yes, you were a nurse up on psych weren't you?"

"That was a long time ago."

"Not that long. I had a placement up there when I was a student."

Johanna managed a smile. "And now you work in the ICU."

"It wasn't for me, that ward. I was terrified to be up there and you were always so calm. Those patients didn't scare you like they did me. You always knew what to do. You never panicked."

"It never does any good to panic around those people. They are very sensitive."

The nurse handed Johanna a plastic cup with her pills.

"What's this?" Blue, green and yellow pills rattled in the cup. It looked like too many.

"That's your antibiotic and your pain medicine and a multi-vitamin. Same as last time. You must be pretty healthy if that's all you need.

Considering what you've been through." She shook the IV bag. "Just one more day of these and you'll be free of all these tubes."

"Good. I don't like that stuff dripping into me."

"It's just fluid and antibiotics. To keep you hydrated."

"So you tell me. It could be anything in there."

"That's right. It could be, but it's not. You're sitting there talking to me, aren't you?"

"Well, I guess I am." Johanna tipped the pills into her mouth and swallowed them all with a drink of orange juice. "If I taught you then I better be able to trust you."

"I think you can, hon."

Hon. It was what Johanna had always called her patients. Endearments went a long way in the hospital. It was a comfort to hear it now. She opened the package of shortbread she had been saving and marvelled at the subtle flavours. Johanna tried to think. She tried desperately to remember that night. But trying to recall those things was hard and her mind wandered to other more abstract notions. She thought about Heinz and Barbara. Both gone now and she thought about them more than ever. What should be done with a life once it's over? Once a person dies, it makes no difference to them what the cause of death is: whether a gas oven, a sudden stroke in the mall or a gun to their own head. Time is only elastic until it snaps and once it is done, the other side emerges, for one as for all. It could be eternity or a brick wall. It is the people left behind who hold the memories of those lives, like slippery beads in trembling hands.

Her mind was still fuzzy but something inside her had changed. The colours in the room were dazzling. Every time she turned her head the lights shimmered with life. She savoured her food – even the simplest consommé. The sheets against her skin made her feel more alive than she had been in a long time. Her entire being felt super-charged. The doctors told her she had been near death and maybe this was what happened when you dodged that fate. Senses became heightened, sharper. You noticed things that before escaped perception. But these surges of energy also wore her out and she was only able to stay awake for half an hour before drifting off to sleep again.

• • • •

When Robert returned in the evening he had his briefcase with him.

"How was work?"

"Oh, fine. Both of my classes had exams today so I had the pleasure of watching the young minds sweat." He pulled over a chair and sat down.

"Why are you so cheery?"

"I have no reason not to be. For one thing you are awake and on the road to recovery."

"I still don't remember everything that happened."

He dug in his briefcase. Maybe he had picked up a magazine for her to read. "My glasses are in the nightstand," she said.

"Good, because I want you to see this." It was not a magazine that Robert pulled from his briefcase. Johanna's face blanched when she saw the leather-bound book and the large manuscript pages. Robert didn't seem to notice. He leaned over the bedrails and gave her a hearty kiss on the cheek.

"Do you remember these? You went down to the basement to get them. Frank gave them to me. I hope he didn't ruin your surprise."

The words reached her but it took a moment to deduce what they meant. It was clear now that she had found them. She must have passed out right then. Something must have made Frank think they were important for him to hand them over to Robert. Once Robert saw what they were he would have assumed they were meant for him. Of course he did. Robert didn't know what her intention had been that night. Her heart sank.

"What's the matter?"

She closed her eyes and bit her lip. Words would not form in her foggy mind. There was no way to prepare for this. It was all a muddy blur.

"Have you played it?" she asked, not able to look at him or the papers he clutched to his chest.

"I have." He couldn't contain his excitement. "I'm working on it right now."

"What do you mean?"

"I'm copying it and filling in some gaps. Heinz wrote it, didn't he?"

Johanna paused. There was a perpetual grin on Robert's face. Of all the things to make him happy, why did it have to be this?

"Parts of it are thrilling," Robert said, guessing that he was meant to fill the silence with his opinion. "Reminiscent of Richard Strauss I would argue. And he must have studied Wagner. There are identical notations." Already he had dissected the work and the journal into sections for an article. The war festivals, the violinist's journal, the opera, and then a brief section surmising the intention of the composer in using the story of Christina the Astonishing in an opera composed in Germany at the end of the war. But most of the article would be about the music.

"I can't wait for you to hear it. Funding requests are due next week. I've been working on my submission to have the parts copied out and printed so it can be produced once I'm done with it. I'm going to rehearse the more polished parts with the orchestra next week! I've just got to hear it. The school will be thrilled to have an original work to produce. Do you have any idea what something like this means to the faculty? It will put us on the map. It will put me on the map." Robert paced around her bed. "It's fantastic, is what it is. And to think your brother sang at Bayreuth! I can't believe it. He actually wrote most of it. It's his writing isn't it? I'm going to apply for a sabbatical, of course. I won't be able to devote the time I need to compose and teach. But I'm sure I'll get it. Something like this doesn't come along everyday. I don't know why you kept it hidden for so long, but that doesn't matter. I'm glad I've got it now. It's amazing. Another composer in the family."

"Stop it!" Johanna hissed. Her hands shook with an unfocussed rage. "You talk about him like he's a hero. He wasn't. Far from it. He doesn't deserve to be glorified."

Taken aback by the intensity of her voice, Robert stopped and leaned against the bedrail. "What do you mean?"

"I never wanted that opera to see the light of day."

"But, why? The music... have you even heard it? It's sublime."

"Do you know how he died?" she asked, ignoring the question.

"In the war?" Robert was sure that's what he had been told.

"He shot himself. He took the coward's way out. Instead of facing the punishment that awaited him, he came running home like a baby and hid, putting both Barbara and myself in grave danger. He was a soulless coward and it was a stupid risk. He left those things there for me to find. What was I supposed to do with them? Did he think it would somehow redeem him in my eyes?"

"Then why did you keep them?" Robert braced himself against the bed, anger and confusion clenched in his throat, like he was four and not getting his way. "Why didn't you get rid of them right away? Why bring them out now? To give them to me and then tell me I can't use them... I don't get it."

Johanna glared at him. "I never meant to give them to you. I was going to destroy them that night. I never wanted you to know any of this. But I didn't make it back upstairs. You just assumed they were meant for you and well, they weren't."

She spat the words out. Robert recoiled from the bed and stared at her, stunned at this revelation. "But, why would you do that?" he whispered. "Why would you keep something like that from me when you know what it would mean to me? This is my past too. I have a right to know about it." His voice shook.

A pained look crossed her face. "Why would you want to know about that? What kind of a mother lets her children know those kinds of things? I can't even fathom what horrors he inflicted on innocent people," she said. "And here he was hiding in my house. I couldn't stand to be in the same room as him. We avoided each other. Not Barbara. She was more forgiving than I. So he sat in the study at the piano. At the time the music that came from in there made no sense to me. I had no idea what he was doing. I had three mouths to feed and food was scarce. I couldn't be bothered worrying about his mood. The war changed him. I could see it in his face. There was no compassion there. There was nothing. Maybe fear, now that he was hunted. But I didn't care if he was afraid. It served him right after years of inflicting the same thing on others."

Johanna turned her head towards the wall and tried to fight back the tears. Heinz had written the opera for her and left it there with the hope she would sing it one day. Now, with Robert slouched in the chair opposite her with a multitude of questions, she wished she had buried everything with him rather than drag it all the way across the ocean with her. She never even glanced at it in all those years in Canada. Why had she brought it?

Robert sank into the chair. His anger subsided when he saw Johanna's tear-streaked face. "But he wrote it for you," he said in a weak voice. "Why was it so hard for you to accept? Albert says you stopped singing right after he came back. I don't understand why you would. It couldn't possibly have helped. It must have felt like sawing off an arm."

Anguish contorted his mother's face. This was exactly the scene she had hoped to avoid. If only she had made it back upstairs then everything would be gone and no questions asked. "I don't care what that opera sounds like. It could be brilliant but it will always be associated with evil for me. The evil that was my brother." She choked on the words.

"How can you say that? Wagner's name is linked with Hitler and the Nazis for all time. He will never escape it. But the music… once that sound reaches your ears, everything falls away. It transcends – that is not even a strong enough word for it. The demons are silenced. Your brother was capable of the same thing. Whatever evil was in him, it is not in his music."

"I couldn't stand to listen to it. How can you ask this of me?"

"How can you ask me to give it up?"

Johanna wiped her eyes. These secrets, so terrible and beautiful – ensnarled in the wilderness of her mind, vines wrapped tightly around ancient trees. There was no possible way to dig them out without pain.

"Did Barbara know?" Robert asked.

"No, I didn't tell her. There was no point. She knew enough. More than I wanted her to."

They sat in silence with the curtains drawn. In that phrase, where Heinz evoked Wagner's famous chord, he must have been tormented over an unfulfilled life and a sister he could no longer love. Alone with the piano, in the house where he grew up but no longer lived. Robert knew exactly why Heinz had chosen those notes. When his mother sang them she couldn't help but get the message. Music reaches greater depths than words. There was an optical illusion that Robert experienced whenever he was at a concert in a darkened theatre. As he watched the stage, everything in his peripheral vision disappeared and all perception of depth fell away so that there was only the stage shimmering in the distance and nothing but infinite waves of music in between. He noticed it now while Johanna rested – the mystic abyss. And he, ever farther from the shore, reached for the fragile thread that connected them.

CHAPTER 16

Exhausted yet unable to rest, Johanna waited for Robert to return. Nothing had been resolved the day before. The nurse had interrupted and maybe it was a good thing. They were both worn out, upset and disappointed. She didn't want to shut Robert out and she was too tired to be angry. It was done now. These things were important to him. That was all he wanted her to know.

She smiled when he came through the door. He seemed pleased to see her, sitting up in a chair beside the bed. Only one IV line dripped into her now. The monitors had been disconnected and turned off.

He placed a package of hazelnut cookies on her tray and opened the coffee he had picked up for her and then quietly placed the manuscript and journal on her table. "These belong to you," he said. "I thought about it a lot and I understand that now. I never should have assumed."

"Don't be mad at me, Robert." She reached for his hand.

"How could I be mad when I nearly let you die?"

"Do you think you did this to me?"

"I think I could have noticed."

Johanna fell silent. Now that the journal and manuscript lay before her she was afraid to touch them. She had kept them hidden for so long, buried as deep as she could dig and now they had surfaced, toxic and exposed.

"I can't believe it either, that I am in here." She waved her good hand towards the ceiling. "I think I went a bit crazy."

Robert pulled a chair over and sat across from her. "Well, you're on the mend. That's the main thing."

"I know how important these things are to you Robert," she said. "But, I can't forgive him. He caused so much suffering. To let you have that opera would mean I forgive him and I can't do it. I just can't."

"I know," Robert nodded. "It's disappointing for me, but I get it. He did awful things. But, Mother, you didn't."

"Didn't I? Not personally, no. But... "

The nurse came to help Johanna back to bed. Robert stood on the other side of the curtain and watched his mother's bare feet step uncertainly across the floor. When the curtain opened she was resting back on her pillows.

"Why did you stop singing?"

"Oh, Robert. I haven't thought about these things in years. I don't know that it was a conscious decision. It just didn't feel the same. There was no more joy in it. The war changed a lot of things." She fumbled with the cookie package and managed to tear a corner free. "Do you think it's good, the opera?"

Robert nodded. "I do. Most of the work is his. It's like that violinist had the ideas but couldn't pull them together. That's why he needed Heinz to play for him. And probably why Heinz ended up with it. There was more of a chance that Heinz would finish it."

"I have a hard time believing Heinz cared anything about that." She slid the cookies over to her son.

Robert shook his head. "I have a hard time believing someone would trouble to finish an opera he didn't believe in, especially given the situation he was in. If, as you say, he was being hunted as a war criminal."

"You're a very forgiving person." Her mouth tensed and she bit into a cookie and chewed hard.

"You haven't heard it. The music speaks for him."

"He wanted me to sing it. He wanted me to be Christina. I thought at the time it was the most hurtful thing he could ask of me." The cookie formed a gritty paste in her mouth. Johanna dabbed at her eyes, overwhelmed and exhausted. She took a breath. "How did you know the music?"

"What?" Robert didn't understand.

"In your apartment, when Albert and I were there for dinner. You sat at the piano and played his music. Where did you learn it?"

"You were singing it one day. I heard you from outside."

It was not possible that he had heard it from her. Singing? Impossible. "I don't think so."

"Well, it didn't just come to me. Some things do but not that. I heard it." An impasse.

• • • •

The sun receded from the room. Robert stared at his mother. Stared at her closed eyes, at her drawn lips, at her barely moving body as she breathed.

"Mother, I understand you feel responsible because of Heinz. You don't want this opera to glorify him and you're right. He doesn't deserve to be. But you choose to tag yourself only to his worst deeds."

Johanna opened her eyes. "I know it's good, Robert. I know he worked hard at it and I know he wrote it for me. Not singing was a way of refusing his gift."

Robert shrugged. "We all have the capacity to create and destroy and we all do both to some extent. But why is it okay for me to know of the terrible things Heinz did but you don't want anyone to know he wrote an opera, or sang at Bayreuth?"

"Because it's easier to hate somebody than to miss them."

The words hung between them – a truth finally spoken. It surprised Johanna to hear it aloud. The joy she used to find in music had always come to her through Heinz. Once he was gone, the sound of music only evoked feelings of loss and pain. It was unbearable.

The music was as familiar to her as her own reflection. Those were the melodies that resounded inside of her ever since she discovered the manuscript on the piano all those years ago. Whether it was buried in the basement or burned to a crisp, it was the treasure she had cached away in the depths of her heart and protected with impenetrable, cold walls.

Johanna turned to her son. "I have to hear it." It no longer belonged to her alone. With Robert sitting across from her, their hands clasped, she knew it belonged to him too and had since the day he was born. Later, after Robert had gone, Johanna picked up the journal and began to read. She flipped the pages randomly, not sure how much she wanted to remember but finding it difficult to tear herself away.

• • • •

> May 17, 1944
>
> Karl and I often sit outside and stare at the brick walls of the lunatic asylum. I used to pity the poor souls inside, but in reality they are insulated from the madness that has befallen our country. The brewery is our only hope for solace in these times. These are the buildings that flank the theatre. With what is going on here this month it may be hard to tell them apart. Troops march

through the streets and we hardly notice anymore. This is not normal, to hear the approach of marching boots and think nothing of it. To gaze into the sky as bombers fly overhead and wonder where they have attacked. Bayreuth is too small for them to disturb. For now they seem more interested in the big cities. Refugees are fleeing to the country to seek shelter and farmers everywhere are forced to take them in. But, they are not fleeing the way one would envision such flight. They meander. Children ride bicycles. Women push baby carriages. They stop on the side of the road and eat a picnic while the planes buzz overhead like flies that they wave away with a free hand.

May 28, 1944

Rehearsals have degenerated into some kind of circus cum parody. The brass section has taken to playing cards while Abendroth rehearses the strings. The strings scratch away at the high tricky parts while the winds are run through their passages and underneath it all is a quiet uproar of a thousand conversations. This will all disappear once we are in the great hall, but until we are in the pit and there is a sense of formality in the air, the rehearsals will continue this way.

The SS has certainly changed the usual atmosphere here. For one, we are all succumbing to their presence and greeting one another with the official *Heil Hitler*. Something that most of us find utterly distasteful, but the tension is fierce and the SS are armed, even at rehearsal and nobody wants particularly to be shot. It will be interesting when the soloists arrive to see if they do the same.

June 8, 1944

Beckmesser gave me a good idea today. He thought the trio would work better with the priest and sisters rather than with Christina and the sisters. And it does. It needed the balance of a tenor voice. The accompaniment is stripped right down to two violas, a cello and a drone through the organ. He is right once again. Sometimes it is painfully obvious to me that his is a greater talent than mine. But then he becomes surly after a few beers and takes his pistol out in the back of the hotel and shoot into the trees, disturbing the sleeping birds. What an ass. It's like watching two personalities wrestle to the death.

August 3, 1944

I've decided to give the manuscript to Beckmesser. It is clear to me that he has far more talent than I. He's not too happy these days, not that his happiness is any concern of mine, but I do see how his face lights up at the sound of the piano and he clearly misses playing for me. My languor in these last days of the festival has prevented me from working and I have come to terms with the fact that my efforts will never make up for my lack of talent for this kind of thing. To finish it would exhaust me and in the end it might turn out to be unplayable. I might as well deliver it into the hands of someone who might finish it and poor Beckmesser will need a purpose after this war is over. My place remains in the second violin section, where, if I am completely honest with myself, is where I am more content. Always striving for more is exhausting. I will leave it to those with the talent and determination to accomplish something. Perhaps within the pages of the manuscript poor Beckmesser will find redemption.

• • • •

Johanna closed the book and set it aside. The violinist was a kindred spirit to her – someone who had known Heinz and had seen the same maddening dichotomy in him. He too had tried to reach out to him and could not get through. He must have given Heinz the opera because he saw the potential, thought it might save him.

It was too late for Heinz, but not for her. It was her choice to make. It was Robert for whom the opera was intended. She remembered how angry she became at the sight of Heinz day after day in that study at the piano. It had incensed her. He had no right. But the thought of Robert seated at his piano, working away the same way did not upset her. She knew it would make him happy.

CHAPTER 17

Leonard sat on the chaise longue, his legs stretched out before him, swirling a drink. "How are you doing?"

"A little confused, to tell the truth."

An hour earlier, Robert had run into Marcelline on the elevator. She had squealed with delight when she saw him and smacked the girl she was with. "This is Robert! My piano teacher," she declared, like he was some kind of celebrity. The two of them were sharing a bag of potato chips, dressed alike in their army fatigues and combat boots. Her friend had spiky hair and a hoop through her nose. Marcelline held the bag out towards Robert. "Have one."

"No thanks. Got the munchies, have you?"

This sent them into spasms of laughter. Once Marcelline had composed herself she said, "Robert, this is Shannon. My girlfriend." Marcelline paused. "The one from Sarnia."

"Oh," Robert stuttered, not sure if she meant girlfriend or friend. His eyes darted between them.

"Remember? I told you about her."

"You did?"

Marcelline punched his arm. "Yes, I did."

"Pleased to meet you." He held out his hand, trying to remember whatever conversation Marcelline was referring to. Girlfriend? He remembered her saying something about a friend visiting. Or had she said girlfriend? Surely he would have remembered something like this. His face reddened. "Well, enjoy your chips."

They giggled all they way to their apartment door. What an impossible old fool he felt. He still had not regained his composure entirely.

"Marcelline is gay," he told Leonard, trying to make his voice sound amused rather than incredulous.

"Of course she is. All the young kids are a little bit gay now. It's very popular. I meant how's it going with your mother?"

"Oh." Robert rubbed his eyes. "It's all coming out now anyway. I still feel guilty for taking those things and reading them when she didn't want me to. I feel like I've invaded her privacy. It was up to her what to do with those things and I intervened."

"I don't think you should feel guilty about this. You didn't intervene. Fate did. You had no idea of her intention. These things needed to play out. If you had never found the journal and the opera then she would have destroyed everything, her arm would have healed and you would never have known the pain she was in. It was either this now or something worse later on."

"It can't just be gone though. The black mark caused by her brother. It can't just be prised out of her like a peach pit and tossed away."

"No, but it can be set aside. If she really had this near-death experience it will make her see things differently."

"She did nearly die. Every time I go to the hospital somebody reminds me of that. As if I would have been at the opening of *The Mikado* of my own free will. She wanted everyone out of the apartment that night."

"You hear about those people. They see the light, they move towards it. They are filled with euphoria, like an opium dream. They let themselves be pulled into the glory. They give themselves over and are at peace at last and then…bam. Welcome back! Nobody is the same again." Leonard sipped his drink and then effortlessly changed the subject. "You didn't have a crush on her did you?"

"Honestly, Leonard. I hardly know the girl. We drink an occasional glass of wine together sometimes. This is a bit of a relief. I thought maybe she had a crush on me."

Leonard grinned. "It happens to the best of us, these cases of mistaken identity. Don't worry about it. If only everyone were that open about what they wanted."

"I guess I can still give her lessons. They have fallen by the wayside with all that's been going on. I mean, it wouldn't do to completely drop her now or she'll think I'm uncomfortable."

"Well, then. Do what you do best."

"It might be easier now. I got so tense thinking she might like me." To his surprise, the thought of teaching a beginner like Marcelline piano made him happy. It would be rewarding to see her progress and she was awfully keen.

Albert swung through the kitchen door with a tray of champagne and crystal flute glasses.

"Ah, the aperitif!" Leonard cried. "I'd have to say this is just like a *Liederabend* at Wahnfried. You're Liszt and he's Wagner, but who the hell am I?"

"You can be Cosima." Albert replied.

"Ha, I knew you were going to say that. Did you hear that, Rob?"

"I heard." Robert grimaced. That Albert knew anything about Wagner irked Robert to no end. He plinked a passage on the piano. They were going to play a piece from the opera for Leonard to hear and after that he was going to work on a section to rehearse with the orchestra. He didn't want to devote too much time to it until his sabbatical was approved. But both he and Albert couldn't resist trying out an aria.

"How about something from the show for me to warm up?"

"Sorry mate. That I just can't do." Robert shook his head. There would be no Gilbert and Sullivan played on his beloved Steinway.

"You know, Robert, Arthur Sullivan was a huge fan of Wagner's *leitmotifs*. Did you notice during the performance? He makes use of them all the time." Albert poured the champagne.

"I hadn't noticed." How would he know of such an obscure connection? When Robert studied music history they skipped over musical theatre. If Sullivan used *leitmotifs* he sure didn't do it very well.

"He actually trained as a conductor in Leipzig." Albert said, studying the music over Robert's shoulder.

"Ha. Wagner's birthplace. What a coincidence." Leonard bellowed and slapped his hand on his knee.

"Are you two trying to depress me? We're having a party here. Sullivan in Leipzig. Sounds like a parody. We could write a pantomime and perform at the nursing home." Robert picked out a romping rhythm on the piano and sung to the tune of "The Yellow Rose of Texas":

"When Sullivan got to Leipzig there was garbage everywhere.
He plucked it up with his baton and flung it in the air.

The people seemed to love it and shouted out for more, and Sullivan
the conductor, wrote trash into every score."

• • • •

Leonard clapped along but Robert could think of no more lyrics. "I had no idea you could sing like that," Albert exclaimed in mock surprise. "Now let me have a turn."

"What are you going to tell me now? That Wagner and Sullivan were long lost cousins?" Robert adjusted the music in front of him.

"Why not? Kind of like you and me."

Robert played the first few bars to test out the tempo. It was the first aria sung by the priest as he tries to convince Christina to come down from the rafters. Albert stood, his hand resting on the piano and nodded his head in time with the intro. Robert settled into the subtle and subdued beauty of the music. The sound of Albert's voice filled the room. It filled every corner and resounded through the piano so that Robert felt it in his fingertips. Never before had these walls experienced such a presence. The music: the voice and piano, together. Robert's chest tightened. His foot quivered on the pedal. Albert's voice soared flawlessly with the piano. The notes and sounds melded into one another. Robert's fingers took over and he hovered somewhere above the piano. This was real music. Its essence intimate, visceral. The harmony and resonance of the piano with Albert's voice were exquisite. Joy surged through Robert. His chest swelled with emotion. Albert hit the high A and the sound ricocheted around the room. The piano arpeggios undulated beneath the held note and in a brief flash Robert felt the infinite overcome the insignificant. This was necessary music. These reverberations sang in harmony with the earth.

The room fell silent as the last notes faded away. Robert's mouth felt dry. He turned to Albert, wanting to say something but didn't know what. Albert clapped enthusiastically. "Bravo!"

Leonard and Robert glanced at one another. "That's quite something," Leonard said thoughtfully from the chaise longue. "To think that was written by a Nazi bastard."

• • • •

Late on the third day they moved Johanna to a private room. Her condition had stabilized and she no longer needed the bed in intensive care. The new room had a window, a telephone and a television. The nurses came around less often, but this suited Johanna fine.

On the nightstand was the photograph Johanna had asked Robert to bring. It was of her and Barbara, taken the last time they were together. Albert had taken it. They were sitting in her garden, laughing at something. Neither one of them looked at the camera, but they were sitting on folding lawn chairs, their hands lightly touching and smiling at each other as though they had a secret to share. Johanna was still getting used to Barbara being gone. It was her fault there had been such a wedge jammed between them and she knew she had been the one to put it there. And it had been stuck between her and Robert too. There was a reason she had passed out in the basement. It was so that Robert could discover the journal and manuscript. There was no other way she would have ever let him see it. The moment had revealed itself. Just as the violinist must have passed it on to Heinz, it was time for Johanna to pass it on to Robert. The tattered thread that connected them could now be mended.

• • • •

There was a knock at the door and someone came in hidden behind an enormous floral arrangement. All Johanna could see were the legs in a pair of jeans and white runners. "Johanna? Am I in the right room?"

Angela moved the flowers to the side so her face could be seen. She grinned at Johanna. "Karen has been champing at the bit to get in here and I convinced her to let me be the one to bring you these. She'll be hot on my heels though. Be forewarned."

"How did you know I was even here?"

"When you missed two shifts Karen called your place and talked to your nephew. He filled us in."

Johanna smiled. Nothing had changed. Karen's network remained operational.

"It's good to see you. Thanks for coming."

"I can't stay too long. I'm on duty you know." Angela settled into a chair. "How are you feeling?"

"Better. Much better, thanks." She recalled the scene on the elevator with Marg and wondered if Angela had heard about it. "How is Marg?"

"She's fine. She did tell me about your encounter here the other day. Doesn't sound like you, Johanna."

"I had a nosebleed and was late meeting a friend. I was in a hurry and you know Marg. She wanted to talk. I know I was rude and meant to apologize the next time I saw her but..." her voice trailed off. She didn't want to explain.

"Oh, she understands. We were all shocked to find out you were in here though. You and your healthy muffins. You could have been eating donuts this whole time for all the good they did you."

"Well, I'm not dead. You don't know that it wasn't my muffins that saved me." Only Angela could get her to joke about something like this.

"I guess you could be right." Angela fussed a bit with the flowers. "Oh – Mr. Korman died."

"Who?"

"Mr. Korman, the patient who attacked you. He died a few days ago."

A muddle of feelings tumbled inside of Johanna at this news. She had forgotten the incident that had put her in this hospital bed. She had been so focussed on the pills and Karen's agenda and the manuscript that she had forgotten that poor man.

"Do you think he suffered?"

"Here? No. Not compared to being in a concentration camp. I'm sure this hospital was paradise compared to that."

Johanna let out a long breath. Angela didn't know of Johanna's past. She thought of Mr. Korman. He would have emigrated from Germany too, like she did. "Do you think he had a good life here? After what the Germans did to him?"

Johanna saw the flash of insight in Angela's eyes. "Well, it wasn't you personally, Jo. Nobody can blame you for that. You would have been a child then. I don't know about your family. You never talk about them."

She could see that Angela wanted to know. Curiosity about Johanna's family – it was natural to wonder. "My brother," she said. It felt like there was a turkey bone stuck in her throat. There was no way those words would come out. Not now. Angela leaned forward and waited.

Johanna rested her head back on the pillow. The scent of the flowers wafted over. Johanna inhaled deeply. "My brother," she began again. "He wrote an opera."

Nothing else would come. A psychologist might tell her it was important to disclose everything about Heinz. To confide in someone the fear that gripped her when she thought of him and what he had done. It was enough for her that Robert knew. Nobody else had to know. She could tell people about the opera. Robert had been right. There were two sides to Heinz.

One did not erase the other and it was up to her what to reveal about him. Angela sat in complete silence and waited, but there was nothing else to say.

"That's all. I've given it to Robert. He may perform it here. Would you come with me? I've never heard it."

"Of course I will. I'll tell Karen you need an escort. That you're unstable or something." She laughed. "That'll get her thinking. Wow, your brother wrote an opera. That's quite something. You'll have to tell me more one day."

Angela stood to go. "Karen will wonder what's become of me. Oh, and that Mr. Korman – there were always visitors in his room, so he had family. I would think he would have come here and made the best of it after what he'd been through. But, who knows? Maybe he was a bitter old man and a grouch. There's no way to know. Nobody can tell a person what to do once they're given a second chance. They can screw things up for themselves all over again. It's a free country."

A free country – that was what Mr. Korman had come for. Johanna hoped with all of her heart that he had found it. That he had made the most of his decision to come here. It was time for her to do the same. She found herself staring into the bouquet of flowers. The longer she took in their fragile beauty, the calmer she felt. Her heart no longer thumped, but beat quietly, imperceptibly. Maybe one day she would tell Angela more. Inner strength was a completely different thing when you were in control of your own thoughts and desires. A triumph, to be able to enjoy a bouquet of flowers simply because the blooms were lovely.

• • • •

When Johanna went back to bed that night, she placed the journal on her bedside table. She still couldn't quite believe how sick she had become. She glanced around her hospital room. It had all led to this. But where had it started? This descent into near madness. Felix talking to her, cursing – she was certain Albert and Robert had taught him. It had all been imagined. The doctor had explained to her it had been the fever caused by the infection that had made her hallucinate. It felt awful to realize how easily your own mind can fool you.

Johanna let the book sit there while she brushed her teeth and adjusted the sheets. She wanted to keep it close by. That was where it had all started.

Years ago with Heinz and that journal. He had ended up dead on the floor of their home and then so many years later she had passed out in the basement with a near fatal infection. Two remote events so definitively linked. It was remarkable how the thread stretched through time. The past exists no matter who was there to witness it. A book filled with lines of words did nothing to change it. It was up to those left behind to either remember or forget. Frank found Johanna lying unconscious on the concrete floor in the basement and at that moment everything changed. Time shifted from the past to the present right there.

Johanna picked up the journal and read:

• • • •

May 16, 1944

This morning Helga had conjured up fresh eggs and strong coffee and some dark bread she managed to bake before dawn. Over coffee Julius imparted some terribly disturbing news. I refuse to believe it until I see it for my own eyes. He says they have brought in Hitler's SS to sing in the chorus this year. He refused to say he was pulling our legs and Helga was no help since there are soldiers and SS all over the place anyway and she has no idea what they are supposed to be doing here other than keeping their eyes open for signs of dissent. So, I have to wait until we get to the theatre to see if it's true. Good God, first they are ordered to kill and now they are ordered to sing. Wagner would turn and flee to have his music performed by that bunch of uncivilised cretins. *Wachet Auf!* Awake! Who in their right mind can sleep through this chaos? It would be a blessing to awake and discover it was all a bad dream. Last year at one performance the chorus of *Wachet Auf!* roused the audience to its feet in a passionate display of nationalism and patriotism and they stood for the remainder of the performance. I don't think anyone feels that way about Germany anymore.

It can't possibly be true about the SS, can it? Rehearsals start tomorrow and then we will know.

May 17, 1944

Julius was right. The SS is here. At first I thought they had been brought in to keep the theatre clean and do the maintenance work but this morning they were a couple of them outside sharing a cigarette at the same time as me and they were studying a score, which I found strange and so I approached them and asked.

"Do you believe it?" they said. "Never did we expect to be singing opera in this war."

They laughed a raucous, harsh laugh and bellowed, "It's not what we signed up for, that's for sure."

Coarse fellows. I hated them on sight. They have been transferred from Dachau, most of them. For the two that we met it was the first time they had been transferred from the camp. Rumours about the camps have been circulating for years, ever since the Nazis started throwing everyone in jail. Nobody ever seems to get out and those who do don't talk. Maybe I'll get up the nerve to ask them, if they ever let their guard down. They seem like typical braggarts and I might not want to ask them anything for fear of what they'll say. This is meant to be a leave for them. Once the festival is over they will return to their guard duties at the camp.

We never expected those thugs to be singing in our operas either but that is what has happened. The chorus for *Die Meistersinger* requires more than a hundred voices for the finale, which is why they are here. There aren't enough musicians left in the country and our beloved Führer will not condone the closure of art galleries or music festivals. He is afraid without culture we will all end up like the Americans, glued to the radio and brainwashed by popular culture.

No one was surprised when the war broke out. It had to all be leading to something, but now even these dimwitted fellows must be wondering how performing as a villager of Nürnberg can possibly fit into their Führer's vision. I could tell by the way they flung their cigarette butts into the dirt that the violent streak that propelled them to the SS to begin with was still in them.

June 15, 1944.

Karl is forever in my debt. I ran into Brigitte and Inge riding their bicycles through town. They had come in search of ice cream and we ended up having a cup of coffee in the back garden. Karl was fast asleep upstairs and I allowed myself twenty blissful moments with both of those lovely creatures and then decided to wake him up. Brigitte fancied him it was clear and we strolled through the public gardens for an hour, Inge on my arm and Brigitte on his. The distance between us grew ever farther and before I knew it Inge and I were lying under a tree kissing. It must have been at least an hour before we noticed the chill in the air and the damp coming up from the ground. I asked her what would have happened if they had found ice cream instead of me and she confessed they had been riding around and around trying to find Karl and me. Even fleeting, sweet love surpasses all.

• • • •

These were the kinds of experiences Heinz had been robbed of because of the war – a chance to be in love, to experience the things common to the human condition, to feel exhilaration and pain any way life throws it at you. She had done the right thing letting Robert have the opera. It did more good for him to have it than for her to keep it hidden away. This time, as she read the journal and came to the awful parts about Heinz, she felt a cool detachment. It wasn't something she did on purpose or anything she tried to do in order to get through it. Instead, as she read, she saw Heinz through the eyes of the violinist. As a lost and troubled soul perhaps, as a despicable human being certainly, but not the main focus of his life. The presence of Heinz did not overshadow this man's love of music and his devotion to his work. If this young violinist could carry on making beautiful music amidst such chaos and in the presence of such brutality, then Johanna should be able to live with him too. Heinz was forever linked to her, no matter what he did with his life, good or bad. He would always be there, hovering at the edge of her conscience.

Johanna re-read the final paragraph in the journal a few times. Where the violinist dismissed all the terrible things the war brought into his life and his country and vowed to continue to do his best. Even in the darkest moments, he spoke with passion of redemption and hope and rebirth – such uplifting and comforting words. Maybe that was meant to be the message all along.

One more day and she would be home. She looked forward to sitting on her balcony and gazing out at the lake, dotted with sailboats and the gulls squawking overhead. Whenever she sat there and stared out at the water she was reminded of her journey with Barbara. She had thought leaving Germany would be the best thing for them, that time and distance would allow the past to fade. And yet, each time she gazed at the horizon she was reminded that the water that touched this shore also mingled with the waters of distant shores. They were all connected to the past as sure as the water touched the land.

• • • •

Just another dress rehearsal, Robert told himself as he paced backstage. The patients started to arrive a half-hour early and filled the seats. The orchestra milled about in their typical pre-concert oblivion that drove Robert mad. Albert had agreed to sing the duet and Robert had spent the last two rehearsals torturing the musicians with hours of nitpicking at Heinz's score. It was just the one piece from the opera they intended to perform and the poor girl singing the part of Christina had nearly quit in despair and he'd had to calm her down after ranting at her about a breath she had to take in the middle of a delicate phrase. Finally he'd consented to let her breathe. His heart pounded whenever he thought about his mother hearing it for the first time. Even though she had been the one to say she wanted to hear it, when Robert had told her of the performance she backtracked.

"You're in the hospital already," he had said. "One of your volunteer friends can bring you. That's what they're there for isn't it? You just have to sit there. What else do you have to do?"

"I am supposed to do exercises three times a day. I like to do them after dinner."

"You can do them while you're listening. That way you won't fidget." Robert was at the window. "I thought you said you wanted to hear it."

"I do. I didn't think it would be this soon. I'm not even out of the hospital."

"Well, music has many healing qualities. It's a well-known fact."

It had to be perfect and the orchestra had suffered by his ragged nerves. A pain shot through his head behind his eyes every time he looked at the score, so long had he stared at it making minor adjustments up until the last five minutes of the last rehearsal. No one dared look him in the eye now for fear of some final instructions.

He paced around backstage among the musicians who idled by the stacking chairs and long wooden tables. A few of them sat around a table and played cards, most sipped from bottles of water or cups of coffee and chatted. Not one of them held an instrument or studied the score. It made him shake when he watched them and yet he knew that the moment he raised his baton that they would be with him. At that moment, the music was in their hands. It was a good sign that they were all relaxed, he told himself. He wandered among them on his way to the room that served as his dressing room and patted a few shoulders and squeezed a few arms. They turned to see what he wanted but he didn't speak. He shut the dressing room door and sank onto the sofa.

It was ten to six. There was a knock at the door and Albert peeked in. "How are you, maestro?"

Robert swept his hair from his eyes. "All right. I think we're in good shape."

"Don't worry, the horns won't miss that repeat in the performance. Something like that doesn't happen twice,"

"I know. They'll be fine. It'll be fine."

Albert sat down. "They are seated in the middle – your mother and her friend Angela."

"I thought she might yet change her mind."

"Hmm. I know." Albert squeezed Robert's arm. "I better go warm up."

"See if you can convince any of the rest of them to do the same. See you on stage."

"Right. Break a leg."

Robert smiled. Albert had called him maestro. He stood in front of the mirror and tied his bowtie. The opening bars played in his mind. The music was in him. The score memorized. It would never leave him now.

In the audience Johanna and Angela watched while the other patients filed into the auditorium. Some on crutches, some led by volunteers or family members. A number of wheelchairs lined the aisles. The orchestra was in place and the players practised little bits of the music. The lights went down and a hush fell over the room.

Robert stretched his arms. It was time. He stood in the wings while the orchestra tuned. Albert and Evelyn Muller, the girl who would sing the soprano part, stood beside him. When the tuning was done he counted backwards from five and then they strode onto the stage. The orchestra rose. The audience applauded. Robert stepped back and let Albert take a bow. Once at the podium he turned and stared into the bright lights. Usually this only took a moment and he could turn around. Not today. He pulled a microphone close towards him.

"Just a few words on today's performance." He wasn't used to speaking when he was up here. His eyes watered from the bright lights. "We are debuting a piece written by Heinz Friedrich, a German composer. The piece we will perform is from a recently discovered opera, written in 1945. The university is very pleased to announce that it will perform a full production of this work next year."

There were people stirring in their seats, waiting for him to get on with it. A normal audience would have applauded this announcement. But here the audience was anything but normal. From somewhere in the darkness came the sound of three loud sneezes. Another patient was asking in a very loud voice what had just been said – hearing aides no doubt left behind. He knew it didn't matter to this audience what they heard but felt he couldn't just launch into the music without saying something. It was after all a world premiere. He hoped the few words didn't make his mother tense. "Anyway, I hope you enjoy it."

He nodded once at the audience and turned to the orchestra.

When Albert and Robert strode out onto the stage Johanna thought she would pass out from anticipation. Her hands tensed around the arms of the seat when she realized Robert was going to say something. But he left her name out of it and nobody seemed to pay attention. He turned around and raised his baton. Angela sat beside her, oblivious to the significance of the moment and waved at a few people she knew. She whispered something in Johanna's ear that she did not hear. Johanna stared at the distant stage. Already tuned in to the music before it began, her vision focussed on the stage, nothing else entered her perception.

The sound of the timpani rolled across the stage and out over the audience. Then, the horn from the back of the orchestra, such soft breath, soothed her ragged nerves. She let it be, let it happen. The clarinets and flutes joined in and then, the cellos, playing the melody, uncertainty and hesitation in the notes supported by the winds. The sound washed over her like a gentle rain. Her head rested back on the seat and her eyes closed.

Robert cued the strings and the first notes caressed her like the hands of angels. Time passed imperceptibly. The student singing the part of Christina had a sure and strong voice that sounded much like Johanna had sounded when she was young and in good form. Her eyes rested on Robert as he conducted and then on Albert as he stood and waited for his entry. Her heart swelled with pride at the sight of them. Such talent and poise. She could hardly believe this was her son and nephew. She remembered the sounds coming from the study at home where Heinz worked behind closed doors. She recognized parts of it, even though so many years had passed since she had lived with him in that house. She hadn't been paying attention, or so she thought, but here were the notes, coming at her with no surprise at all. She knew every phrase. When Albert's voice joined in, the harmony of the two voices carried her away. Behind closed eyes Johanna returned to the study where Heinz waited by the piano for her. He sang his part and played while she stood behind him and waited for her entry. This time she knew the words and sang with him. It would be the last time. Their voices united, rang through the walls of the house. Powerful and resonant, in perfect harmony.

The soprano's voice trilled on a high note – clear, precise and flawless. It jolted Johanna from her daydream. She stared at the girl who sang the part that Heinz had written for her. The program said she had won a scholarship to continue her studies at Julliard. Such a voice, Johanna thought. It was right she be given an opportunity to develop it. For certain she would continue on to many great moments on the stage. It was not for everybody, to stand upon a stage and sing.

As she relaxed, she heard the flute play a distant melody. It was the time when Heinz dragged her into the study and wanted her to sing and she had ran from the room in a rage. The moment she vowed never to sing another note. And here it was, that same music, quenching her withered heart like rain on a long neglected garden. The soprano's voice floated up to where she sat. The notes bathed her in a silvery light. Johanna's head fell back and her eyes remained closed. He was there, touching her hand, imploring her to hear. To listen to the music he had written for her. Tears winked at the corners of her eyes. If he were here he would understand that this was what she had wanted – not to sing, but to be sung to.

When the piece finished on a soft timpani roll, the audience responded with a smattering of applause. Johanna smiled at Angela's enthusiastic clapping and shouts of "Bravo" that inspired a few people to join in. Robert's eyes searched for hers but she was lost in the lights. There was more music on the program and Johanna settled back to listen. After a moment Albert sidled up the row and sat in the seat next to her and squeezed her arm. In the darkness he whispered, "That came off quite well, I thought. Did you like it?"

"I loved it," she whispered back. She pretended to conduct with her bandaged arm. "I think I'm cured."

They sat in the darkened theatre while the orchestra played a Beethoven overture. Johanna stared at the back of Robert's head while the music washed over her. Nothing terrible had happened. At last she sensed some calm – calm where she had been so certain catastrophe would fall. It had not devastated Robert to learn the truth. There was light in his eyes again. And to think it was a man who did the devil's work who put that light there.

Magdeburg, Germany, 1945

In the end Heinz has given Christina a bird, one that sits and flits up among the leaves and branches, something to keep her grounded, to keep her company while she inhabits the physical world. In the final scene, everyone gathers as she is laid to rest, at peace at last. The chorus sings a haunting Agnus Dei to the memory of a tormented life. The second violins take over the melody in unison. A distant sound swells from beneath the stage and rolls infinitely forward. One voice sings over them all. There is a hush as the last note is sung. Then silence. Before there is any movement a sound can be heard coming from the rafters. It is Christina's songbird – a low G sounded on the flute, followed by a single cello – E flat, and then viola and muted horn enter on B flat. On the stage, heads turn from the coffin and faces are uplifted to see where the sound is coming from. A shaft of light illuminates the upturned faces. There is a swell of music as the trumpets repeal and the orchestra crescendos. The sound fills the small church. The brass blazes and the timpani thunders, carrying the spirit of Christina heavenward. Then, the music slows, the sound fades. One by one the chorus leaves the stage. The set is dark except for a single beam of light and the hushed tone of one flute playing – E-flat. Two half notes. Then, one. And… curtain.

Thank You

To the Enfield & Wizenty staff for their encouragement and time spent: Gregg Shilliday, Ingeborg Boyens, Maurice Mierau, Catharina de Bakker.

To Frederic Spotts for writing the illuminating books that helped guide this project: *Bayreuth – A History of the Wagner Festival* and *Hitler and the Power of Aesthetics*. And for providing me with further details and cast lists for the war festivals.

And to the following people for their unwavering support and enthusiasm: Tammy Bentley, Karen Csoli, Ellen Reid, Andrea Smits, Caley Strachan, Micheal Teal, Anita Turner, Ricki Valcourt, Erika von Kampen, Margaret Wilding. You always say the right things!